Read...

Even though all of my books can be read on their own, they all exist in the same world—regardless of series—so for reader clarity, I have included a recommended reading order to give you the ultimate experience possible.
This is also a timeline accurate list.

Lucky Hit (Oakley and Ava) Swift Hat-Trick trilogy #1

Between Periods (Novella) Swift Hat-Trick trilogy #1.5

Blissful Hook (Tyler and Gracie) Swift Hat-Trick trilogy #2

Craving The Player (Braden and Sierra) Amateurs In Love series #1

Taming The Player (Braden and Sierra) Amateurs In Love series #2

Vital Blindside (Adam and Scarlett) Swift Hat-Trick trilogy #3 (Coming Sept 2022)

Playlist

Exchange — Bryson Tiller	3:15
Single Saturday Night — Cole Swindell	3:08
LOVE IN THE DARK — Jesse Reyez	4:14
Hold You Tonight — Gryffin, Chris Lane	3:39
Love You Still — Tyler Shaw	2:30
As I Am — Justin Bieber, Khalid	2:54
MIDDLE OF THE NIGHT — Elley Duhe	3:04
Every Kind Of Way — H.E.R	2:40
Know No Better — Justin Bieber, DaBaby	2:42
If It Weren't For you – FINMAR	3:16
One More Night – Maroon 5	3:39
Kiss You Inside Out – Hedley	3:37
High For This – The Weeknd	4:07
Still Into You – Paramore	3:36
I Don't Do Drugs – Doja Cat, Ariana Grande	3:09

Taming the Player

HANNAH COWAN

Portions of this book are works of fiction. Any references to historical events, real people, or real places are used fictitiously. Other names, characters, places and events are products of the author's imagination, and any resemblances to actual events or places or persons, living or dead, is entirely coincidental.

Edited and proofed by: Sandra at One Love Editing @oneloveediting

Cover design by: Acacia Heather @everaftercoverdesign

Special Edition

ISBN: 978-1-990804-007

For those who have taken a huge risk despite fearing what could come after. You're kick-ass. Give yourself a pat on the back.

PROLOGUE

THREE WEEKS AGO

Braden

Sierra's gone. Her apartment is empty, her car is in storage. All I have left of her are a few hair ties on my bathroom counter and the smell of her shampoo on my pillow.

My chest feels hollow. Like she took my heart with her and left me an empty husk.

Tyler sits across from me on my unmade bed. A thick stack of papers rests between us, a blue pen placed on top. He's saying something, but I don't listen. I'm too far inside my own head, lost in a colossal mess of potential plans and self-deprecating thoughts that I've been tormenting myself with.

Sophie's voice plays on repeat in my thoughts every time I pull one of those potential plans out and focus on it. *"I'm going to help you fix this."*

I hear it over and over again but don't reach out. Don't ask for her help. Without any plans of my own, there's no point. It's only been a day, and I feel the heavy weight of defeat on my shoulders.

Tyler snaps an impatient finger in my face, and I blink a few times, clearing my head. "Yeah?"

He sighs, annoyed. "Did you hear anything that I just said?"

"No."

With a roll of his eyes, he picks up that thick stack of paper and holds it up in front of me. Narrowing my eyes, I focus on the word *sale* written across the top before looking at him.

"What is this?"

"It's a plan. One that's going to get your ass out of this room and on a plane."

"Don't be vague." I can't handle the false hope right now.

"Alright, I won't." Setting the papers back down, he hands me the blue pen. "Sell me the gym. Take the money and buy something in Toronto. Start a new life there with your girl. Let me make this happen for you."

"*What*?" I ask again. "I'm not sure that I heard you right."

"Sell. Me. The. Gym."

"It's not mine to sell." I swallow the lump in my throat. "It's Dad's."

The corner of Tyler's mouth tips up. "It was. Until he suggested transferring ownership to you."

I scoff. "Why the hell would he do that?"

Tyler stares at me with a look that says, *You're an idiot.*

"Because it's been yours, more or less, for the past ten years. Dad's old. He doesn't want it anymore. He wants to close this chapter of his life and start a new one with Lana. This is the easiest way to do that. I had my lawyer draw everything up. We just need you to get on board. Accept ownership, sell it to me, and then take the money to start something new."

"You're crazy." A warped laugh escapes me.

This sounds fucking nuts.

"Maybe." He shrugs. "But it's a damn good plan. Stop letting this goddamn city hold you back. Take the money from the sale and create a future for yourself somewhere else. If it doesn't work, you can always come back. It's not life or death. You'll always have a place here. But don't miss this opportunity."

"It's not going to be that easy," I say.

"So? Is that supposed to mean that you shouldn't do it? That's pussy mentality, man."

He has a point. I'm being handed the perfect opportunity here. A chance to get my girl back. I would be an idiot not to take it. But doubt is a nasty bastard that loves to play mind games. What if I do this and she turns me away? What if there's no second chance for us?

I can barely think past the raging sound of my own heartbeat in my ears.

Opening my own gym . . . fuck, I don't know if I could even do it. It could either be the biggest mistake I've ever made or the best decision of my life. But I won't know until I actually take the jump and risk landing on my face.

When I don't reply, Tyler says, "I've seen the way she looks at you. It will take some time and a fuckton of work on your end, but she'll forgive you. She loves you just as much as you love her. Just take the fucking chance."

His words light a match inside of me, and before I realize it, I've grabbed the pen.

"Where do I sign?"

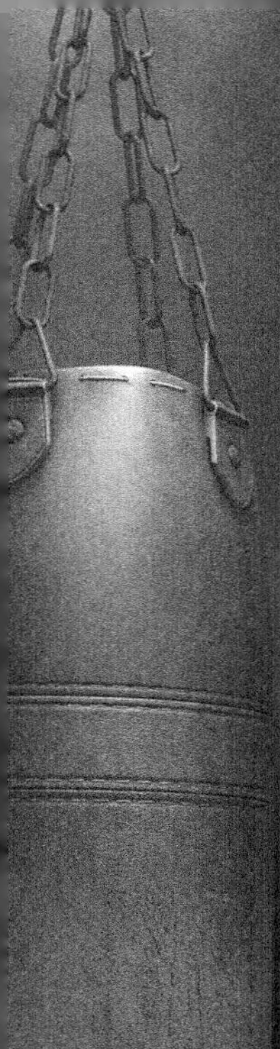

1

THREE WEEKS LATER

Braden

The door behind me creaks open slowly, tentatively. The *click-clack* of high heels on the roof drowns the thumping heartbeat in my ears. With my shoulders pulled back and my confidence teetering on the edge of completely fucking imaginative, I turn around and smile, any previous thoughts clearing from my head like a break in a heavy fog.

"Hey there, my little fighter," I say through an emotion-clogged throat. It's only been a few weeks, but seeing her in front of me again is enough to cut me down at the knees.

My fingertips tingle in the front pockets of my jeans. I want to close the distance between us and take her in my arms. The need to promise never to let her escape them again is earth-shattering, nearly debilitating. My ego is a thing of the past, nothing but a memory of the terrified little boy I was before Sierra stormed into my life like a category five hurricane. Fuck pride. I want her to know exactly how badly I've missed her. Rejection be damned. Anything would be better than living every day with broken pieces and an ache that only she can soothe.

Sometime before she left, Sierra managed to pry her perfectly manicured, french-tipped nails deep into my chest cavity and grip my beating heart with punishing strength. What she didn't know before hopping on that plane was that I would have held her wrist and helped her yank the bloody thing from my body with the promise of forever.

If she had known how I felt, maybe she wouldn't have left without me. And maybe I wouldn't have let her go, my heart tucked unbeknownst in her suitcase. But she didn't know how much I love her, and I've spent the past three weeks planning how to fix what I broke between us.

Everything inside of me is begging me to storm over to her and feel her soft skin against my fingertips. To kiss her lips and breathe her in. But I know I can't push it. Can't push *her*.

The ball in my throat threatens to cut off my air supply seconds before her feet move, jerky at first before forming a desperate stride in my direction. I catch her easily when she jumps into my arms, fitting perfectly against me like she always has, even when I wished she felt wrong. My hands grab her thighs as they lock tight around my waist, keeping her as close to me as possible. A gush of air is pushed from my mouth as relief flows through my tight muscles, relaxing them.

"You're here. You're in Toronto." Her words kiss my throat, dripping with surprise. The arms she has looped around my neck loosen. Her face leaves the crook of my shoulder, and shining silver eyes fall on my face, wide, familiar, and so fucking warm.

"I'm here, baby."

I hope to God she can see everything I haven't said yet in the way I devour her with my stare and press my forehead to hers. My chest is tight, so full of unspoken truths and feelings, but my tongue lies limp in my mouth.

"How are you here?" she asks a heartbeat later, watching

me, her expression so full of hope yet dampened by something I can only assume to be heartbreak and fear.

Sweat breaks out on the back of my neck as I drop her to her feet and push my hair back for no good reason, instantly regretting letting her move from my arms. I play off my nerves with a sarcastic reply that I realize right away she doesn't appreciate.

"A plane."

Her eyes harden, jaw setting. I want to tell her everything that's happened in the past three weeks. Every tough decision and goodbye. She deserves to know what led to this meeting, but will she forgive me afterward for everything that came before?

"*Why* are you here? Why now?" Her words lack emotion, but I'm not surprised nor offended by it. She has every right to keep me at arm's length.

My hands shake at my sides, but there's no stopping what comes next. Fear be damned.

"I should have been here three weeks ago, Sierra. I know that. I should have told you how desperately in love with you I was in that fucking bar and never let you leave me in the first place. But I was a coward, baby." I grab her face in my hands. There's shock in her eyes, but I beg her to stay silent with the look in mine.

"I don't deserve your love, but I'm a selfish bastard who's going to take it all anyway. Every single last fucking ounce of it until there's none left. And I want you to do the same with mine because there's so much of it that I felt like I was going to explode these last three weeks with nobody to share it with. I love you so goddamn much, my little fighter. And as long as you'll have me—*if* you'll have me—I'll be here."

Sierra blinks, lips slightly parted. I'm winded, overwhelmed with relief and a hint of nausea sparked by her silence.

A thousand questions tumble through my head, making me wonder whether or not I should have waited to tell her how in love with her I am, if I'm too late, or if, by some fucking chance, there's someone else in the picture now. If there is, it's absolutely a test from God. One that I'll fail with a smile when I kill the guy who thought for even a second that he could have my girl and dump his body in the ocean.

Shark food, Sierra. Don't test me.

My thumb runs over her bottom lip, pressing gently. The adoration I feel for her is written all over me; I know from the way she's watching me, like I'm a creature she can't quite figure out but desperately seeks to. There isn't anything that I wouldn't tell her right now when she's looking at me like this, all wild-eyed and flushed. I would allow her full access into my head and let her sift through my thoughts for anything she wanted to know.

It's a dangerous, terrifying realization, but one I've prepared myself for.

"Say something," I whisper softly.

"I don't know what to say. I'm so surprised that you're even here, let alone saying all of this," she finally says, sounding just as out of breath as I feel. For some reason, that thought helps calm me. "I've wanted to hear you say all of that for weeks."

"And do you believe me?"

She doesn't hesitate. "Of course I do. You're not exactly the most outspoken about your feelings. I can't see you lying about them."

A breath of relief escapes as I nod, my gaze unwavering. A warm feeling settles in my stomach as my heart rattles my ribs like the bars of a prison cell, desperate to burst through my chest.

There's a spark of doubt, though, somewhere deeper in my mind. "I sense a 'but' coming." The words taste rotten.

Sierra's the first to break eye contact, heaving a sigh. She turns slightly to the left, toward the blanket laid on the rooftop. The sudden movement forces my hands to fall back to my sides, and the warmth that once filled my stomach turns to lead, sinking deep.

It was Sophie's idea—the romantic gesture, that is. I've never done anything romantic a day in my life. I don't know my head from my ass when it comes to romance, so I didn't argue with her when she said I should go all out. So I spent far too long this afternoon hanging twinkly lights and ordered too much food for the both of us.

I can't be sure if it helped any with getting me back in Sierra's good books, but it was worth a shot anyway. Even if it makes her feel appreciated and not want to gut me like a fish for the slightest moment.

"I believe that you love me. I think I always knew that you did, you just weren't ready to accept it. But how are we supposed to do this? You've already made it very clear that long distance won't work. So what? Now it will? You haven't reached out to me in three weeks and what? Now you're ready for a relationship? I'm confused, Braden."

I can't blame her for being frustrated. It was *my* fuckup and inability to open myself up to the possibility of a future with her that planted the seeds of doubt inside of her head. I let her feel unwanted and like she wasn't worth it. I'm the one who told her she was nothing more than a fuck buddy when she was always so much more than that. Even when I was incapable of seeing it.

There's only one thing I can do now that has a chance of helping anything, and that's to tell her the whole truth about why and how I'm here.

Closing the distance between us, I grab both of her small hands and squeeze them before bringing them to my chest, desperate for her touch. Her breath hitches while she presses her palms against my pecs and stares up at me with guarded eyes.

I have to fight back the urge to curse at myself for being the cause of the wall she's put up between us. Shoving away the anger that's started heating my blood before I let it show on my face, I grip her hips and pull her body flush to mine.

"Sit and have dinner with me, and I'll tell you everything about how and why I'm here. I'll answer any questions that you have. I promise."

I'm pleading with her, but I'm too antsy to care. I'm aware of how small my window of opportunity is here.

Sierra isn't the type of woman who needs a man. If she doesn't think I'm worth it, she'll toss me out on my ass with both her middle fingers raised. I know how well she's been doing for herself out here, and the last thing either of us wants is to ruin that.

She lifts a brow and looks between me and the food that's in desperate need of being reheated with a strong sense of contemplation. I can practically hear the gears turning in her head as she thinks about whether to tell me to fuck off and never show up here again or take the chance on dinner.

Luck seems to be in my favor tonight because she nods and says, "I'll have dinner because I'm starving and you brought enough food to last me the entire week. But as pretty as it is up here, we're not eating in the cold."

I almost bend down to kiss her before thinking better of it, opting to grin and squeeze her hips instead. "Done. No eating outside."

"I would say that you can follow me down, but it seems

Sophie has already taken care of letting you know which apartment is mine."

I gulp before Sierra shakes her head and smiles softly to herself.

"I prefer to follow you. The view is better that way."

She steps back and looks away in an attempt to hide her blush from me, but it only makes me feel a heavy sense of pride to see that my words still affect her just as strongly now as they did before. Nothing has changed in that regard.

"Help me pack this up," she mumbles before rushing to collect the containers of food and placing them in the basket I set off to the side of the blanket.

Her thick pink coat covers her thighs, resting just above her knees, but paired with her skirt and thin black tights, it leaves her lower body completely bare to the early December chill. I scowl but decide not to chastise her for walking home in the low temperature without proper clothes on and help her collect the food in silence instead. She won't be walking to and from work alone anymore now that I'm here anyway.

Usually, I would have pushed my luck, unable to keep myself from poking at her, but this is just yet another reminder of how badly I need this night to go well.

Sierra has to forgive me. I don't want to think of what I'll do if she doesn't.

2

Sierra

After three weeks of silence, Braden told me that he loves me. Yes, *loves* me.

Talk about a shock to the system. The last thing I expected today was to find the man who hasn't made a single effort to reach out to me after discarding my heart like a dirty sock on my roof with a grand romantic gesture and a love proclamation. I'm still trying to catch my breath.

His presence presses against my back, warm, heavy, and confident despite the nerves I noticed on the roof. Nervous. Braden was *nervous*. I'm not sure whether knowing that I brought out that side of him should make me feel proud or guilty. Considering it's nearly impossible to catch a glimpse of that part of Braden through the heavy armor of arrogance he wears on the daily, I should feel accomplished seeing him sweat. But at the same time, my damn feelings for him have my stomach in knots at the mere thought of him being upset.

My apartment in Toronto is only a bit bigger than my old one in Vancouver, but more expensive considering the location is in the city centre, only a few blocks from work. With two bedrooms, one bath, and a small yet open-concept kitchen and living space, Braden's presence is nearly suffocating.

The living room seems to shrink in his company, forcing me to feel closer to him than I really am from my place on the couch. Braden sits with his legs splayed out on the cushion closest to me, refusing to move to the far cushion like the stubborn ass he is while I sit with my legs tucked under my body, chewing on a bite of chow mein.

It's hard not to see the similarities between us before and now, with the scattered tins of Chinese food on the coffee table and the feelings threatening to pop like an overfilled balloon between us, but it's different now. That's why I didn't let him turn on *Law & Order* after we sat down, opting for the evening news instead. I won't be able to stand my ground if I let us fall back into that routine. *Our* routine. The memories of past nights spent together have my throat tightening and an unsettling feeling coiling in my stomach.

With that thought, I'm putting my food down on the table, not hungry anymore.

I avoid looking at Braden, knowing that he's been watching me slither back in my head to hide. But it's his hand on my thigh—the touch so gentle and reassuring—that sends me over the edge. Suddenly, I can't see past the unshed tears blurring my vision or breathe past the thick lump in my throat.

The hollow ache in my chest that I've fought so hard to dull comes back with a vengeance. My heart splits again, both halves too fragile and sore this time around to stick together by more than a frayed string.

"Fuck, baby," he curses before eliminating the distance between us and pulling me into his lap. He binds his arms around me and holds my body so close to his that I can feel his heartbeat against my cheek when I press my face to his hard chest.

I welcome the familiar smell of his cologne, and a shudder racks through me at his next words.

"I tried to get to you the day you left. I was too late, though." A large palm traces the ridge of my spine in soft strokes, not stopping even when I grow rigid beneath it, my breath catching. "I was with my dad hours before your plane took off, trying to convince him not to move away with his new wife. It was such a jackass thing to do, but I didn't care. The only thing I could think about was making him stay. I was terrified of how lonely I would be without him. Without *you*."

Braden's heartbeat keeps thumping away in my ear, and I find myself rubbing my cheek against his chest, as if that would somehow help calm him down and help him continue his story. It's rare for him to open up like this, and regardless of how I feel about everything that's happened, I want to help him in any way that I can.

"I was a pretty lonely kid my whole life, but especially after my parents divorced. They hated each other for the majority of my childhood. The fights were ruthless, both of them so angry with each other for things I never understood. I was hardly even a teenager when my mom took off for two years. She barely waited a day after the papers were signed before she went to 'find herself' in a completely different country. My dad didn't know how to deal with me on his own, so we barely spoke.

"I spent the rest of my teen years getting my ass beat in fights and doing the stupidest shit. I was so desperate for my dad's attention that I would have done anything to get it. It wasn't until I graduated and started university that I grew out of it. Once I became an adult, it was easier for my dad to talk to me. I wasn't as hotheaded and dramatic as I was as a kid. We got along."

"All kids are attention seekers, Braden. Even more so when

they feel invisible to the people they care about. There was nothing wrong with how you reacted to something so drastic and life-changing." Leaning back in his arms, I slide my hand up his chest to hold his jaw. The skin is prickly under my fingertips, showing his lack of shaving as of late.

He leans into my touch, eyes clouded and dark with something that looks a lot like regret. I want to smack him for carrying this feeling of self-loathing with him for so many years.

"Don't feel bad for me, Sierra. That's not why I'm telling you this."

I glare, pinching him in the side with my free hand. "I'm allowed to feel bad for you. I know you're not telling me this so that I'll pity you. But I'm not going to pretend that I agree with the weight you've been carrying all these years."

He sighs and turns his head to kiss my palm. "I was an awful son to him when he met Lana. I didn't understand their relationship—hell, I still don't—but I took it too far. I didn't realize that until I found myself in his exact position. I spent months criticizing something that I didn't understand until I met you."

My stomach flutters before I can control my reaction. "What are you talking about?"

His stare is so intense I feel it everywhere. It steals my breath, holding it hostage. "My dad was willing to risk everything to follow the woman he loved across the country. He was planning on following Lana here, to Toronto. For months I told him that he was making a mistake. That no girl was worth leaving everything you've ever known behind. But I was so fucking wrong, Sierra. Even after flying all my shit out here and renting an apartment that is honestly pretty embarrassing compared to this one, I still can't believe how wrong I was."

I suck in a sharp breath, tears welling in my eyes for the second time tonight. They spill when I shake my head and raise a shaking hand to my chest. “Don’t lie to me right now, Braden. It’s not funny.”

He laughs, rough and familiar, and swipes my tears away with his thumbs. “I’m here to stay as long as you’ll have me. There was nothing keeping me in Vancouver, not after you left. I was fucking blind not to see that earlier.”

“What about your brother? Clayton? Boxing?” I push at his chest and stand, my fingers winding through my hair, scratching at my scalp. *Distance.* I need distance to think.

I start pacing around the living room.

He didn’t really move out here for me. There’s no way. He’s about to be an uncle—now isn’t the time for him to be making rash decisions. His family is going to need him. I can’t stand back and steal him from his family. Even if his dad is moving out here for his wife. Tyler is going to need him. His mom—regardless of how close her relationship is with her son—will need him. Right?

There’s movement by the couch, but I avoid looking toward it, scared I’ll completely lose it once I look into those brown eyes I love so much.

“Dammit, Braden. Why did you do this?” I spin around, my arms flailing in the air before coming down on a hard chest.

My eyes widen in surprise when I register Braden’s closeness. I exhale slowly and curl my fingers into the soft material of his sweatshirt.

“Relax, fighter,” he coaxes, his strong hands rubbing my shoulders and upper arms in soothing motions. “You need to calm down before you have a panic attack.”

My eyes narrow. “Don’t tell me to calm down right now. And don’t call me that. This is serious!”

There’s a twitch in his brow as he watches me with heated eyes. It’s like he wants to pick me up and toss me on the bed so he can fuck my worries out of me. Usually, that would have worked, and I would have let him without a second thought. But not now.

Sex is completely off the table. Even if I'm so completely sex deprived that the thought of being punished by Braden has me rubbing my thigh together.

"Do you not want me here? Is that it?" The heat in his eyes is washed out by something deeper, anger maybe.

"Of course I do! I've been asking Sophie every single day for three weeks for updates on you and your whereabouts. But that doesn't mean that I'm not worried. I can't just not worry about something so monumental just because you tell me everything's okay, Braden. That's not me."

"I know, and I don't want to change that about you. I'm just asking you to trust me when I say everything will be okay. Better than okay, actually."

Sliding my hands to his shoulders, I press my forehead to his chest. I'm being weak, I know that. I should be putting up a bigger fight, kicking and screaming and telling him how badly he hurt me. But instead, I whisper, "Tell me how you know everything will be okay."

His arms engulf me like my own personal shield. "The flight time from Toronto to Vancouver isn't even five hours, sweetheart. It won't be impossible to fly home and visit. Not to mention Tyler will be playing here a few times this season. I know you're worried about me not seeing my niece or nephew, but I will. If it makes you feel better, I promise that I'll go home after Gray gives birth and stay with them for a few days.

"Clayton is a big boy. I wouldn't worry about him. I'm sure Sophie will keep his ass in line for me. And as far as boxing goes, you'll just have to believe me when I say I have it figured out. That's all you're getting from me right now."

His tone is final, and I find myself nodding. I know better than to push my luck with him, even if the mere thought of not knowing absolutely everything settles in my stomach like a puddle of vomit.

The tension leaks from my muscles as I replay everything he just said. He's right about the distance not being as big of a barrier as I thought. But I can't help but wonder why he's okay with being away from them but not me. I mean, he *moved* here. He very well could have just come back for a weekend and tried to get me to agree to a long-distance relationship after telling me all of this. He didn't have to get up and move here for me. Especially knowing that he did it with the chance I could tell him to leave me alone for good.

A gentle finger is placed under my chin and tilts my head so I'm forced to meet Braden's stare. It's like he's in my head, reading my thoughts. I don't have a chance to tell him what's bothering me about all of this before he's speaking.

"I know exactly where you're taking this conversation, and I'm putting an end to it right now. If you think that I would be content with seeing you merely a few times a month, not touching or witnessing with my own eyes that you're okay and happy, you must have forgotten who you've fallen in love with. There was nothing but an old boxing gym tying me to Vancouver. I had no plans, no dreams, no fucking anything."

He bends down, hovering his mouth over mine. We're close enough that I can feel the brush of his lips but so far that I can't taste him like I'm dying to after weeks apart.

With eyes unwavering, he says, "The weeks without you were hell on fucking earth. I'm not doing that again. Ever. You're mine, little fighter. And you have no idea what you've gotten yourself into. I've never done relationships before, but that changes right now. With you. You're never going to be free of me again."

His words crash into me like waves on a cold, windy day. They knock me over and drag me under. No matter how hard or fast I swim, I'm stuck under their pull, drowning beneath them as they force me to surrender.

And I do surrender—mind, soul, and definitely body as I push up on my toes and connect our mouths, stealing from him like he did from me. He's gentle, but I'm rough, desperate, *hungry*.

He tastes me while I devour him.

The heaviness of how sudden the roles have reversed doesn't go unnoticed. If anything, I focus on it, taking my fill while I have the chance.

My hands grasp his nape and hold him to me. I'm overwhelmed with the sensations swirling in my veins and clawing at my insides. It's intense, almost too intense as I lose my balance and lean against him, stabilizing myself.

He catches me with ease and holds me tightly against him before pulling back. Braden's pupils are dilated, the black nearly engulfing all of the warm chocolate brown. His breaths are hot puffs of air on my pulsing cheeks.

"Things are going to be different this time, Sierra. If I'm going to get another shot at this—if you'll give me one—I'm going to do it right. And fucking you on the floor of your living room after a reheated dinner and an emotional talk is not what I had in mind when I came here today."

I stare back at him, trying to blink away my surprise. He shakes his head and laughs, grinning so wide his dimples show on both cheeks.

"I'm going to go back to my apartment before it's too late, and after I'm gone, you're going to go to sleep and dream of me. I'll be back in the morning to walk you to work, and you can let me know what you've decided then."

I hold my breath as he places a kiss on my cheek, followed by one on my lips, and walks to the front door. My first instinct is to ask him to stay, not wanting him gone again after finally getting him back, but I push back that urge. If he were to stay, we wouldn't make it five minutes without having sex.

If Braden of all people wants to give this a real try, I'm going to at least *think* about it. Everything that he's done to win me back has to count for something. I mean, he moved across the country for me, knowing that I might never forgive him.

If I were a different person, someone less hard-headed and stubborn, maybe I would have forgiven him the moment I saw him on the roof. But that's not me, and I can't find it in me to hate myself for it.

Over the past weeks, I've hated him, begged for him, and mourned the future we could have had if things had gone differently. But still, after the tears and anger fade, I can't deny that being with Braden is still something that I want, crave, and sometimes feel like I *need*.

Love doesn't disappear overnight, not when you feel so strongly about somebody. But it does take shelter, hiding from anything that could possibly shred it with unforgiving claws again.

Love becomes wary, fearful after heartbreak. It doesn't throw out forgiveness or second chances. It has to be earned, and if Braden is willing to work for it, I'm not going to tell him no. Although, if I'm being completely honest with myself, I don't think that I ever could.

"So, you want to be my boyfriend now or something?" I ask, watching him slip his sneakers on.

He shoots me a proud wink and opens the door. "Or something. Boyfriend doesn't even come close. But I'll take it until I can think of something better. Oh, and wear pants when you walk to work from now on. It's cold out. Good night, my love. Dream of me."

“Good night,” I mutter, holding a hand to my chest as he leaves, shutting the door softly behind him.

I’m in a state of shock as I do as he says. I get ready for bed before crawling under my sheets, falling asleep quicker than I have in weeks, and dreaming of what the future could hold for us. All night long.

3

Sierra

True to his word, Braden shows up at seven thirty with a Christmas-themed Starbucks cup in his hand and a thin coat stretched across his shoulders.

His smile burns bright as he stands on the other side of my door, foot tapping the carpet, oblivious to my peeping. I'm grateful he hasn't noticed that I'm currently peeking at him through the tiny peephole in my door instead of inviting him in and examining him face-to-face. I have no doubt he would tease me for it if he did.

Blowing out a breath, I step back and wipe my sweaty palms down my thighs.

There was a part of me that didn't believe he would actually show up this morning. I mean, it's easy to make promises in the heat of the moment just to realize after a good night's sleep that maybe you shouldn't have.

I don't want to have doubts about his intentions or spend the time preparing myself for the possibility that once he leaves my side, he won't come back, but once trust is broken, the scar left behind never fully fades.

I don't know how long it will take for that trust to grow again, if it ever will.

"Are you going to let me in anytime soon? I don't have a problem with waiting, but your coffee is going to be cold, and I know how much you hate cold coffee," he calls through the door, a hint of amusement in his voice.

My lips tug up at the corners with the knowledge that he remembers something as small as how I like my coffee. Maybe that's ridiculous—okay, it totally is.

"One second!" I flatten the hairs at the top of my head, button up my jacket, and slip my work bag over my shoulder before opening the door.

Braden's presence is commanding and intimidating as it swallows me. The way he carries himself even in unfamiliar territory has always made me jealous. He has the type of aura that you either gravitate toward or get owned by. Depending on the day, I've done both.

Today, it owns me.

"Good morning, gorgeous." He extends the Christmas cup toward me. I grab it eagerly, stepping into the hall and taking a sip of the latte.

"Good morning. I suppose I should be thanking Sophie for making sure you got here on time? It was her that told you when I leave for work every day, right?"

His grin is wicked. "You're not wrong."

I lock the door behind me and raise a brow when I catch Braden's heated stare on my legs.

"You're wearing pants." It's a statement, one full of something dirty and knee locking. I'm proud to have received such a reaction from him. Bringing a man like Braden to his knees over something as small and ridiculous as wearing pants just to appease one of his concerns is enough to make a girl too cocky for her own good.

Snapping my attention to the legs I purposefully covered in fleece-lined leggings, I nod. “It’s cold.” *And you said to wear pants.*

He brings his eyes to mine, and I shiver from the heat flaring in them. My chest rises and falls rapidly, and I squeeze my coffee cup tighter.

Familiar tension crackles and sparks in the air between us. The feeling grabs me by an invisible, silky thread and pulls, attempting with every bit of its strength to make me tumble into him even as I straighten my spine and repeat the word *no* in my head.

Braden steps toward me, and I step back, my back pressing against the door. He places a hand beside my head and leans forward, kissing me softly before pulling back, eyes still closed.

“That’s my good girl.”

My eyes nearly roll back in ecstasy. With legs like Jell-O, I focus on keeping my balance and my heart from fluttering out of my chest. “We need to leave. I can’t be late for work.”

A hint of a smile pulls at his mouth before he’s kissing me a final time, this one hard, possessive, and *final*, leaving my lips buzzing with the feel of him when it’s over.

“Let’s go, then.”

I wait for him to back up, to give me room and air to breathe, but he only watches me with lust-drunk eyes. It’s like he’s trapped in my atmosphere just as much as I am his.

Thankfully, he doesn’t make me beg and steps back after a few more seconds, leaving me with just enough room to slide around him and lead the way to the elevator.

His stare is a brand on my back the entire way to the elevator. It’s not until the doors slide open and we’re caged inside the metal box, side by side, that he looks elsewhere. I don’t torture myself by trying to find what now holds his attention.

"How long have you been in Toronto?" I ask after a few silent heartbeats. My fingers tap the strap of my bag resting on my shoulder as I watch the numbers light up with every floor we pass on our descent.

Without hesitation, he says, "A week."

"A week?" I gulp. "Has everyone known, then? That you've been here?"

I look at him and frown, recognizing the look on his face: contemplation and a flash of fear.

"I asked them not to say anything."

It shouldn't bother me that his arrival was kept a secret, but Sophie should have told me. As my closest friend, she should never keep secrets from me, especially not ones containing info about my . . . ex? Whether he asked her to stay silent or not, it shouldn't matter. She knew how devastated I was. The rejection and self-doubt that I was living with every day.

Betrayal winds in my gut regardless of my inner pleading.

It took every sliver of my self-control not to respond to her calls or texts after Braden left last night, not wanting to give her any sort of false hope or talk about feelings that I couldn't even figure out myself. Now, after finding out that she knew about his surprise arrival all along, I'm glad that I didn't.

If she had lied to me last night, I don't think it would be as easy to forgive her.

"Don't, sweetheart." His voice rips through my head, yanking me from my thoughts. I blink back my hurt and cock a brow. "If you're going to be upset with anyone, be upset with me. Not them, and especially not Sophie."

I square my shoulders, lifting my chin. "You don't get to tell me what to do. Not anymore."

He grimaces but nods in agreement. "You're right. I just want you to know that even though Sophie kept this from you, she's also the reason that I was able to get here so quickly. Without her help, I probably wouldn't have made it here for at least a few months."

"I don't like secrets."

"I'm sorry." Braden swallows thickly, his Adam's apple bobbing.

It looks like he wants to say more, but the opening of the elevator doors has him choosing to drop the conversation. His hand falls to my lower back as he leads me silently through the lobby and into the nipping winter wind.

A shudder moves through me, the surprisingly low temperature chewing through my jacket and brushing my skin. It's not even a second later that a heavy arm drapes across my shoulders and pulls me close to a warm body.

"You need to start driving or taking a cab. It's fucking freezing." It's almost a scolding yet somehow carries a flicker of amusement.

"Are you telling me this jacket isn't warm enough for you?" I bite back my laugh and grab a handful of Braden's thin, army green bomber jacket. "You're dressed for mid-fall Vancouver, not for early winter Toronto."

A flick on the arm makes me squeal.

"Keep it up, little fighter. Keep it up." His voice rumbles, deep and strong.

"Was pulling me close to keep me warm or you?" I flick him back, grinning when he winces. "Or neither?"

I know that I should stop teasing him. Stop playing everything off as back to normal, but it feels too good, too *natural.* It seems almost criminal to stop in hopes of keeping up a rough exterior.

Besides, playing with him is harmless. It's something that we used to do back before it became more than just sex. It doesn't have to mean anything more than what it is.

"What if I said both?" he asks. I lean my head against his bicep and shiver when he places a kiss on my hair.

"I would say that you're pushing your boundaries."

"That so?"

His eyes burn into me from above.

"It just seems like a very . . . boyfriend-y thing to do." Can he hear how fast my heart is beating?

"Yeah, it does," he says confidently, not even a flicker of indecision in that raspy voice of his.

Blushing, I drop my eyes to the sidewalk, watching my feet tap the concrete with every step. Braden's huge feet somehow match my pace. I swallow my laugh.

I wonder how hard he's trying to slow his stride and walk at the speed of my much smaller legs.

Braden clears his throat, and I shove the stupid thought from my head to look up at him. "This is it, right?"

Turning, I realize we've made it to our destination. The towering forty-storey building that now houses the new offices of Brenton and Thompson is, in simple terms: really fucking intimidating.

I remember standing in this exact spot and nearly painting my brand-new pair of open-toed heels in vomit on my first day.

Maybe the intimidation stems from the new territory or from the fact that none of us have yet met the infamous Mackenzie Thompson, the new second half of Brenton and Thompson.

From what I've gathered, Mackenzie was in Vancouver the day the announcement of an expansion was made, having just finished signing all of the legal crap for the joining of companies. He was expected to make an appearance but decided to fly back home instead.

Clark and Mackenzie—according to Gretchen, Mackenzie's receptionist and my newest friend in this still-unfamiliar town—grew up together in Toronto before Clark moved to Vancouver after graduation. Clark built Brenton Marketing while Mack attempted to build Thompson Marketing.

Clearly, one fared better than the other.

I assume that it was Mack's idea for us to expand and merge companies here after he nearly went bankrupt on his own just a few months prior to our merger announcement. Again, office gossip and rumours. I'm not sure that I'll ever know the full story, nor do I really care to.

I'm here for one reason. Experience in a more decorated position that under different management, I may never have gotten this quickly.

As soon as I've spent enough time working under Cole Travis to fill that empty space on my resume, I'm gone.

Hasta la vista, baby.

See you *never*.

"Would you like me to walk you in? Or is that too boyfriend-y for you?"

I snort in the most unflattering way possible but can't find it in me to shy away.

"I can walk by myself," I reply, grinning at the humour twinkling in his eyes before gulping back the majority of my warm coffee.

"Fine. I'll be back at five thirty to walk you home."

My breath clots in my throat when he pulls me into his arms, our chests pressed firmly together and my empty coffee cup mashed between us. Then he claims my mouth in a kiss that should belong solely in the bedroom.

I let my eyelids slide shut and focus on the feeling of his lips on mine, so warm and familiar. They're as addictive and thigh clenching as I remember them to be late at night. When I'm alone, two glasses of wine deep, and can't help but think about him.

Braden draws out a breathy sound from deep in my chest while branding his name on my mouth in an invisible claim that I'll have no choice but to carry with me all day.

His hand slides up my back to cup my nape and tilt my head. The move drips of possessiveness in a way that has my mouth opening for him, as if he just commanded me to allow his tongue to stroke mine. And when it does, he groans, the deep, strained noise shooting like a zap of electricity to my clit.

We separate when the honk of a car horn blares somewhere close by, reminding me that we're in front of my work and, in fact, *not* in the bedroom.

Fuck.

Suddenly deadly aware of what I just let happen—*again*—I push at Braden's chest and stumble backward. "I have to go." The sense of déjà vu is sickening.

I swallow when I meet his stare and see the utter frustration etched in the smooth edges of his face. No doubt my rejection scratches at his pride.

But just as quickly as it appeared, the frustration is gone, replaced by a mask of easy confidence that I recognize quickly. Too quickly.

"Text me if you get finished early. Please don't walk home without me."

Simply knowing that he worries so much about my safety is enough to have me agreeing to just about anything that could come from his mouth, but I don't say that. Knowing Braden, he would hold that against me for as long as possible.

Braden waits for me to acknowledge him with an easy nod before he's gently grabbing my wrist and tugging me back toward him. I don't fight him when he kisses my forehead or lingers a few seconds longer than usual before pulling back and walking back the way we came, hands tucked away in the pockets of that stupid jacket. I watch him, laser focused on the quick stride of his legs until he turns the corner and disappears from view.

Sucking back a few deep breaths, I dump my empty cup in a nearby trash bin and head inside Brenton and Thompson.

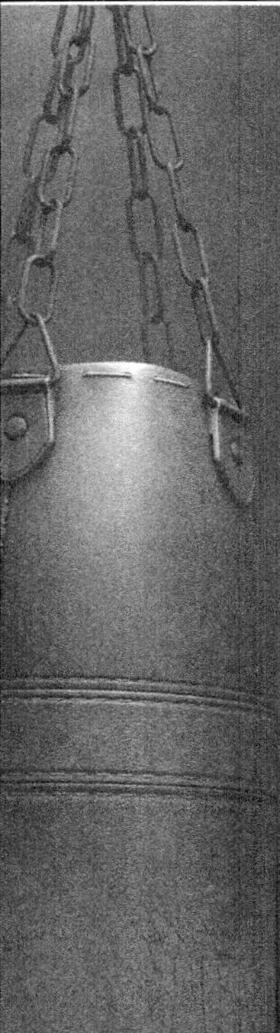

4

Braden

I hate watching Sierra pull away from me—both emotionally and physically.

The realization and regret that filled those big beautiful eyes seconds after we broke apart might as well have been the nails in my fucking coffin.

There's no mistaking who should bear the fault for those walls she's rebuilt around herself, but they still act like a dagger to the gut regardless. I desperately want to go back to how things were before shit hit the fan, but with every conversation we have, I feel the weight of my mistakes heavier than the last. At this rate, it won't be long until I'm crushed beneath it.

My apartment is not much warmer than the air outside as I slam the front door behind me and lock the three separate locks.

Dad hasn't stopped digging into me about my choice of housing—given the sudden influx of zeros in my bank account—but I began viewing anywhere without Sierra a formality a long time ago. Plus, I've been crashing in his new house every night for the past week while it sits empty, waiting for their arrival.

I imagined my first few days here to be lonely and quiet while I got everything figured out, but although it was lonely, it was a far cry from quiet.

The new Lowry boxing gym, while still an empty, nameless shell, has begun to take shape and for the past week has occupied ninety-nine percent of my spare time. With buying a completely empty building in a new construction area, we're starting from scratch, but it'll be worth it, however long it takes.

That doesn't stop me from thinking about how permanent this all feels now, though—owning my own gym in Toronto. All too quickly, I have something else tethering me to this city. Something that I won't be able to just up and leave behind, regardless of what the future holds.

Sierra was the reason I came here, the reason I pushed myself so far out of my comfort zone that I couldn't climb back in no matter how hard I tried. But it's quickly become deeper than that. I can only hope that when I show her how serious I am and that I'm not going anywhere regardless of if she forgives me, that that damn armor of hers will slide off her shoulders and bare her to me again.

There is no going back for me. I just have to convince her of that.

My phone sings in my pocket, drawing me out of my head. I cringe when I realize that I've been standing by the front door in my snow-soaked jacket and shoes that began making awkward squelching sounds on the way home.

Kicking off my sneakers, I shrug out of my jacket and answer the phone, tucking it between my shoulder and ear. "Hey."

"Please tell me that you've gotten back in Sierra's good

graces because her demon twin is going to be the reason I become a liquor store regular."

I sputter a laugh at Clayton's venomous words. "Sophie is not that bad."

"Not that bad?" he echoes incredulously. "She broke into my car and dumped glitter all over the seats, Braden. It's been a week and I'm still picking glitter off my pants every time I get out. How old is she? Twelve?"

"You spied on her date with that Jarod guy and then told him that she had genital herpes."

"I didn't spy on them. I was picking up food for my mother."

"At a Thai restaurant? Your mom hates Thai food. She told me it gives her heartburn."

He's silent for a few seconds before he grunts, "It doesn't even matter. Point is, I need her to leave me alone, and until you fix your relationship, I'm stuck with her coming around, bugging me for updates. Actually, why don't you just text her yourself? Last time I checked, I wasn't a messenger pigeon."

I fight the urge to tell him that I do, in fact, text Sophie updates and have been for the past few weeks because I don't want to fall in the middle of whatever game these two are playing.

If I didn't know better, I would have started to think that they were into each other.

"I'll text her later," I choose to say instead. My breath escapes in a *whoosh* when I flop down on the cheap couch I found on Kijiji.

"Thanks. But really, how is it going? Did she kick you in the balls?"

I scoff. "No. She didn't."

"But?"

"But it's going to take time. Like I told you it would before

I left. Sierra is almost as stubborn as I am. I told her that I wanted a real relationship, and I saw how that affected her. She wants it too, but she's hurt. *I* hurt her."

"I'm surprised she even let you speak. I owe Sophie twenty bucks."

"You bet against me?" I gasp, although I feel anything but surprised by that.

Clayton abandoned me to join Team Sierra after the whole club fiasco, alongside pretty much everybody else I know. Their side swap didn't hurt me in the slightest, but it did make asking for help a bit harder. Clay was the easiest to convince, though, considering I was offering him something he wasn't expecting.

The entire apartment to himself.

"Technically, I suppose," he replies. Something clunks around in the background, sounding like somebody banging pots together.

"If I was a lesser man, I would be offended by your betrayal."

Clayton laughs loudly. "If you were a lesser man, I would have bet more than twenty bucks."

"Careful, you'll make me swoon." My eyes fall shut as I rest my head against the back of the couch.

The moving boxes that I know are still lined up along the walls of the living room make the place feel almost claustrophobic. It's usually stuffy on a good day, but my skin almost feels slick with sweat as I sit here.

I need to go work out, maybe run a few miles to burn off some energy before I combust and destroy the place. I've fallen off my training with everything going on, and while it doesn't look like it, I'm definitely beginning to feel it. I'm embarrassed to admit that I got winded after running up the stairs the other day. Dad would never let me hear the end of it if he found out about that.

There's a loud bang that shakes through the call. It has me pulling the phone from my ear and wincing. Clay's shouts follow close after, the octave they hit surprising me.

His next words are rushed. "I gotta go. Keep me updated, and text Sophie. Stay positive."

The call ends before I can reply, so I throw my phone down on the cushion beside me. Groaning, I run a hand through my hair, slightly pulling on the ends before standing.

I know full well that I won't be staying here tonight, so I spend the next few minutes collecting another few days' worth of clothes from packed boxes and shoving them in my duffel bag. After the bag is full enough that the zipper barely holds together, I sling it over my shoulder and head back out into the cold.

Growling under my breath at the cold, I make a promise to myself to buy a fucking winter parka and slide inside the first cab that I can find.

5

Sierra

Toronto is a gorgeous city. More so after the sun has set and the buildings light up the dark like stars do the night sky. My heart skips a beat each time I see the skyline—an unfortunately rare occurrence—and the bright streaks of colours that reflect off the water like melted crayons on a black canvas.

While I know how to appreciate it, art was never my strong suit. It still isn't. Not in the generic sense.

I was never creative enough to create something beautiful out of lead and paper or paint and a blank canvas. I remember the art projects we used to do in school and how I dreaded every single one of them.

My silhouettes looked like blobs, my landscapes wince-worthy at best. I didn't have a real passion for anything back then, but I knew art was a definite no go.

The only thing I gave a shit about back then was the sometimes overwhelming need to get the hell out of Parkridge High and the plan to use the next four years at Vancouver University as a reason to piss off my parents, even if the thought of marketing classes had dread hovering over me like a dark storm cloud preparing to piss rain.

Imagine my surprise when I began to enjoy the marketing classes I took each day enough to look forward to them every day. It wasn't exactly the art that I thought I *should* love, but art nonetheless.

Suddenly, I was coming up with themed advertisement ideas and logo designs that filled countless notebooks to the point half my minuscule paychecks from my part-time job at a local college coffee shop went toward new ones.

As my grades rose, my enthusiasm skyrocketed. By the time four years had passed, I was attending interviews with a dozen firms willing to give me even five minutes of their time. More than half of them were just being nice, I realized later on, but by then, I had already accepted the job working for Julia Stroll. The woman I thought would help me reach my potential, but instead ripped my confidence to shreds before feeding it to her stupid little dog that she brought to work with her every day.

I was naive when I worked for Julia, and even more so when I started with Clark and that man whore Cole.

Some days, I don't know what would have been worse: staying to work with Julia and being treated like a rabid dog or working with Cole and being treated like a piece of property that he can't wait for the sale to go through on.

"Knock knock, baby doll. I brought lunch," Gretchen says from the doorway to my office, her thick curls a vibrant shade of red.

Her mossy-green eyes hold a heavy sense of calm that settles me the moment I look her way. She reminds me of home in ways that have helped tremendously during this move. It's almost like Clare is here with me.

I close my laptop and grin. The white takeout bag from our favourite sub shop rests at her side.

"Meatball?" My stomach growls audibly.

"With green peppers and extra mozzarella."

Slim fingers wrap around the back of one of the plush grey chairs in front of my desk as she pulls it back and sits down. A white-wrapped sub is placed in front of me alongside a bottle of Pepsi, and my mouth waters instantly at the smell of food.

"Mack let you go for lunch early today? I thought he was still being a massive alphahole," I mumble, tearing through the wrapping of my sub before taking a massive bite. The moan that escapes me would usually embarrass me, but for some reason, nothing I do around Gretchen makes me feel embarrassed or weird.

She rolls her eyes at the topic of her boss. "His mother came by and stole him for the afternoon. I made the executive decision to take an early, long lunch break as a reward for entertaining her until he finished up a meeting. If he has a problem with it, he can take it up with me later."

I shake my head, smiling at her confidence. If anyone can grip the balls of a man who believes he's larger than life, it's Gretch. Although, I'm sure it helps that she's actually held Mack Thompson's balls in her hands before, but that's a story she doesn't like retelling unless she's wine drunk.

"He's lucky to have you. You deserve a lot more than a long lunch break considering everything you do for him," I say honestly.

Gretchen snorts. "You're right. Maybe one day he'll realize that."

"Maybe he does and he's just picking on you like schoolboys do to the girls they like," I tease.

"Then he's got another thing coming because that shit has never ever worked." She takes a bite of her sandwich, glowering at me from over the top of the bread.

"I would say to tell him that, but it's probably safer if you don't say anything. Knowing you, you'll end up handing him his ass, and I can't risk you getting yourself fired. There's no way I could deal with Cole without having you to vent to afterward."

"That's because Cole Travis is a pig, Sierra. If you went to HR, you could probably get him fired. I would go with you if you wanted."

The food in my stomach turns to lead as I set my sub down on the wrapper and take a large gulp of my drink, desperate to wash away the spoiled taste in my mouth.

The reminder of Cole's hands on my ass, gripping and pulling at it like it was his to touch, makes everything I've eaten today threaten to come back up as I pale and exhale shakily. "You don't really think that they would believe me over him. It would only make things worse."

The frown on Gretchen's face is prominent as the sad reality of how the world works sets in. "We won't let him get away with how he's treating you, Sierra. I promise."

I don't want to talk about it anymore, so I nod in agreement. The bile burns in my throat as the smell of food continues wafting around me. With sweaty hands, I push my office chair away from my desk and stand on wobbly legs.

Gretchen is following suit before I have a chance to excuse myself from the room like I planned to, saying, "Let it out now, and then lock that shit right back up. Don't let him see that he has any effect on you."

Arms wrap around me, and the smell of greasy meatballs is replaced with eucalyptus and mint. My stomach settles slightly, and I allow Gretchen to hold me tight, to become my shield from the world for just a few moments.

"I saw Braden outside this morning," she whispers, tightening her grip on my shoulders briefly before pulling back and running her hands down my arms. "When did he get here?"

I swipe away a stray tear and take a step back, steadying myself. She must have recognized him from the pictures she saw on my phone. Yes, the ones I couldn't bring myself to delete. What can I say? I'm a glutton for punishment.

Her sudden interest doesn't sneak by me, however. She's far too clever.

"Don't even think about it, Gretch. He can't find out."

The idea of Braden finding out about Cole's behaviour since I arrived in Toronto is enough to strike fear deep in my bones. But it's not fear for myself or for Braden. It's fear for Cole.

There is not a sliver of doubt in my mind as to how Braden would take care of him. It would be cruel, painful, and *bloody*. The worst part is that if it came down to it, I would stand back and let him do whatever he saw fit to that asshole. That's why I can't give him the chance in the first place.

"How long is he here for?" she asks after a long pause.

"He said for good."

Her eyes bulge almost comically. "Oh, wow."

"I know. I was up all night replaying our conversation. When he showed up at my apartment this morning to walk me to work, it really threw me for a loop. He told me he was going to be there, but a part of me didn't believe that he would actually show up." That's an understatement, and the bags under my eyes would agree.

"That's a good sign, right?" she asks. I nod, and she blows out a dramatic breath and wiggles her brows. "The pictures didn't do him *any* justice, by the way. How do you plan on staying strong when the guy wanting back in your bed looks like that? I couldn't do it. I would let that man break my back right in half and thank him afterwards."

A smile breaks out on my face as I throw my head back and laugh. "I actually *did* try to get him in my bed. But in my defense, I've been so damn horny lately, and Braden has some weird juju claim on my vag that makes it nearly *impossible* not to want to jump his bones."

"Juju claim?" she sputters, looking like I just called myself the queen of fucking England before pouting and adding, "I'm jealous. I want a man to own me like that."

"It's not exactly ideal when falling into bed so quickly is exactly how we started and ended up in this mess in the first place. We need a new beginning. Even *he* wants to start fresh. Do this the right way, you know?"

She stares at me sympathetically but not in a way that makes me feel pitied.

Gretchen doesn't know everything that happened between Braden and me, but she knows the most important parts. She was the one rubbing my back and sliding scoops of ice cream in my mouth while I sobbed over the loss of someone who I was never even able to fully claim as mine.

"Then that's what you do," she says, ever so confident in me. "No more screwing that god of a man until at *least* the third date."

Third date? I can do that. That's how normal people date, right? Shit, I don't even remember how to date.

I've gotten over my initial surprise of him turning me away last night and have quickly sunk into a small pit of embarrassment when I think back on it.

I couldn't have done anything more desperate than practically climbing him like a tree before we had even managed to have a decent conversation about the future. But I was just so happy to see him, so overtaken with the need to be close to him again, to touch and feel him, to think of anything but doing just that.

He was right to stop us when he did. Everything he said about starting over and doing this the proper way was exactly what we should do. Regardless of what happened before I left, I can't pretend that my feelings aren't there, that I'm not head over heels in love with him when I so obviously am.

We didn't do things right the first time. We were both too stubborn and jaded about the idea of love and relationships that by the time we both got there, it became too much too soon. For Braden especially.

I don't know exactly what it was that seemed to pull Braden from that noncommittal fog of his, but I plan on finding out. I plan on learning *everything*.

We have a second chance here, something so many people don't get. And I plan on doing right by it.

I owe it to myself to at least try.

Who knows what I might be giving up if I don't.

6

Braden

I STRETCH OUT MY FINGERS IN THE POCKETS OF MY new jacket as I wait for Sierra to finish work. It's just after 5:00 p.m., but with how dark it is, it feels way later.

The whole Christmas vibe going on downtown is eye-catching, I'll give it that. With the yellow lights wrapped around the lampposts, freshly fallen snow, and wreaths hung on seemingly every business' door, it looks like the setting of a Hallmark movie.

Christmas was never a huge event when I was younger. Mom became a modern-day Scrooge after the divorce, forcing us to spend Christmas eating pasta at Antonio's restaurant like any other day, while Dad was too emotionally closed off to offer me much more than a brief "Merry Christmas" and a bowl of bland oatmeal.

And while it's still a little over two weeks away, I want to know what Sierra does to celebrate. Was it a big deal for her as a child? Does she have any traditions that she's held on to over the years? We're here together now, and there's a giant piece of me that wants to spend the holidays stuck to her side like a damn leech.

Lana and Dad won't be here until a few days before Christmas, but I know that my new "mommy" will want to do something to celebrate her first major holiday as an official member of the Lowry family. I just have to cross my fingers and hope that Sierra will join me and save me from a few hours of Lana-induced torture.

I hear Sierra's laugh before I see her. She's the first through the door, jacket hugging her body like a glove, that fucking gorgeous smile of hers beaming right at me. I ache to have her in my arms and have to fight to stay where I am on the sidewalk so that I don't up and steal her away.

Her eyes, so warm and gentle, are locked on mine as she lifts a hand and waves almost shyly. I'm no longer surprised to find myself missing her whenever we're not together. It's become like second nature to me, and I don't hate it either.

It isn't until the person beside her waves a hand in her face that she looks away from me, shaking her head and saying what I can only assume to be an apology. The woman beside her has flaming orange hair that's whipping furiously in her face as the wind picks up. She's small in size, almost elf-like. I could easily bench-press her without breaking a sweat.

Both of them turn to me then, and Sierra's small friend eyes me threateningly yet carefully, like a predator does its prey. It's like she's assessing me, learning the best form of attack to cripple me in one go. I feel a sense of approval toward her, knowing that she's protective of my girl. That she's looking out for her when I'm not around.

They both head my way soon after, their cheeks already pink from the cold.

"If it isn't the infamous Braden Lowry," the redhead says,

crossing her arms and pinning me with a glare. "I have to admit you're shorter than I expected."

Well, that's a blatant lie. I cock a brow. "Sorry to disappoint. I'll try better next time."

I feel Sierra's warmth against my side and wrap my arm around her, pulling her as close as possible. I grin when she doesn't fight me on it but relaxes against me instead, like being held in my arms is exactly where she wants to be.

Fuck, that makes me happier than it probably should.

"Braden, this is Gretchen. Gretchen, Braden," Sierra introduces us with a wave of her hand and a stern look shot at her friend, almost like a warning.

"Gretchen," I echo, biting back a snort. "Like from Mean Gi—"

"If you say *Mean Girls*, I will cut you," Gretchen cuts me off, her words like a whip. I blink a few times, too stunned to speak.

Sierra steps closer and places a hand on my chest, laughing under her breath. I look down, sucking in a breath when I find her already staring at me. Her eyes are my favourite shade of melted silver. The intensity in her stare hits me low in the stomach.

"You got a new jacket," she states on a breath, fiddling with the bottom hem. Her fingers have always been slim and dainty, but for some reason, it's more noticeable to me now.

My attention becomes laser focused on the slight shake of her hands and how red they've gotten from the cold. I immediately grab her hands in mine and bring them to my chest, brushing her knuckles with my thumbs. "I did."

She swallows. "It looks good."

I smile at the compliment. "Thank you, beautiful."

Gretchen's snort reminds me that she's still here.

"Ready to go?" I ask Sierra, tucking a piece of her unruly

brown hair behind her ear. "You're already freezing, and we still have to walk."

As if she's just remembering the time and place, her eyes widen slightly, and she nods, turning to her friend and wishing her a quick goodbye before I do the same.

Once we're alone again, I tuck one of her hands into her coat pocket, keeping the other linked with mine and sliding them into my pocket. I set a mental reminder to bring her gloves tomorrow morning.

We walk for a few minutes in comfortable silence, both of us trapped inside a web of our own thoughts. It doesn't last for long, though. Mostly because I don't want to waste my time with her not speaking.

"How was work?" I ask, immediately cringing at how fucking lame I am.

Thankfully, Sierra doesn't seem to mind because she replies without hesitation.

"Frustrating. One of our newer clients is refusing to raise their advertisement budget regardless of how many times I tell them that what they're offering isn't enough to get them anything better than a bus stop ad in a low-density residential area." The last sentence comes out in a grumble that has me fighting back a smile.

"What is the product?"

"Pine-tree-scented men's soap."

I can't hold back my laugh before it escapes me, loud enough that it draws attention from the people around us. "You're shitting me."

Sierra's annoyance is gone just as quickly as it appeared as she says in a voice far too deep, "Are you ready to find your inner lumberjack?"

Fucking brutal.

My chest shakes as I pull my hand from her and maneuver

us around a group of men. Throwing my arm over her shoulder, I pull Sierra closer. "Was that slogan your idea?" I already know that there's no way in hell she came up with that lame-ass jingle, but I won't miss a chance to poke at her.

Sierra plays along. There's no way that she doesn't know what I'm doing.

"What if it was?" she throws back with ease, peeking up at me through long, snow-coated lashes. A lump gathers in my throat, and everything dims around her.

I wait for a halo to appear above her head and wings to spread at her back.

Sierra is an angel made of everything pure and fucking holy, and I'm more than ready to finally get down on my knees and worship her.

My next words come out with enough sincerity to shock me.

"Then I've never heard anything better in my entire goddamn life."

Sierra

My breath catches at the way Braden looks at me. Like I'm the most precious thing in the world to him. It should hurt —how deeply he's dug himself beneath my skin—but all there is is a searing bliss that I can't seem to get enough of. He managed to get deep enough to wrap himself around my soul and brand his name on it, and I wouldn't have it any other way.

As quickly as someone taking a hammer to a brick wall, I

crumble beneath the love I see bleeding from his stare. Love for me and what I hope he imagines our future could hold.

"Then you'd be a liar," I tease lightly, grabbing his side when a shoulder knocks mine on the crowded sidewalk and I stumble slightly.

His hold on me becomes stronger, like an anchor. "Meh, it would be worth it. At least you'd be happy."

The heaviness of those words hits me harder than I expected. I hide my blush behind the collar of my jacket. "Stop saying stuff like that."

"Why?"

I know that he's looking at me. His curiosity is a heavy weight between us. I look straight ahead and say as calmly as I can manage, "Because you're making me want to skip the first three dates and invite you upstairs."

A giddy laugh escapes me when he scoops me up and takes off down the pavement. I bury my face in his shoulder to keep the wind away while he laughs, the rough sound of it making me shiver.

"What are you doing?" I shriek.

"What does it look like? I'm taking you home, my little fighter."

7

Sierra

My giggle can be heard for miles as Braden fumbles with my keys, trying to unlock the door to my apartment. I don't tell him that sometimes it gets sticky and you have to jiggle the key at a certain angle to get it to work because watching him get flustered is far too entertaining and rare of a chance to pass up.

"Stop laughing at me and help," he grumbles, attempting to sound annoyed with me but failing miserably. I couldn't pretend not to notice that smile on his face, even if it wasn't one of the most beautiful things in existence.

I palm his jaw—the rough stubble bringing back memories that make me rub my thighs together—and force him to look at me. His lips part, nostrils flaring, and I know that he can see the heat in my eyes and flush on my cheeks. "Hurry."

Half expecting him to set me down on my own two feet so that he can concentrate, I'm surprised when his grip only tightens as a new look of concentration washes over him. It's only a few heartbeats later that my door flings open and he walks us inside.

I vaguely hear the door shut behind us before I'm on my feet and pressed against a wall, gasping. My eyes zero in on Braden, on his intimidating presence that has wetness pooling in my panties and eyes so dark with his want for me that I subconsciously lick my lips in a silent invitation.

He watches my tongue slip back inside my mouth and groans so deep that I feel the vibrations of it in my stomach.

I want him closer, pressed against me so that I can feel his heartbeat. Has his chest ached like mine? Did his heart break like mine did?

"Every single day without you was torture," he admits, his words like gravel.

My breaths are shaky, weak. I'm aware of the way my palms are pressed to the wall when they become slick with sweat. Braden takes a step toward me, followed by another, and another, until his warmth wraps around me like tendrils of smoke.

Fingers brush my cheekbones, and I arch my back, desperate to feel more of him as he murmurs, "So beautiful."

With shaky fingers, I unzip his jacket and slowly push it off his shoulders, feeling Braden's stare like a brand on my skin. When the jacket drops to the floor, neither one of us makes a move to pick it up.

Braden simply moves it aside with his foot and closes in on me, so close that I can't help but look up and meet his soft, unwavering stare. I swallow the emotions bubbling up before they overwhelm me.

His fingers drag from my cheek to the pulse thumping in my throat. They dance over the smooth skin before dipping lower to the collar of my jacket. Braden toys with the lining for far too long, almost like he likes the way I'm growing more and more anxious too much to stop.

Just as I'm about to say something, he's unbuttoning my

coat with a surprising swiftness before sliding it down my shoulders and tossing it away. I'm left in my peach blouse and these damn fleece leggings that I put back on in exchange for my pencil skirt before leaving work.

He pinches the silky material of my blouse with a reluctant sigh before saying, "I'm sorry."

I don't have a chance to ask what he's apologizing for before he tears it open, the buttons scattering along the floor. *Holy shit.* Need rages inside of me like rough, windy waters as I grab him by the front of his shirt and pull him toward me, close enough that I can kiss his waiting lips.

He doesn't waste any time before responding, kissing me back roughly, so desperately that my knees shake, seconds away from giving out completely. Like he already knows, Braden grabs me by the back of my thighs and lifts me. I tighten my legs around his hips and cry into his mouth when he thrusts his erection between them.

"Do that again," I gasp, running my hands all over him, taking my fill. Taking and taking and taking. He presses against me harder this time, sending my eyes rolling back at the friction.

The ache between my legs is all-consuming. I'm hyper-aware of my breasts in my bra, how my nipples swell and harden, scraping against the material. I feel like a starving animal, and Braden is my next meal.

"*Fuck*. Look at you," he says while leaning down and nipping at my throat before soothing the sting with his hot tongue. "You're soaking, aren't you, baby? Does your pussy ache for me?"

There's no point in lying. I'm too far gone for that. Nodding frantically, I whimper, "Touch me. Please."

Cold air nips my back as he pulls back and moves us around before dropping me on the couch. I sit there in front of him, my sore lips puffed and eager and my chest rising and falling rapidly as he watches me with a look of pure savage hunger.

My head hits the back of the couch as I wait. Each second that passes by is pure and utter agony. Thankfully, he doesn't wait long before dropping to his knees in front of me and taking hold of my thighs in large, warm hands, kneading the skin and muscles with powerful fingers.

Suddenly, I realize that in these moments, when all of Braden's walls are down and he's baring himself to me completely—jaded soul, wild heart, and all—I fall even deeper in love with him. So much so that I know without a doubt that I would do anything *for* him and anything *with* him, by his side.

The sharp edges that protect that mushy, warm centre of his don't scare me anymore. Not when I know that he won't allow them to touch me.

It's times like this when I'm reminded of the way he keeps himself hidden from others. Right now, I see the side of him that would rather cut himself open and bleed himself dry just so the person he loved could see that giant heart of his without risking them so much as pricking themselves on his serrated exterior.

The weight that I've been carrying on my chest evaporates, taking with it the fog in my mind. There's a rattling behind my rib cage as my heart acts like a bird trying to take flight. I suck in a confident breath and speak without hesitation.

"I want to do this. Us. I don't want to waste any more time," I say frantically. His surprise is written all over his face, but I don't let it affect me or keep me from saying what I need to. "I know that we did this backwards, and that as much as we both want it to, it might not work out anyway. But I also know that I love you. And I don't want to throw what could be our only remaining chance away because of hurt feelings and a messy past."

My cheeks are on fire by the time I finish baring my heart to him. I'm too aware of Braden's firm grip on my thighs and the way he hasn't so much as blinked since I began speaking. The weight of his reaction—or lack thereof—is hung above my head by a thin wire just waiting to be cut loose and crush me to a pulp.

He must finally register the alarm on my face because he pulls his hands away from my thighs and places them on my cheeks instead, leaning into me with a look of complete bliss.

His eyes search mine, for what I'm not sure, but when his face fills with my favourite dimpled grin, I know that he's found whatever he was looking for.

"I'm so fucking happy to hear that, Sierra. But now I really, really need to kiss you."

"Kiss me, then, Braden," I whisper.

He does without hesitation. His mouth takes mine in a kiss so powerful I feel it as an ache in my bones. I wind my fingers in his hair and attempt to pull him closer, to take back some of the power I can feel him stealing from me, but he nips at my bottom lip in response, like a punishment.

I break our kiss with a near painful gasp when his fingers brush my hardened nipple through my bra. The sensation is heightened tenfold by how turned on I've been the past few minutes, and I wonder if I could come like this, with nothing more than his fingers brushing my nipples. By the state of my underwear, I'm not sure if I'm willing to rule out that possibility yet.

He discards my shirt and pulls my breasts free from my bra. The peaks of my chest tighten and swell under his stare before he's pinching the left one. I whimper his name, my head falling back again.

"I won't let you leave again, baby," Braden groans, the words heavy with lust and a promise that doesn't slip past me. He twists and pulls my nipple between his thumb and forefinger. "I couldn't let you go again even if I tried. You're fucking mine."

Nodding, I arch into him, desperately trying to get more contact. My brain is short-circuiting, and every fuse inside of me blows, leaving me desperate for more.

"I still have some apologizing to do."

I hear the words but don't register them, too far gone to even begin trying to understand. My head shakes furiously, though, as if it knows what to do all on its own. "No."

"Yes." He presses his face in my neck and kisses my flushed skin, inhaling deeply before leaning back and sucking my nipple into his mouth. My fingers find purchase in his hair, scratching at his scalp when his teeth close around the sensitive flesh and bite down just hard enough for me to feel the throbbing increase between my legs.

My nipple is wet when he releases it with an audible *pop* before nipping at the other one, making my toes curl.

"Braden." The word is nothing short of a plea for more. More friction, more of the feeling flaming inside of me.

His hands fall to my thighs again before he pushes them apart. "I'm going to make it up to you, my little fighter. But first"—he slides his fingers under the waistband of my leggings before yanking them down swiftly—"I need you to come on my tongue."

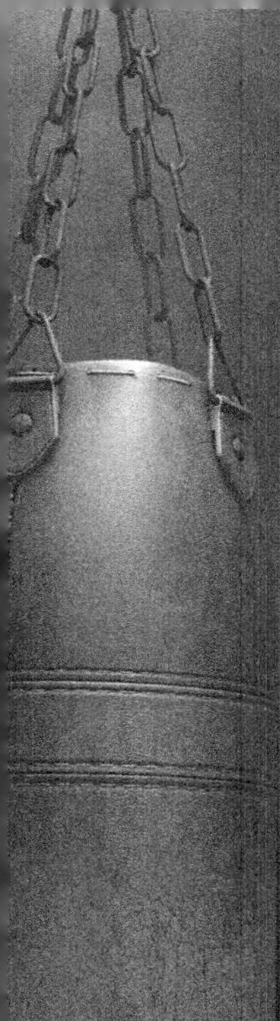

8

Braden

Sierra's muscles quiver beneath my fingertips. They actually quiver, and fuck if that doesn't make my already aching cock throb and push against the zipper of my jeans. I can feel the wetness collecting on the tip, wetting my underwear, and it only makes me want to yank it free of its restraints that much more.

My dirty words have her whimpering and grabbing at me like I'm a tall glass of water she's finally found after being stuck in the desert for days. I love it when she gets like this. All wild eyes, flushed cheeks, and no inhibitions. Like she's completely let go and has handed over control of her mind, body, and soul to me and me alone.

Swallowing a possessive growl, I remove her leggings from around her ankles, dropping them beside me. I squeeze her thighs one final squeeze before trailing my hands upward, stopping just before my fingers make contact with her panties.

Biting down on my tongue, I stare in absolute awe at the simple white underwear and how they've become so wet they stick to her pussy, exposing how swollen and ready she is for me.

"Just like I thought. You're soaked," I say breathlessly, my voice thick with desire.

Sierra nods again, like that's the only thing she's capable of. She's too turned on and lost in the feelings that we undoubtedly share to even attempt to speak.

I swipe a finger along her slit and unleash the groan that I've been trapping down when my finger meets the slick material. She shivers, sucking in a sharp breath when I tug her panties to the side and expose her glistening pink pussy.

My dick is so hard it physically hurts as I take my fill of her, but I don't make any move to touch myself and alleviate the pain. In all honesty, I deserve it. I deserve a lot worse.

Right now, this is all for her. I wanted to worship her, and now I have my chance.

Already on my knees, I lean further between her legs and spread her with two fingers. A string of curses slips from my mouth before I press my tongue flat against her heat, slipping it between her folds and circling her entrance. She bucks her hips at the sudden intrusion, gasping a string of breathy words that I can't understand.

I raise my eyes to watch her, expecting to find her staring up at the ceiling in bliss, but find her staring at me instead, eyes burning so bright that I feel their heat licking my skin. The urge to take a picture of her so that I can have this image with me whenever I please beats at my chest, but I shove it aside and slide a finger inside of her instead.

"Braden," Sierra chokes, gripping my hair and arching into me again, stronger this time. I press a hand on her hips and hold her still. "Please."

"I know, baby. Just a little longer. I haven't had my fill yet."

Her clit must be throbbing horribly by now, with how I've

been ignoring its presence, licking and sucking everywhere else, knowing that she'll come the moment I touch it. She's on the edge already from all of the teasing earlier, so I know that it won't take much more to set her off. But I want to delay her orgasm as long as possible. It'll make it that much more explosive, that much more *memorable*. Maybe that makes me selfish, but I don't give a fuck.

I trace circles around her swollen clit with my tongue, continuing to tease her. My face is soaked in her arousal as I replace my finger with my tongue, fucking her with it. I use my wet finger to continue circling her swollen bud at a quick pace.

Her grip on my hair becomes painful, letting me know that she's close.

"I need you to come for me now, Sierra." I'm sucking her clit between my lips and shoving two fingers inside of her as soon as the words hit the air. Her walls grip me like a fucking vise, and her clit begins to throb as she cries out for me.

"Braden. I'm coming! Oh my God, *Braden*." Her legs tense and lift from the couch. I remove my hand from her hips, letting her press up against my mouth.

"That's it," I hum in approval, lapping at her entrance and revelling in the way she quivers around my tongue.

Sierra rides her orgasm beautifully for a few seconds before her legs fall limp and the fingers in my hair relax, leaving behind a dull ache. There's the slight sheen of sweat on her forehead that makes her hair stick to her flushed skin, and her bare chest rises and falls at a speed that at any other time would have had me worrying.

She looks well and truly sated.

"Are you okay?" I ask, fighting back a grin as I sit back on my heels and use the bottom of my shirt to dry my face.

A flicker of amusement passes across her face as she wipes

the hair from her forehead and exhales slowly, nodding once. "More than."

I nearly beat at my chest like a fucking gorilla but opt for a crazy grin instead.

She must notice my confidence rising because in Sierra-like fashion, she half-heartedly scolds me in an attempt to keep my head from inflating too much.

"You're ridiculous."

"That I am, little fighter. You should have hidden while you had the chance."

She contemplates my words for a few seconds, like I've just spoken some riddle that I want her to solve. Her brows furrow as she asks, "Would that have stopped you? If you didn't know where I was?"

I don't have to think about it.

"No. I wouldn't have stopped looking until I found you." I'm moving closer and holding her face in my hands now, my thumbs brushing across her lips. "I might have gone crazy, though. Depending on how long it took me to find you."

Molten silver eyes blink back at me, eyelashes sweeping across the skin beneath them that hints at several sleepless nights. A sharp pain grows behind my ribs at the knowledge that she hasn't been sleeping. I wonder how long it's been since she's had a good night's sleep. For me, it's been weeks.

Those same eyes travel across my face, searching for something. The possibility that I'm lying, maybe. Whatever it was, she doesn't seem to find it.

"As opposed to what? How crazy you already are?"

I shrug. "Crazy for you, yeah."

Her mouth falls open, a loud laugh falling between us as she shakes her head and pushes at my shoulders. I take the hint and pull away from her again, even as every fiber of my being scolds me for it. She reaches down to fix her underwear.

"What are you? A teenage boy?"

I smirk. "Fuck, I sure hope not."

Her lips twist to form a scowl, and she gestures for me to get up. "We need to work on your after-sex talk."

"If I remember correctly, you were the one who insulted *me*."

Holding out my hands, I help her off the couch.

"Somebody has to keep you grounded," she states like it's common knowledge.

When she tries to pull her hands free, I tighten my grip on them, not ready to let her go just yet. The minute that I do, it'll sink in that I need to go home. That I need to leave her here alone. A muscle ticks in my jaw, and before I can hide it, Sierra's kissing me.

The kiss surprises me so much that I don't respond for a few seconds. She threads our fingers together and squeezes, finally drawing a response from me. I pull our joined hands so that they rest against my chest and kiss her back, trying to shove my thoughts toward her as if our minds are connected by an invisible thread.

Her touch calms me, my frustration slipping away. I want to wrap myself in this feeling, want to curl up in her arms and stay there forever. But that's not taking it slow.

She might have agreed to give me a second chance and to do this over again, but that doesn't mean that she's ready for everything that I'm ready for. We need to move at her pace, and I plan on respecting that.

Gently pulling away, I let go of her hands and tuck her hair behind her ear. "I should go."

"Okay," she whispers, watching me with a sadness that acts like a dagger between my ribs.

"I'll be back in the morning. Please try and get some sleep."

I sweep my thumb beneath her eye, on the blue-tinted skin. "Call me if you need me."

She nods, swallowing so hard her throat bobs.

"I mean it," I push. "Doesn't matter how late it is."

"Are you okay?" she asks cautiously. Sierra knows me better than she probably thinks she does. I used to see that as a threat, but now I recognize it as a blessing. She understands me completely. There's no reason to hide anything from her.

"I don't like leaving you. Not normally, and sure as shit not somewhere I'm not familiar with. Call me overprotective or whatever you want, but it's true. Toronto is new territory for me. I'm going to start worrying about you as soon as I walk out that door just like I have been since the minute I left you in that stupid fucking club." The words come out in a rush. My cheeks burn. I'm fucking embarrassed.

Sierra's eyes soften instantly. "I'll call you if I need you. I promise. Plus, my building is incredibly safe. You really don't need to worry so much."

I roll my eyes and pull her in for a hug. "Tomorrow morning. Check the temperature before getting dressed, would you? Or should I take a cab here instead?"

"I'll let you know." Her laugh vibrates along my skin, permanently marking itself along my body like a damn tattoo.

It's not long after we pull apart that I'm kissing her goodbye and walking back out the front door. A familiar sense of excitement—like the one I get before every fight—dances in my stomach, buzzing in my ears like a swarm of angry bees when I think about seeing her tomorrow.

The last thought that I have before I leave is that I never want this feeling to go away.

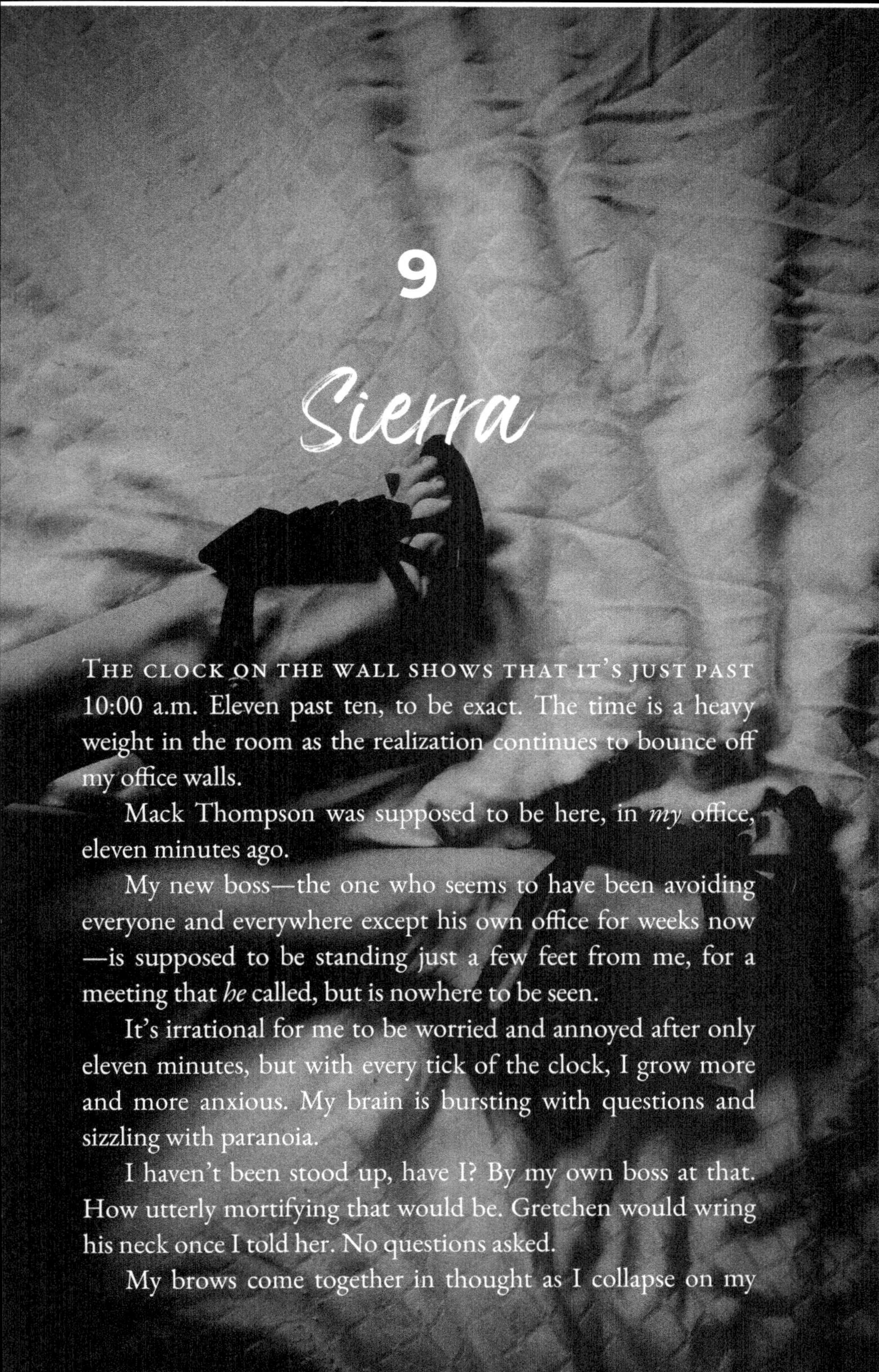

9

Sierra

The clock on the wall shows that it's just past 10:00 a.m. Eleven past ten, to be exact. The time is a heavy weight in the room as the realization continues to bounce off my office walls.

Mack Thompson was supposed to be here, in *my* office, eleven minutes ago.

My new boss—the one who seems to have been avoiding everyone and everywhere except his own office for weeks now—is supposed to be standing just a few feet from me, for a meeting that *he* called, but is nowhere to be seen.

It's irrational for me to be worried and annoyed after only eleven minutes, but with every tick of the clock, I grow more and more anxious. My brain is bursting with questions and sizzling with paranoia.

I haven't been stood up, have I? By my own boss at that. How utterly mortifying that would be. Gretchen would wring his neck once I told her. No questions asked.

My brows come together in thought as I collapse on my

fancy leather chair. Dropping my elbows on the desk in front of me, I shut my eyes and groan.

There's no way Gretch would have worked for Mr. Thompson for so long if he was a complete and total asshole. She might act as if she can't stand him, but I think that has more to do with their unresolved sexual history than his behaviour at the workplace.

If she truly thought he was that bad, she would have jumped ship the minute Mackenzie Thompson's firm tanked, not stuck around to see if there was a chance to save it.

A small sound of surprise escapes me when a rough chuckle echoes through my office. My attention snaps to the owner of such a gruff laugh—one that sounds as if it hasn't seen life in years—while I slide my sweaty palms down my navy blue dress pants and rush to stand.

He stands in the open doorway, a slight sheen to his dark brown skin. It looks as if he had chosen to run up all twenty-seven flights of stairs instead of taking the elevator up. "Are you okay, Ms. Caster? You seem a little . . . agitated. Should I come back in five minutes with a latte?"

I gape at who I can only assume to be Mackenzie Thompson and the way he holds his large, suit-tailored body with such ease. He's unfamiliar yet speaks to me as if he already knows me. Either he's just very confident, or he knows more about me than I thought.

A lightbulb goes off in my head. *Gretchen.*

Clearing my throat, I round my desk with an easy smile and extend my hand. He takes it without hesitation. "Mr. Thompson, I'm assuming?"

"Oh God. Call me anything but Mr. Thompson. Mack or Mackenzie works fine." I attempt to hide my surprise, but he notices, adding, "The only two people who call me Mr.

Thompson are my assistant and my mother. Both opting to do so only *after* I've done something to piss them off."

"Gretchen may have mentioned that that is a very common occurrence." I laugh and make note of the way his emerald-green eyes spark at the mention of my friend. "Would you like to sit?"

Stray pieces of thick black hair fall to his forehead as he nods and sits down in one of the two leather chairs opposite my desk. "You're probably confused as to why I asked for a meeting."

"More curious than confused," I reply, settling back behind my desk.

"Gretchen tells me that you're working on a difficult project at the moment."

It's a statement worded like a question, so I reply as if it were the latter. "That's right. I am. There have been a few snags along the way, specifically regarding money on their end, but I'm hoping to have that resolved by the end of the week."

It's a pipe dream, in all honesty. It's already Wednesday, and the Waterton Brothers have no intention of giving me what I have assured them over and over again that I need for all of this to succeed. They might be content with having their advertisements plastered on broken bus benches and shattered store windows, but our company is not.

There's no way that I can run this by anybody above me as a serious option without it looking horribly on my reputation and future here. Not to mention Cole would use it to his advantage. A shiver racks through me.

Mack scratches at the dark stubble covering his jaw, looking as if he's fighting back a smile. My face pales, and I know instantly that Gretchen has told him far more than I initially thought. *That damn traitor.*

"You can be honest with me. I'm the last person who

would think less of you because of an idiot, tight-pocketed client who thinks they live above reason. We've all had them." He pulls at the knot in his tie and sighs in relief when it loosens slightly. "If I'm being honest, I did request this meeting because Gretchen asked me to help you, but I didn't come here planning to do so unless I thought you deserved it. I don't put my back out for many people, let alone a new hire who I have never met and certainly don't trust."

Sweat breaks out on the back of my neck as I register his words. It would seem that my dear friend has a lot more pull with her boss than she let on. I'm not sure whether to be grateful for that or a bit embarrassed that she felt the need to ask for help on my behalf. I know that it wasn't with ill intent —quite the opposite of it, actually—but I'm not somebody who is overly happy looking like a helpless puppy in the eyes of my superiors.

The way Mack is looking at me right now doesn't scream pity or disappointment, though. If anything, he seems to be . . . curious? Maybe a bit cautious?

It's clear as to why Gretchen has deeply scarred feelings for this man. Some reasons are the same as to why I love Braden. There's something undeniably sexy about a confident, straightforward man. They make you weak in the knees and your heart flutter wildly like a baby bird trying to learn to fly. It's nearly impossible to get over them once you offer them a piece of you.

"Okay." I straighten my back and meet Mack's confident stare with my own. "What do you want to know?"

Approval flashes across his face before it fades away to nothing. "I'm assuming you have plans—ideas, and a way to execute them. So tell me what you need from those buffoons, and I'll get it done."

I blink once, twice.

His pink lips part with a grin. "That surprises you?"

"I thought you said that you didn't know whether or not I deserved your help."

"I did. And I've decided."

"So quickly?"

He chuckles, pushing back the hair that continues to flop across his forehead. It's cut in a way that would hint at a daily use of hair gel. I'm assuming he skipped that step today.

"Is that a problem, Ms. Caster?"

"No," I rush out. "I'm just surprised. I figured that you weren't awfully involved around here anymore." Wincing, I tell myself that I should have stopped while I was ahead.

The amusement I watch flicker to life in his eyes has me floored.

"All of you transfers seem to have the impression that I either don't know how to do my job or that I simply hate it."

"Is that why you haven't been around, then? The judgment?"

He seems to like it when I'm blunt, because his smile reaches his eyes, and the skin beside them crinkles, making him look older than I first thought. Maybe late twenties or early thirties.

"I'm far past caring about other people's judgment, darling."

My eyes narrow as I say, "Then why not introduce yourself sooner? It would have been nice to receive some sort of welcome when we arrived."

I scowl as I begin to recognize how the bitterness toward this move, and what it cost me is clouding my judgment. Being a bitch to the one person here who wants to actually help me—favour or not—isn't going to get me anything but fired. When I turn back to look at him, I find him in thought, as if he's silently chewing on the words I've rudely spoken.

"I can see why my assistant is so fond of you, Ms. Caster."

Mack's face is stoic, yet his words are almost tender. It's a weird paradox that I don't understand, but I smile anyway. "Do you have my email?"

Is that a serious question? "I do, yes."

"Send me everything in the Waterton Brothers file, and I'll look it over tonight. It was nice to meet you."

He gets up and leaves without another word, the reality of the situation really dawning on me for the first time.

First, I just met Mack Thompson. And second, he's going to help get my ass out of some serious hot water. After I chew her ass out, I definitely owe Gretchen an endless tap of tequila for this.

10

Sierra

"I've never been so turned on in my life as I am watching you eat those noodles," Braden says, his body shaking beside mine on the couch. He's laughing, nearly in full-on hysteria as he watches me with glittering eyes.

The Chinese food that we ordered after work is nothing but empty boxes stacked between us. The TV plays a Hallmark Christmas movie with a cowboy and a wedding planner returning to her hometown. The originality of it was what sold me. *Not*.

In all honesty, I nearly turned on one of my recorded episodes of *Law & Order* before I caught myself and gripped the remote so hard the buttons left imprints in my palm. I didn't feel like opening up that can of worms and digging into all the reasons as to why I haven't been able to watch the stupid show in the past three weeks.

"Keep making fun of me and I'll kick you out in the snow." I wipe away the grease on my cheek before reaching across the chow mein box in my lap to swat him in the arm. Swallowing the rest of the food in my mouth, I narrow my eyes on his dimples.

Braden cocks a daring brow while setting his food down on the coffee table. Patting his spread thighs, he says, "Try me, fighter. I'll go willingly if you can get me off the couch."

"Having me splayed across your body isn't much of a punishment, now is it?" I laugh before shoving the last forkful of noodles and chicken in my mouth.

I feel his smile deep in my chest.

"Fuck no it isn't. Having you on my lap and in my arms is a fucking reward, never a punishment."

"Then no." I place the empty box beside his on the table before moving to sit back down. My eyes fly toward him when he grabs my wrist and pulls, sending me toppling toward his thighs. "Braden!" I squeak. He ignores me but drops my wrist, giving me false hope before he's gripping my hips and situating me so my legs hang on either side of his.

His body heat wraps around me, his smell flooding my senses. I place my hands on his shoulders and watch through thick lashes as his warm eyes slither over my torso, snagging on the white scar I know lives along my left collarbone.

"I fell out of a tree when I was ten," I murmur, shivering at the feeling of his calloused fingers rubbing the bare skin above my hip where my shirt must have ridden up. His eyes meet mine with an intensity that nearly steals my breath. "There was a big oak tree in front of our house, and Clare double-doggy-dared me to climb as high as I could. I only made it a few feet before I slipped and fell. I broke my collarbone pretty badly, and they had to stabilize it through surgery. My mother was livid. She grounded us for two weeks and called some guy to come and cut down the tree the next day."

"She grounded you for falling from a tree?"

I smile sadly and press my thumb to the creases between his

brows, trying to smooth them out. "That's my mother for you. If we were having fun, we were being too rowdy, and if we were too quiet, we were being sneaky and deceitful. There was never a middle ground. I learned young that it was impossible to please her, yet I couldn't help myself from trying."

The fingers on my hips tighten their grip and guide me further up Braden's thighs until I'm so close to him that my nose brushes his chest, and I can feel the bulge in his pants brush my centre.

"Your mother sounds awful," he says, voice full of gravel. "What about your father? Was he just as bad?"

I shake my head but frown. "He loved to play games with us when Clare and I were younger. Hell, he encouraged us to laugh and yell when we were having fun. But then he started letting Mom walk all over him. He never told her to back off or that we should be allowed to act like kids."

"You resent him for that." It's not a question, and there's no judgment in his words. Nodding, I close my eyes and try to think about where to start.

I want to deny it, to stand up for my father in ways he never thought to do for us as children, but I do resent him. I blame him for never being around the same way that I blame his job for taking him away so often. Hating a job, an organization, that does so much good in the world never fails to make me feel like a piece of old gum underneath a running shoe, but I won't torture myself by forcing myself to feel differently.

My parents spent their lives helping other people's children while their own grew up alone. It's a sick twist of fate, I guess.

I think the worst part of it all is that we could have dealt with the distance between us, the lack of family dinners and no "I love you's" at night if they had both cared enough to try when they weren't away working. Even when the distance was no more than a few feet, my sister and I ate alone before it was her that tucked me into my bed at night.

There are so many questions that I want to ask them but never have the guts to do so. Did they even want kids? Were we really a burden that they didn't want to feel the weight of? Is that why they found a job where they could pretend we never existed?

A soft touch on the wet skin of my cheekbone pulls me from my thoughts. I open my eyes, realizing through blurred vision that I've started to cry and that Braden is wiping the tears away.

There's a thick ball in my throat that I try to swallow past. "I'm sorry."

"Don't apologize for things you can't control, Sierra. And never for how the actions of somebody else affect you. Your parents let you down. It's as simple as that. You don't need to feel guilty for being upset about the way they've treated you."

I exhale slowly. His eyes narrow and blaze with something that looks a lot like anger and frustration as he watches me fight a silent battle. The way that he can tell exactly what I want to hear has me wondering how he knows all of this. I want to ask if he's speaking from personal experience or if he's just become incredibly wise over the past few weeks.

Almost like he can read my thoughts, he says, "You're not the only one who's spent years resenting your parents, baby."

I want to push him, want to tear open the small hole he's exposed in his close-kept past for me, but fight against the urge. If I touch that opening, he'll stitch it shut before I have the chance to mangle together an apology.

Instead, I slide my hands to his trim waist and hold him, pressing my cheek to his chest. I debate on whether or not to say anything but decide to keep quiet and hand the invisible reins over to him.

His heartbeat quickens beneath my cheek, and I recognize the way it skips and rams against his rib cage, trying to burst free, because mine does the same all too often.

Fear is an all-encompassing emotion. It fills your stomach with acid and spikes your blood with adrenaline. Fighting against fear is like going up against the boss at the end of a video game without actually playing a single level.

I tighten my grip on him and kiss the centre of his chest, then the burning skin beneath his Adam's apple. He shudders, breathing deeply and licking his lips.

"I didn't grow up around love. I grew up with two parents who fought so often they forgot what it was like not to fight. When I was ten, I watched my mother throw an empty bottle of vodka at the TV after Dad got home too late from work."

My sharp inhale is obvious enough for him to briefly pause and drop his chin to the top of my head. I squeeze him in response, and he continues his story.

"My mother disliked vodka the way she did my dad—with a passion that burned so bright the line between love and hate often blurred. She didn't drink often, but when she did, you wouldn't dare reach for her glass in fear of how deeply it would upset her. It was the same way with my dad. When she cared for him, he would be the only one she could see in a crowded room. But when she hated him . . . he learned over time to try and keep a lengthy distance between them.

"It never worked when he would stay away, though. It was like she craved the high that came with winning a fight between them and always sought him out just to have a go at him. It was impossible to understand why my parents went from smiling and laughing one second to cursing and screaming the next. To this day, I still remember begging Dad to make it stop. He was tucking me into bed the night that I told him they were tearing me apart. Two days later, my mother told me they were getting a divorce."

"Do you think that he told her what you said?" I ask gently.

Braden nods once, and a strong breath of air ruffles my hair. "Yeah, I do. They never told me what the final straw was, but I've always thought that it was what I said that night."

I think back to the night of Brooks' and Lana's wedding and how different Braden's relationship with his mother looked than how he's describing now. From what he's told me, it's been over ten years since she left him behind and took off to Europe, so I suppose I shouldn't be surprised. I for one know how hard it is to continue holding a grudge against someone that you love so deeply. It's the reason I struggle so badly with the relationship I have with my dad.

There's a pang in my chest at the heavy sadness that's found a home in his words. If I could shoulder the hurt and betrayal that he's felt for the past decade as my own, I would. The decisions that he's made in our relationship are starting to make more sense to me as the different parts of himself that he's shown me form a much clearer image. It's still fuzzy around the edges, but progress is progress. Especially when it comes to someone as steel-walled as Braden.

I nuzzle my face against the spot in the centre of his chest and ask, "How is your relationship with her now? It seemed good at the wedding."

"I love my mother, I do. And we're much better off now than we were a few years ago. But it took me a long time to forgive her for everything that happened to our family and how she decided the only way she could repair what was broken inside of her was by abandoning me for two years. My father was far from perfect in their marriage, but it's no secret between both of them that I chose his side, regardless of what feelings I held against him and his part in everything."

The warm breath on my head becomes laboured slightly, so I look up, my stomach turning sour instantly. I'm not surprised to see the guilt that's sunken deep into his features, but it still upsets me nonetheless.

"The last thing that you should feel is guilty, Braden," I say, a bit harsher than I intended, but I don't dare take it back. I don't want to. "You were a child forced to watch the two people you love destroy each other. Choosing a side was inevitable, especially when you had to choose between someone who had stayed with you and somebody who had left."

Braden's lips part, and his eyebrows stitch together. I watch something dangerous, something tipping on the edge of becoming out of control, spark in his whiskey-brown eyes seconds before he takes my mouth in a searing kiss.

The kiss doesn't last long, but it leaves my insides simmering by the time he pulls away to mumble low words across my lips.

"Thank you."

11

Braden

I'VE BEEN HERE IN TORONTO FOR JUST OVER THREE weeks now, and although my gym is still nameless, it's no longer empty. The training equipment was brought in yesterday, and the crew finished up the locker room this morning. We're still a few months away from opening to the public, but it's progress.

It doesn't matter how much time I spend here, I still can't believe how far this place has come in such a short time. I'm incredibly grateful. Each day that passes is another day that I have to bite my tongue to avoid telling Sierra about this place.

It's not that I don't want to tell her; it's that I don't want to tell her *yet*. Not until it's finished. I want her to see it for the first time with just me. Just us, alone. Is that stupid? Probably. But I'm selfish that way. When her pretty pink lips part in shock and she turns to me with surprise in her eyes, I want to feel that same rush too. In private, with the girl that helped me realize I'm capable of doing something bigger.

For now, she knows that I've started working at a local

boxing gym. It's not technically a lie, but it still makes me feel a bit guilty regardless. *It'll be worth it,* I remind myself.

I'm flipping my newly built desk over onto its legs when I hear a set of familiar, low voices carry to the room that will soon be my office. Dropping the screwdriver that I borrowed from one of the crew members out front, I push my hair out of my eyes and head out to meet the guys.

When Tyler called me yesterday and told me the Vancouver Warriors would be in town for their last game before Christmas break, he pretty much invited himself over. I didn't mind, seeing as how I've actually missed the asshole, but I will admit that I got a bit nervous. It was Tyler's money from the sale of the old gym that helped make this possible in the first place, so I guess I just don't want to disappoint him. If he knew that I was thinking this way, he would undoubtedly kick my ass—or try anyway.

It doesn't help my nerves any that he also invited his brother-in-law and team captain along. Oakley Hutton has seen more athletic gyms and training centres than most people ever will. It's not shocking, considering he's the face of the professional hockey league, but it still makes my small, unfinished gym feel tiny and forgettable in comparison.

I'm still trying to shake off my nerves when Tyler pops out from behind the small wall separating the front entrance from the main gym, spotting me at the same time that I do him. He doesn't exactly grin, but he smiles in that familiar half-assed way while bumping Oakley on the shoulder.

The move pulls Oakley's eyes from their intense sweeping of the gym as they land on me. "Well, well, well. If it isn't Braden fucking Lowry. Long time no see, buddy."

"You're telling me," I reply while eating some of the distance between us and pulling them both into quick hugs. "How was the flight?"

"Restful. Slept the whole way." Oakley says, squeezing the brim of his hand between his hands. I could count on one hand the number of times I've seen him without a hat on and messy brown hair peeking out from beneath it.

"Snored like a fucking pig too," Tyler grunts.

I slant my brother a look. "I have it on good authority that you snore loud enough to make Gracie contemplate buying earplugs."

"She said that?"

I toss him a wink.

"I believe it. She used to complain every morning about my snoring when we were growing up." Oakley chuckles.

My grin is evil. "At least I know what to get her for Christmas."

"Has anyone ever told you that you're an asshole?" Tyler asks, scowling right at me.

"Once or twice." I shrug. "What time is the game tonight?"

"Eight. You want tickets?" Tyler asks.

I shake my head. "Nah, I already have plans."

"Speaking of," Oakley says, the corner of his mouth twitching. "When are we gonna meet these 'plans'? Gracie's been going on about your girl since they met at your dad's wedding. It's made my wife incredibly jealous."

Tyler snorts. "It's not Gray's fault that you've been too busy to meet her."

Oakley pins my brother with an exasperated look before turning to me again. "This guy hasn't invited us either."

"I've only been here for three weeks." Throwing my hands up in front of me, I shake my head and scowl.

It's Tyler that speaks next while patting me on the shoulder with fake sympathy. "Plus, he's been grovelling for those three weeks. I doubt Sierra would have agreed anyway with how bad Braden fucked up."

I want to step into a pit of quicksand and let myself get pulled under. Talking about my rocky relationship with Sierra is not how I planned on starting this reunion. It's not a conversation that I had planned for today at *all*.

The past two weeks have been anything but easy. Sierra and I have made leaps and bounds in our relationship, but trust takes time to rebuild. I've walked her to and from work every day, and each night she invites me inside for dinner. We talk about things so trivial and childish while learning about each other in ways that I never wanted to learn about somebody before.

I know the way she likes her eggs in the morning—runny and drenched in ketchup—how she only wears mismatched socks because "the dryer eats the matches," and what three things she would take with her on a deserted island. She looked almost giddy when she told me her list.

"Obviously a water bottle for water, a magnifying glass to help start a fire, and a black Sharpie."

When I asked why she would bring a Sharpie, she said, "So that I can draw a penis on your forehead and laugh to distract myself from the fact that we're going to get eaten by animals and die on a stranded island."

I didn't tell her, but the fact that she imagined herself there with me kept me up all night with a smile on my face.

There's still that same buzzing attraction between us that seems to only intensify as time goes on, and every night we fight it like high school virgins scared of our parents catching us making out on the couch.

We eat whatever takeout I've ordered before picking her up, or if she's not too tired, she'll teach me how to cook something easy that won't lead to me burning the house down. Then we cuddle up on the couch and watch TV until she passes out in my lap, and I carry her to her room before letting myself out.

It's become a routine, something that I look forward to every day after working at the gym. I can almost see the broken pieces of our relationship gluing themselves back together. If I wasn't terrified of speaking anything into existence, I would say that we might be even better than we were before.

I fall back into the conversation happening around me when Oakley throws a teasing dig at my brother.

"He's not the only one of us that's fucked up something great because his head was in his ass, Ty." Oakley chuckles before adding, "At least he didn't sleep with her best friend."

"He's got a point," I say in easy agreement, ignoring the evil side-eye from Tyler.

Gracie kicked her ex-best friend/roommate out of their shared apartment the same day that she found out about her secret one-nighter with my brother. It had happened way before Tyler and Gracie got together, but it caused quite the ruffle between them. The fight didn't last long, though, before Ty was declaring his love for her and promising a happily ever after.

"Whose side are you on?" Tyler asks, still glaring at me.

I sling my arms around both of their shoulders and tighten my grip. They both stiffen but don't fight to break away as I say, "Whoever's paying for pizza."

"Who said anything about pizza?" Oakley ducks under my arm before tilting his head to the side, cracking his neck.

Tyler shoves his elbow into my ribs, forcing me to let him go and clutch my side with a pained wheeze. "Can you even have pizza, Lee?" He flicks his amused gaze to me. "Oakley here is on some fucking vegan diet now. Can't even have real cheese anymore."

My nose scrunches. "You're kidding."

Oakley rolls his eyes, as if he's already tired of this conversation, and casually lifts one shoulder. "Some of us actually listen to our trainers."

Tyler scoffs, and a muscle in his jaw pulses. "Here we go again. I'll continue to eat my real fucking food and avoid becoming a scrawny shit like you."

"You're no bigger than me. If anything, you're smaller. I have at least two inches and ten pounds on you. Plus, that's not how it works. You don't just get skinny because you choose not to eat real dairy or meat products."

Tyler's scowl only gets more intense. "Keep telling yourself that, string bean."

My brows are raised as I watch the two guys, bemused by the sibling-like bickering going on between them. Tyler may be my blood, but they're just as much siblings as we are. It gives me some sort of peace knowing that he has a family that loves and cares for him outside of just Dad and me. He damn well deserves it.

"Do you guys want a tour?" I ask, hoping that my suggestion will help draw their attention away from whatever argument I can sense brewing. If I had to guess, I would say Tyler's asshole ego has been getting him into trouble at work. It wouldn't be the first nor the last time.

Their attention snaps away from each other and falls on me. Excitement passes across Tyler's face, and I'm happy when he doesn't bother hiding it from me.

Oakley smiles wide, nodding. "Please."

I lift my arm and gesture for them to follow me as I move us away from the front doors and past the hallway leading toward the two large locker rooms and my office. Coming to a halt where the old tile flooring meets the newly laid laminate, I look toward the empty open area bordered by floor-to-ceiling mirrors with a prideful smile. Soon this entire room will be fully equipped with the array of workout equipment we got this morning, punching and speed bags, and a training ring.

"There will be a room for those who want to train privately as well. The goal is for anyone to feel comfortable working out here, not just boxers," I say, looking at them from over my shoulder.

"How many trainers are you considering having?" Oakley asks as he steps up beside me, his arms crossed and eyes carefully working their way across the room.

"Two boxing trainers other than myself and one personal. Right now, it's hard to tell how many I'll need. I don't have any clients here yet," I answer. There's a subtle hint of nerves in my voice that I try to ignore.

"And when are you estimating you'll open? February? Early March?"

It's Tyler who speaks next, sneaking around me and walking toward the tape stuck to the floor where the training ring will eventually sit. "It was March, right?"

I nod. "Yeah. There's only a few more cosmetic things left before the ring can be placed. The equipment will be moved in soon."

"I think you should look at hiring a few more personal trainers. I know a lot of the guys train with a bag but not in a ring. They don't wanna take the risk."

"Bunch of pussies," Tyler grumbles.

I ignore him as my brows stitch together in confusion. "What guys?"

Tyler simply laughs at me while Oakley slaps my shoulder, saying, "I've been talking you up to Kyle Davies, and he said that he and a few other guys from the team might be interested in swapping gyms. He wants to come check it out before opening."

"Kyle Davies as in the captain of the Toronto Timberwolves?"

"Yes. That is if you want a bunch of puck-twiddling assholes in your gym," he replies, squeezing my shoulder before dropping his hand and joining Tyler by the ring markings.

"Adam has a few past clients from WIT that live here now too. He told me to tell you that he can send you their numbers anytime," Tyler throws in.

One of our college friends, Adam White, owns an ice hockey training arena in Vancouver. I'm not surprised in the slightest that he has clients way out here. He's made quite the name for himself after graduating college. Especially when it comes to players in the hockey world.

Adrian Loskowski, the first pick of the draft this past season, spent the last four years of his junior-league career training alongside his coach *and* Adam at White Ice Training.

"I'll call him today," I reply, still a bit dumbstruck. My stomach is twisted and knotted to the point I'm beginning to wonder if I'll be able to undo all the damage.

"You've done a great job, Braden. This is going to be huge." Tyler's tone is so light and airy that I nearly stumble backward in surprise. His pride is openly scrawled across his features, like he couldn't hide it even if he wanted to. I soak it up, knowing that it's a rare occurrence.

"Toronto was the right move, buddy. You're going to make a name for yourself out here," Oakley chimes in, wearing a similar look to Tyler's.

"Thank you. Both of you." My chest is tight, nearly painful even. I rub my palm above the ache before I can stop myself.

"Okay, let's go eat before we all break down into fucking tears," Tyler grunts as his mouth forms its usual scowl again.

I can't help but laugh and nod in agreement. It will be a cold day in hell before the three of us snuggle in a circle and let our walls down enough to cry together. But fuck, our joint laughter is more than enough.

12

Sierra

"Come to dinner with me on Christmas Eve."

I lift my eyes from the bowl of spaghetti in my lap to stare at the giant man stretched out on my couch. Braden's watching me intently, cautiously, as if he really believes there's a chance that I'll say no to him.

Setting my bowl down on the coffee table, I readjust myself so that I'm facing him on the couch, my legs tucked under me, knees brushing his thigh. "You know, usually the guy *asks* the girl to have dinner with his family, not orders it."

He visibly winces, and an apologetic smile pulls at his mouth. Clearing his throat, he asks, "Would you like to go to my father's for Christmas dinner with me?"

"I would."

My insides turn to mush when he grins so wide his dimples pop. He looks like a kid in a candy store, and it amazes me that it was me that put that look on his face.

Before Braden, I viewed dating through a black-and-white lens. There were set criteria and a list of do's and don'ts to follow before you could consider yourselves a society-approved relationship.

Obviously, having sex with a stranger and then falling in love with them in three months was not a part of that plan.

I never would have thought that I would be so eager to spend a holiday with a guy and his family after only being on a single date, but here I am, completely accepting of the idea—excited, even.

Braden and I didn't spend time at restaurants and bowling alleys getting to know embarrassing childhood memories or our biggest pet peeves before deciding whether or not to continue a relationship. Instead, I learned how easily Braden falls asleep when I play with his hair and how he drinks his coffee black and piping hot in the morning.

As time went on, I started becoming proud of him over small things and frustrated for him over others. It didn't take baring my soul and all of its dark secrets to get to that point. It just happened.

We didn't fall in love the "right way" when it comes to society and its standards, but we did it *our* way—tangled up in sweaty sheets and drowning in denial.

"Okay," Braden replies, almost to himself, before setting his bowl on the table and grabbing my hands in his. "Okay."

"How are they settling in?"

Brooks and Lana only arrived in Toronto three days ago. Five days later than what they were hoping. Turns out Lana's modelling career is a bit more serious than I previously thought. Serious enough that she got called for a shoot in Vegas the morning before their original flight and had to postpone the next one for four days later.

A familiar stiffness pulls at Braden's shoulders, and I know right away it's because the topic of his new stepmom isn't his favourite one. Not by a long shot. His attitude toward her has definitely gotten better—more accepting and less cruel—over the past few weeks, but it's going to take a while for him to fully accept her into his family. Nobody, not myself, his father, or anybody else, can judge him too harshly for that.

"It looks like they've lived there for weeks already. Lana didn't waste any time."

His thumbs roll circles on the top of my hands as he rests his cheek against the couch, watching me with a calmness that I welcome wholeheartedly. I want to curl up beside him, so I do just that. Scooting closer, I press my front to his side and lay my cheek on his chest.

Expelling a quiet puff of air, Braden drops my hands and grips my thighs, laying them over his lap. It's only after I'm as close as possible that he wraps an arm around my back and asks, "Is this good?"

"Very good," I hum in satisfaction while looking up at him through a curtain of mascara-coated lashes. The idea of having to get up and leave the warmth that is Braden just to take my makeup off makes me want to throw a fit like a small child.

"Are Clare and Liz still coming on Boxing Day?" Braden asks, tracing designs on my hip with the calloused fingers that I've grown to love so much.

Excitement blasts through me at the mention of seeing my niece and sister for Christmas. We've never not spent the holidays together, and although I offered numerous times to be the one to fly back home, Clare was insistent that she and Liz needed a change of scenery. Whatever that means, I have no clue. But I'm sure I'll find out.

"They are. I'm excited for you to meet them." Probably a bit too excited, but oh well.

When I first asked Braden whether he would want to meet my family over the holidays, I was pleasantly surprised when he said yes, not a twinge of hesitation in his voice. In a way, it also helped reassure me that I made the right decision in giving our relationship another shot.

"I'm excited too, fighter. And pretty scared, if I'm being honest. I can barely handle one Caster woman, let alone three."

My eyes roll. "I would be more scared of Clare's cooking than anything else. She hasn't been able to perfect a meat dish in her entire life. So I hope you like overcooked, rubber-like turkey."

Braden doesn't have a chance to reply before my body is flushing cold, and sweat breaks out on my neck and chest. I push away from him, swatting at the warm hands wrapped around me and placing weak legs on the ground. One hand flies to my mouth while the other presses against my stomach, eager to calm the churning sensation I feel forcing my dinner back up.

"Sierra? What's wrong?"

That stupidly warm hand touches me again before I'm pulled against an equally warm, if not hotter, hard body. I shove at Braden again, but it doesn't do anything. I'm too weak to fight him as he guides my hunched-over body to the bathroom.

"Jesus Christ," he mumbles. His voice sounds higher-pitched than usual.

"Get out," I groan before sinking to my knees in front of the toilet bowl. Reaching behind me, I wave my hand in the air. "Go."

He doesn't listen, and before I can protest again, my throat is contracting and my dinner is coming back up. I heave into the toilet bowl, my arms shaking and nose burning.

"You're okay, baby." Braden's presence moves from behind me before I hear the sound of drawers opening and closing. I shiver when fingers brush the back of my neck and my hair is pulled back into a loose pony.

He rubs circles on my back until the nausea passes, and I fall back onto my feet, my head lolling to the side, hitting his chest. A shaky breath escapes me as I wipe my mouth with my arm and attempt to climb to my feet before swaying too much and sitting back down.

"Let me help you," Braden orders gruffly, flushing the toilet. He moves behind me and slips his arms beneath my armpits before pulling me up easily, like I weigh nothing at all. "Do you want to shower?"

I debate saying no, but the thick layer of sweat covering me makes me reconsider. "Yes. But I can do it myself. Go. I'm disgusting right now."

"Stop telling me to go, Sierra. I'm going to fucking help you whether you like it or not."

"But you don't need to. I'm more than capable of showering myself."

He sighs, exasperated. "Let me help you, dammit. I *want* to help you."

"Fine," I snap through gritted teeth. Pulling free of his supportive grip, I sit down on the toilet, shooting off a quick, silent prayer that the seat wasn't up. I've been embarrassed enough for one night without adding falling into a toilet bowl to my resumé.

Braden doesn't say anything else as he moves around the bathroom, his shoulders and back tense, brows pinched together in concentration. He turns the shower on as hot as it can go and digs through the cabinets before finding fresh towels.

I'm being a complete bitch right now, but the part of my brain that would usually tell me to suck it up and accept the help seems to have been brought up with tonight's dinner and flushed down the toilet.

"Let me take off your clothes," he orders in a rough tone,

daring me to argue. I don't have the energy to fight him on it anymore, so I don't.

I dip my chin and stand. "Okay."

With my approval, Braden drops to his knees in front of me. The backs of his fingers brush my knees and the tops of my thighs before he's reaching for the waistband of my sleep shorts and swiftly pulling them down to my ankles. I step out of them and watch him drag his intense gaze up my bare skin before he presses a soft kiss to the inside of my thigh. My chest throbs at the gentle gesture that I wouldn't have expected from him a few months ago.

I want to tell him how much those little things mean to me, but when he backs up quickly and rises to his feet, I keep my words to myself. He's silent as he removes my tank top and drops it beside my shorts.

Braden moves to the shower and tests the water as I wrap my arms around my naked chest and watch in slight wonder at the way he so easily fills the small bathroom. When he stops a few steps in front of me and starts taking his clothes off, I blink at him.

"The tub is smaller than both of our old ones," I mumble half-mindedly, too busy staring at the strong rippling of his thigh muscles as he lifts one leg at a time and steps out of his pants. "I doubt you'll fit."

His grin is crooked and beautiful. "Have a little faith, sweetheart. It might be tight, but I'll fit."

I release a puff of air and smile slightly, meeting his glittering stare. "Does your head always go straight to sex?"

"You're almost naked, Sierra." He shrugs, moving his eyes along my body. I'm fully aware of how my nipples tighten beneath my arm and goosebumps slither up my bare skin. "But you need to get in the shower before you pass out. Up," he orders before reaching for my hands and pulling me up.

The sigh that escapes me as soon as I step under the water is one of pure relief. My arms hang limp at my sides, and my forehead touches the tile while the hot water pelts my neck and upper back, seeping deep into the tight muscles.

I feel Braden step in behind me before the shower curtain slides shut. Fingers brush my spine, moving higher and higher until strong hands grip the skin of my shoulders. "How are you feeling?" he asks in a deep, gravelly tone that makes my belly tighten. I can feel him completely bare behind me, so he must have shed his boxers after I got in.

"Tired," I reply, my voice a bit strained. Tipping my head back in the water, I reach for my shampoo, but my arm stills in the air when his fingers close around my wrist.

"Let me."

Blinking a few times, I drop my arm.

More than a few moans spill beneath the water when he slides soap-lathered fingers against my scalp and massages my head for probably far too long before nudging me forward to help rinse it out. I fight back a whimper when he coats my loofah in bodywash and moves it along my body in a way that I'm positive isn't intended to be sexual but feels incredibly intimate. By the time I shut off the water and we step out of the tub, there is way more than a slight tingle between my legs.

Tucking in the end of the towel I just wrapped around myself, I walk the few steps to the sink and grab my toothbrush. After squeezing out a hefty amount of toothpaste on the bristles, I shove it in my mouth and meet Braden's eyes in the mirror. They're dark, half-lidded. The toothbrush in my mouth feels unnaturally heavy as my stare travels down his bare, damp chest, past the collection of dark hairs gathered in the middle of his Adonis belt, and falls to the thick, hard cock between his legs.

I quickly look away and force myself not to gulp, spitting a mix of toothpaste and drool into the sink instead. His presence behind me couldn't be any harder to ignore than it is right now. If I didn't consider myself totally unfuckable tonight, I would have already dropped this stupid towel and let him have his way with me.

I hear him moving around behind me before the bathroom door creaks open and his footsteps fall on thick carpet. With a shake of my head, I'm pulling myself back together despite the ache between my legs. *Get it together, Sierra.*

Braden doesn't return from whatever he was doing until I'm dressed in a baggy shirt and plugging my phone into its charger by the bed.

"Is there anything you need before I leave?" he asks, fully dressed in his hoodie and jeans from earlier. Suddenly, a feeling of dread hits me. I don't want him to leave. I haven't wanted him to leave a single night since he's been back but haven't found it in me to ask him to stay. Before tonight anyway.

"Stay," I blurt out. "If you want to."

Lines stretch the length of his forehead when he lifts his brows. "You sure?"

"I'm sure." I pull the comforter back and slide into bed.

Braden's surprise doesn't last long before he's shedding his clothes again and joining me. He's warm, like always, but instead of turning to his side and curling around my body the way I became accustomed to in Vancouver, he stays on his back. If I had to guess, I would say that this is his way of being respectful and not stepping over the boundaries he assumes I still have in place.

With a small smile, I make the move and turn to him, resting my head on his chest and sliding my arm along the hard grooves of his stomach. Tapping my fingers against his side, I tilt my head and press my lips to his jaw.

"Thank you for taking care of me. I don't know what the

rules are when it comes to what we're doing, but I love you. Good night, Braden."

His swallow is audible as long, strong fingers intertwine with mine. He dips his chin, and his mouth brushes the top of my head.

"I will always take care of you, little fighter. I love you."

13

Sierra

I'm having a meltdown. A full-blown, sweaty-pit, stomach-collapsing meltdown. I've burned holes in the carpet from my pacing, I just know it.

Oh my God.

Nothing. Fits. *How* can nothing fit?

My entire closet is scattered across the carpet in my bedroom. Not a single one of my dresses zips up past the middle of my back, and my skirts—even my favourite, five-season-old stretchy one—won't make it up past the ass that has seemingly grown double its size overnight.

I'm too young to be having a heat flash, but I feel like I've been shoved inside of a damn oven. Pulling at the neck of my tank top, I let the cool air hit my damp chest and sigh, tipping my head back.

My panicking isn't helping matters; if anything, it's only making it worse. If I don't calm down, I have no doubt that I'll end up sweating off the entire face of makeup I spent far too long doing this afternoon or yanking out the fancy braided bun I glued to the back of my head with an entire package of bobby pins.

It's Christmas Eve. I can't lose it on Christmas fucking Eve. Especially not when I'm supposed to be spending it with my boyfriend and his closest family members. Not to mention that I can't exactly show up in my underwear and a sweat-soaked tank-top either.

I'm too scared to check my phone to see what time it is. Braden is supposed to be here at four thirty, and I'm almost certain that it's way too close to that time. I've spent at least fifteen minutes just standing here freaking out.

Raking my eyes over the mess of clothes on the ground, I fist my shirt so tight my fingers burn. "Screw it."

The bottoms of my feet hurt as I stomp my way to the closet and pull the accordion-style door as open as possible without ripping it off the hinges. There, hiding behind a bagged pantsuit and the dress that I wore for my high school graduation—not sure why I still have that one—is the only article of clothing that my mother ever gifted me.

A knee-length maroon dress with long, lace sleeves and a plunged yet modest enough neckline that keeps enough chest to the imagination, made by a designer that I've never heard of before.

This dress was my gift for graduating university, and it would have been a great gift had she not bought it a size too big and in a colour that I've avoided like the plague my entire life, knowing how badly it washes out my pale skin. I kept it anyway, since it was one of the nicer gifts she had ever thought to buy me, but it hadn't seen the light of day since it left the store four years ago. Well, until tonight.

Tonight, it's the only thing big enough to fit me. Talk about a blow to the old pride and confidence.

Yes, I tend to wear more formfitting outfits that don't technically leave a lot of room for . . . growth, but it still sucks big-time to try on dress after dress with not a single one fitting the way they used to.

I rip the dress from the fabric hanger and throw it toward the bed before taking off my tank top and dropping it on the floor. The bra I slide on is nude and strapless and matches the plain cotton underwear I've been strutting around in all afternoon. It's not a sexy set by any means, but I'm hoping it won't stay on long after dinner. At least I *was* hoping to have Braden strip me naked and have his way with me as soon as we got home, but that was before I realized I had gained more than just a few pounds of happy weight. Now I'm not sure if I want Braden anywhere near me after I pound back turkey and potatoes and fall into a food coma.

Shit. What has he been thinking these past few weeks? How long has my ass been growing? Also, how is it growing in the first place, considering how sick I've been the past few days?

Stopping my hands before I rub at my face, I pick up the dress, feeling the silky material between my fingers. With one long exhale, I slip it over my head—careful not to wreck my hair—and pull it the rest of the way down. It fits almost perfectly, only slightly loose around my waist and shoulders and formfitting everywhere else.

Three hard knocks on the door have my heart in my throat. With shaky hands, I grab my phone, jacket, and black ankle boots off the bed and stumble over my own feet as I walk out of my bedroom, flicking off the lights as I go.

My palm is sweaty when it closes around the doorknob, and I open the door.

"You really need to give me a key to this building if you're not going to answer your buzzer or cell phone. I had to slide through a closing door after an old couple came inside. I'm pretty sure whoever watches your security feeds has my face plastered on a 'keep an eye out for' poster in their office," Braden says, half scolding and half teasing me. He grins brightly down at me, chin to his chest.

There are big fluffy flakes of snow in his gelled-back hair, and his cheeks are pink, looking wind bitten. Moisture collects on my tongue as I rake my eyes along his body in an anything-but-subtle way. I've seen Braden in dressy clothes a few times, but I can't say that I think that I'll ever get used to how well he can pull them off.

The thick wool jacket stretched across his wide shoulders and brushing the top of his knees hides most of his outfit, but with the top few buttons undone in typical Braden fashion, I can see the hint of a black dress shirt and the knot of a . . . tie? Blinking back my surprise, I lower my eyes to the black slacks and shining black dress shoes peeking out from beneath them.

"Oh crap. I didn't hear anything," I mutter apologetically and start to fiddle with the jacket in my hands. "Are you wearing a tie?"

His chest shakes with a laugh that brushes my warm cheeks. "My dad threatened to beat my ass if I didn't. I had to watch a few YouTube videos before I figured it out."

I'm far from surprised by that. If I was a betting woman, I would put money down on either Gracie or Tyler being the one who tied Braden's tie for his father's wedding.

"I'm sure that he'll be happy you listened to him," I assure him. It's so obvious how badly Brooks wants his son's approval in all aspects of his life, but said son just so happens to be too much of a stubborn ass most of the time to see that.

"You look beautiful, Sierra." He reaches forward and traces the neckline of my dress with gentle fingers. A thick brown brow lifts. "You never wear red. I assumed you hated it."

I hold back a snort. "I do." Confusion twists his features

before I shrug and nod to the open door behind him. "It's a long story. We should go."

"Right," he says, like he's just remembering we have somewhere to be. "The cab driver is a real prick, by the way—just a heads-up in case he's gone when we get downstairs."

I slip into my jacket before picking up the bottle of wine I set by the door and asking, "Wouldn't you be if you had to spend your Christmas Eve driving people around town?"

Braden contemplates it for a second, his mouth twisting before replying, "You have a valid point. I can't say that I feel like testing the bounds of his patience, though. We'll be lucky to get another one here before dinner if he leaves without us."

With my keys and a bottle of wine in hand, I step into the hallway beside him and lock the door before we head downstairs. Braden lets out a triumphant holler when we near a yellow cab waiting by the curb. The passenger window rolls down, and an older man, probably in his late fifties, glowers at my boyfriend as if he just tossed his only child out of an apartment window.

"I leave in two minutes," the driver snaps, frowning in a way that reminds me of an angry man in a cartoon.

Braden must think something similar because he places a hand on the small of my back and laughs a bit too loudly. "Got it, Mr. Fudd."

THERE'S A SLEEK, black SUV with overly tinted windows parked in Brooks' driveway when we arrive. Beside it, an old, lifted truck with chipped cherry-red paint and badly rusted rear wheel wells sits, hugging the pavement with thick, well-treaded tires. I know just about nothing when it comes to vehicles, so I won't embarrass myself by trying to guess what year or model it is.

Catching on to my gawking, Braden presses his fingers a bit deeper into my lower back to get my attention. When I look up at him, he's already watching me with a look of amusement.

"That's Dad's. I swear he loves that piece of shit more than me," he says, humour thick in his words. His fingers slide up and down my back through my jacket, pulling a sound of appreciation from my throat.

"How long has he had it?"

"Since I was small enough to need to be lifted into it."

I smile at the idea of a toddler-sized Braden having to be lifted and set inside of the large truck. "You probably hated not being able to jump in yourself."

His grin is affirmation enough. "I did. But after I pitched enough fits about it, he started carrying a step stool in the box—oh, don't give me that look, babe. The old asshole already has one young woman chasing his heels. He doesn't need another."

I swat at his chest and try to snuff out my swoon. "I can't help it if your dad is a DILF."

Braden's hand stills on my back. My eyes bulge.

There's no possible way that I actually said that out loud. Clearly, I've been on the receiving end of far too many of Sophie's gushing rants about Brooks and how he's complete DILF material. *Oh God.*

"Did you just call my dad a DILF?"

My cheeks have their own heartbeat at this point as I flush from head to toe. Avoiding eye contact with Braden is incredibly hard, especially when he's looking at you as intensely as he is me right now. Rolling my lips, I nod, not daring to move my eyes from the patch of ice below the drainpipe on the side of the house. "Yep. That I did."

Braden hums, deep and loud, as his fingers resume their exploration of my lower back. He's so close to me that the heat from his body soaks into my side. I suck in a breath when his other hand lifts to stroke my jaw and cheek, his thumb tracing the edge of my bottom lip. "I'm not above being jealous of my own father, Sierra. Don't make me put on a show with you."

"What do you mean?" is my reply, although I'm sure I can already guess what kind of show he's talking about. I'm stuck between wanting to laugh at how easy it was for him to believe there's a single man that could compete with him and slapping him silly for it.

One second, we're standing in the open on the sidewalk, and the next, we're hidden between the shadows of the side of the house and the garage, visible only through a small window that I assume leads to a bathroom.

My heart thumps against my ribs when the fingers beneath my chin tilt it up, and he bends down enough to hover his mouth so close to mine, close enough that if I just pushed up on my toes the tiniest bit—

"You're mine," he rasps before slamming his mouth to mine.

I gasp against his lips, and he uses my surprise to slide his tongue inside my mouth, tasting, exploring, taking. My eyes slide shut, and my toes curl in my boots as I respond, turning my body so that my front brushes his front and then moving even closer until we're as good as fused together.

With the hand I don't have clutching a wine bottle, I touch his waist before moving to his back and sliding up to his strong shoulders. The cold bites at the bare skin of my fingers, but I only press them into his well-earned muscles, using them as a way to anchor myself.

There's an audible smack when he pulls his mouth from mine and lets out a long, deep breath that fans across my swollen lips. I'm still regaining my bearings when he says with an obvious promise, "Next time, I won't stop. I don't care where we are."

I blink once, twice, three times before swallowing and dipping my chin in acceptance. Braden places a soft, quick kiss to my cheek before grabbing my hand and threading his fingers through mine. "Let's go before they send out a search party."

"The SUV in the driveway." I clear my throat. "Are Tyler and Gracie here?"

Braden pulls on my hand lightly and starts walking toward the house. I catch up to him quickly and walk by his side. "Yeah. They got here this morning."

I run my free hand along the top of my head and over the bun in the back to make sure I'm not going to be walking in looking like a mess. When everything is still in place, I let out a sigh of relief. "That's exciting. I thought they weren't going to make it."

Braden makes a sound in his throat. "Tyler didn't want Gray flying out here, but from what he told me on the phone yesterday, she threatened to name their baby after Harry Styles unless he let them come. Her doctor also assured him that she's safe to fly for another few months, so I think that helped."

"She's six months along, right?"

He nods and grabs my forearm to help me up the porch stairs that shine with the look of fresh ice. "Careful." He mutters something under his breath that sounds like a curse toward his father for not salting earlier before swinging open the front door.

Braden ushers me inside the warm home before following right behind me. There's Christmas music playing and voices twirling and mixing together as we shed our coats and shoes in the front entry.

My stomach gurgles at the array of different smells from

various foods, but I shove the uncomfortable feeling away. I just have to make it through dinner.

"You okay?" Braden asks quietly, rubbing my arm with one of those large hands of his.

I plaster a smile on my face that I wish was completely genuine and place my hand over his, squeezing it. "It's Christmas. Of course I am."

"If I find out that you're lying to me, I'll spank your ass as soon as we're done here. I don't care if I have to do it in the cab."

"Merry Christmas to you too, son."

14

Sierra

Lana Lowry is a Christmas elf. And I mean that in the most flattering way possible.

From the moment Braden and I were ushered inside—our cheeks beating with embarrassment after Brooks heard his son threaten to spank my ass—and glasses of apple cider were shoved in our open palms, Lana hasn't stopped twirling around the house either singing a Christmas tune, fluffing at her overflowing tree, or passing around plates of homemade gingerbread men.

I've found her love of Christmas quite adorable, seeing as how I've never witnessed anyone with so much holiday spirit that hasn't been on a television screen before. Braden, on the other hand, looks like he hasn't gone to the bathroom in a week.

He's seemingly oblivious to the way I'm watching him from where I'm sitting with Gracie in the living room, which is probably why he hasn't felt the need to mask the annoyance written all over his face and body.

Brooks' and Lana's new house is incredibly charming.

From the wood-burning fireplace beside me, the original oak floors, and massive windows that must let in so much morning light, I feel rather comfortable here. It's exactly the kind of place I would picture a man like Brooks living.

Lana obviously had some say in the place when it came to decorating. I can't imagine Brooks willingly purchasing a beige, faux-fur rug, a tall lamp with a beaded lampshade, or the painting of the Santa Monica Pier sunset that's hung above the fireplace. They must have compromised, and that makes my heart warm.

"How long do you think it will take before Braden tells her to go stick her head in the snow?" Gracie asks quietly, leaning over just enough to ensure I'm the only one that hears her.

Lana continues to babble on about something, either not noticing the exasperation on Braden's face or just not caring. His hands are shoved deep in his pockets as he leans against the archway separating the kitchen from the living room and mumbles something back to her.

"I'm surprised he hasn't already. I was prepared to jump in five minutes ago."

Laughing under my breath, I steal a glance at Gracie's hand as she rubs soft, slow circles on her swollen stomach. She hums in response to me, but it's clear that her attention has fallen elsewhere.

As if sensing my stare, she turns to me, all blue eyes and slightly flushed skin. "Do you want to feel? Baby hasn't stopped moving since we got here this morning."

I blink at her, taken aback by the offer, before managing to recover with an eager nod. She smiles wide and grabs the hand I don't have wrapped around a glass of water, pressing it down flat on her stomach, just above her belly button.

I nearly drop my glass when something pushes against my palm. My eyes bulge when it happens again, stronger this time, even through her dress. "How is it so strong? You feel that all the time?" My mouth is hanging open when I drop my hand back in my lap.

Gracie laughs gently. "Yeah. Mostly while I'm trying to sleep or after I eat ice cream."

"And you don't want to know the gender?"

She straightens out her back before starting to rub her stomach again. "I did at first, but we've made a bet out of it instead. I'm positive it's a boy, but Ty is certain it's a girl."

I tap my fingers on my thigh before saying, "I'm with you. I think it's a boy. Call it a gut feeling."

Gracie's smile is beaming as she grabs my hand again, this time leaving it where it is but just holding it in hers. I find myself smiling too and give her fingers a squeeze. "You're awesome, Sierra. I'm so happy that everything worked out between the two of you. Braden was absolutely terrible without you—don't tell him I told you that."

My eyes find him again so easily. There's a lurch in my chest when our gazes meet, and I realize that he's been watching me. I smile softly and watch the tightness in his shoulders disappear.

Brooks and Tyler have joined him and Lana, but I know that he would rather be over here with Gracie and me than in the middle of whatever they're talking about. I purse my lips and kiss the air, earning a swift eye roll and wink from him before I turn back to Gracie.

"Was he really that bad?" I ask her, chewing on the inside of my cheek.

I'm not sure why it's still hard for me to imagine Braden struggling so hard after I left. I've heard it from Sophie before and from Gretchen during all of the nights she spent trying to make me feel better. Even from Braden himself. But it feels so much more real hearing it from someone who knows him so well. Someone like Gracie.

Her grip on my hand tightens, a sigh spilling from her glossy lips. "He got better every day, once he knew that it was actually possible for him to go after you. But he wasn't ever fully himself."

"What do you mean?" I mumble, feeling an ache build at the centre of my chest.

"See, I've only known Braden for five years, but there was never a time where he wasn't wearing arrogance as a shield for whatever parts of him were broken inside. Tyler and Braden are very similar in that sense. It takes a lot for them to open up, and even when they do, it's like pulling teeth out of someone who hasn't had their mouth numbed. I think that's why it hit me so hard when Braden would come to the house and just . . . sit there, silently, like he couldn't be bothered to try and act like everything was fine.

"He didn't even look like himself. I was staring at someone who had lost everything while also experiencing an epiphany at the same time. It all hit him at once. You were gone, he was realizing how in love with you he really was, while also figuring out his past and how to move forward with that."

There's a burn in the back of my eyes that has me grinding my teeth in frustration. Hissing out a breath, I set my glass down on the floor and swipe away the tear that escaped with the back of my hand.

Suddenly, both of my hands are in Gracie's. "I'm sorry," she apologizes quickly. "I didn't mean to upset you."

Her apology only frustrates me more, knowing how ridiculous it is that I'm getting so worked up. The ache in my chest has expanded to my entire upper body now, and my stomach coils around itself. *What is wrong with me?*

Once a sob builds in my throat, I'm pulling at my hands,

pushing off the couch with an apologetic glance at Gracie, and heading down the hall to where Lana told me earlier the bathroom would be. I grab at my chest as if I'll be able to rip the ache away before falling into the bathroom and shutting the door with my back.

My breath is shuttered as I rip off a piece of toilet paper and hold it beneath my eye, hoping to avoid ruining my makeup. What a disaster. This isn't me. I don't get so emotional that I go off so easily. Especially not in front of so many people.

Maybe I really am sick. I've been pushing away the possibility due to the fact I hate going to the doctor's office and avoid doing so like the plague. But I haven't been myself for a few weeks now at least. The vomiting I brushed aside as anxiety and moving stress, which I suppose could be the case for my emotional changes as well, but it seems more serious than that.

I jump at the soft knocks on the bathroom door before running furious hands over my hair and throwing away the wet, mascara-stained toilet paper. "I'm almost done," I say, loud enough that it's way too easy to hear the wavering in my voice.

"Can I come in?"

Relief washes through me when I hear Gracie's voice instead of Braden's. If Braden isn't here, hopefully that means that he didn't see what happened. I doubt that he would have let Gracie come see me instead of himself.

Instead of replying, I pull open the door. Gracie's guilt is obvious as she frowns, her blue eyes dull and avoiding mine.

She steps inside the bathroom and shuts the door behind her before turning back to me. The bathroom isn't exactly small, but with one of us sticking out more than the other, it's pretty crowded with both of us. Her belly is only a few inches from brushing mine when she asks, "Can I ask you something pretty personal?"

Swallowing back my fear, I nod once and rub my palms along the front of my dress.

"Do you get regular periods?" Her question comes out of left field, stunning me. I stare at her blankly as she continues. "If you don't want to answer that, I totally understand. I just want to help." She looks just about as nervous as I feel. "Braden called me the other day to ask for advice on what to do to help you feel better when you're sick, and after I asked what was wrong, he told me that you've been throwing up a lot recently."

"I don't get my period anymore. My doctor said that it's because of my birth control," I mumble, my body flushing cold. Sucking in a shaky breath, I tuck an invisible hair behind my ear.

Gracie watches me intently, like she's evaluating my answers and coming up with a hypothesis. That only makes me more nervous.

"Okay," she says, and it's only now that I spot the purse hanging from her shoulder. "I know this is probably overstepping my boundaries, and you can yell at me and tell me to screw off if you want and I won't be mad, but I checked and there's a gas station open a few blocks away. I think we should go get you a pregnancy test."

I barely manage to drop to my knees and lift the toilet bowl lid before I'm heaving into it, tears freely streaming down my face. A hand touches my back as Gracie sits down beside me, staying close but not too close as I lose everything that I managed to eat today.

"I'm going to text Tyler and let him know to keep Braden busy, okay?"

I nod quickly, my throat burning too much to try and speak.

"How long has this been going on?" she asks, and I lift three fingers. "Three weeks or three days?"

"Days," I croak and lean back on my feet, pressing my chin to my chest.

Gracie holds a wet wipe and a piece of gum out in front of me, both of which I accept eagerly. After I wipe my mouth and pop in the gum, she holds out a hand, and I take it, standing up on wobbly legs.

"Thank you," I whisper before washing my hands in the sink. She checks her phone.

"You're welcome. Are you ready to go out there? Tyler has the guys in the basement doing God knows what so we can sneak away, but he insists on driving us. Is that okay? I can tell him to suck it up."

Yeah, right. There's no way I'm going to stand in the way of Tyler's protectiveness over his pregnant wife and unborn baby because of my own problems.

"It's okay," I assure her. "Do you really think I'm pregnant?"

The question sits heavy between us and even heavier on my shoulders. I'm happy that my brain is still playing catch-up and I haven't fallen into a full-blown anxiety attack yet.

She chews on my question for a few seconds before saying, "It's very possible. But we should get you a test before anything else."

And so we do.

SNEAKING out of the house was easy, as was sitting in complete silence as Tyler drove us to the gas station that wasn't even five minutes away. The lack of conversation didn't even faze me. Not when I couldn't bring myself to speak even if I wanted to.

But things only got harder.

I bought three pregnancy tests, a toothbrush, and a tube of toothpaste before carrying everything into a dirty bathroom to avoid having to take the pregnancy tests at my boyfriend's father's house. Then I took each one of the tests, hovering over the germ-infested toilet as I did so before washing my hands until they were raw and brushing my teeth until my gums started to bleed.

Yet that was still nothing compared to now. I stare at the freshly taken tests and wait for the results to show—alone because I'm too stubborn for my own good and refused Gracie's company when she offered it.

Before I got out of the SUV, she told me waiting would feel like an eternity, especially if I stood and stared at them for the entire three minutes, but I'm doing exactly that anyway.

My stomach is weak, still sore from earlier and even more painful now as fear sinks its claws into it and threatens to tear it to ribbons. I've been avoiding thinking of what comes after. What I do or say once the results flicker across the little screen.

I'm twenty-six, far from incapable of raising a child. I have decent savings and a job that I might have a love/hate relationship with but still provides a secure income. My apartment is small, but at least there are two bedrooms.

That's all that I'm allowing myself to think about. Not the fear of Braden's possible reaction or what might come from it. And definitely not what my parents will say.

I will those worries away and force myself to glance at the tests on the counter. My knees buckle, and I have to grab the edge of the sink in a white-knuckle grip to keep from collapsing. My vision blurs as I read the results staring back at me.

Pregnant. 3+ weeks.

15

Sierra

From the moment Gracie, Tyler, and I got back to the house, Braden hasn't left my side. I've taken full advantage of his attention, needing him now more than ever, even if he doesn't know what's weighing on me yet.

With a steadying hand on my thigh, he strokes my skin with his thumb and throws his two cents into one of the various conversations taking place around the dining room table.

My dinner plate is empty besides the half-eaten dinner roll that Braden's been picking at over the past few minutes. He finished eating long before me—even after refilling his plate with overflowing stacks of turkey, potatoes, and a puddle of gravy for a third time—so he opted to help me polish off my food. The same food that now sits like lead in my stomach.

Gracie and her husband have been shooting me cautious, borderline terrified looks ever since I slid into the back seat of their rental car and we drove back in complete silence. I don't blame them for being curious about how I'm feeling about all of this. I haven't given them much to go off, considering how I've taken to hiding behind phony smiles and forced laughs.

This is not the time or place to deal with something this important, and the last thing I plan to do is ruin Braden's Christmas with his family because I can't shoulder this alone for a few hours. We can talk about this when we get home. It won't be long now.

The thought has me pushing out a long breath and reaching for Braden's hand, desperate for his support. His eyes flick to me, and he smiles so sweetly that I can almost feel my blood sugar spike. He makes my worries disappear so effortlessly. It seems borderline unnatural.

"Do you want anything else to drink? It's Christmas, baby. You don't have to drink water," he whispers, leaning over to brush his nose along my cheekbone. His sudden closeness has me shuddering in my seat, a sound of satisfaction daring to claw up my throat.

"I'm good with water" is my fumbled reply. I forget to breathe when his palm slides up my thigh an inch, and he cups my skin like he's scared it'll fall apart in his hand.

He must notice my sudden breathlessness, because he says his next words in a low, husky rasp. "Do you want to leave soon?"

My skin is burning when I nod. As if acting on their own command, my thighs squeeze shut, sandwiching his hand between them. The black rings on his fingers are cool against my skin as he wiggles them between my legs, and his left brow twitches in amusement.

"I hope that you'll consider coming with me sometime, Sierra," Lana says, her high-pitched voice distinct enough to pull me from my lustful haze. I blink a few times as I try to recall what she's talking about.

"Sierra's really busy with her new promotion, but I'm sure

that she'll try, right, sweetheart?" Braden cuts in, sending me a smirk that heats my blood.

I clear my throat and say, "I would love to go," hoping to the gods that I haven't just agreed to spend an afternoon at a tennis club sipping on nonalcoholic martinis or something. I'm atrocious at anything sports related.

The smile that lights up Lana's perfect complexion is enough to make it worth it if that were the case, though. She has a million-dollar smile. One that hits you right in the gut.

"Speaking of your promotion, Sierra. We both wanted to congratulate you," Lana adds. Brooks grunts his agreement, too busy shovelling food into his mouth to speak. I bite back my laugh.

"Thank you." My lips lift in a genuine smile. "It's a definite change of pace."

"I hope you don't mind, but I threw your name out to my modelling agency. I'm not sure if your firm takes on agency clients, but I figured I would give it a shot." Lana mentions it so subtly, so calmly, that I take a second to digest her words.

Of all the things that I was expecting her to say, that was not one of them. My appreciation and respect for her grows tenfold. Every day, it becomes clearer to me just how little you know a person until they do something that takes you by surprise.

After what seems like an eternity later, I respond. "Wow. That's amazing. Since we just expanded into a new city, we're looking for a bunch of new clients. I'll keep an ear out."

She clasps her hands together in front of her. "Perfect."

I sit up straighter in my chair, gasping when fingers travel higher between my legs and knuckles brush the seam of my underwear. I reach beneath the tablecloth and pinch Braden's wrist.

He laughs under his breath and does it again, this time

twisting his hand and running a fingertip along my slit, using enough pressure to have my legs begging to open back up. I press my tongue to the roof of my mouth and attempt to calm my racing heartbeat. Thankfully, the conversation has moved on, and the eyes that were just settled on me fall elsewhere.

I wrap my fingers around Braden's wrist and tug, but he only continues to rub at my centre, teasing me to the point my arousal wets my underwear and my clit throbs, pleading for attention.

"Something wrong?" he asks, that stupid arrogance dripping from his words. I want to reach over and smack him but somehow reel the urge back in. "Do you want to go home now?"

"We can't leave yet," I hiss, wishing it was that easy. My head is foggy, my thoughts jumbled. I can't focus on anything but the touch of his fingers between my legs and how long it's been since I've had him inside of me. My cheeks flare at the thought. I wish I had left my hair down so that I could have hidden behind it.

"We can." He toys with the side of my underwear, pulling it to the side before letting it settle back in place. "We've been here for hours."

"Your dad is still eating. And it's rude not to help clean up."

His next words brush my ear. A whispered promise. "The only mess I'm going to clean is the one I've made between your legs, baby. It's up to you whether I do that here or at home. Choose carefully."

I'm shooting up from my seat not even a second later, smoothing down my dress as five sets of eyes fall on me. My fingers shake at my sides as I place one foot over the other and stare down at the man grinning like he won the fucking lottery. "I don't feel well."

His bottom lip slips between his teeth while he watches me with lifted brows. "Really? What's wrong?"

I won't stab him. I won't reach down to my plate, pick up my fork, and stab him in the crotch. I won't do it again, and again either.

My eyes narrow as I glare at him, hoping that every ounce of my anger is clear on my face. His Adam's apple bobs as he swallows, and his grin falls.

"I'm going to take her home," he rushes out, standing up beside me and sliding an arm around my shoulders, pulling me so that I'm forced to lean against his body.

I hear somebody choke on something and see a red-faced Tyler with a fist over his mouth while his wife pats his back, looking just as red. Braden mutters something under his breath that sounds a lot like a string of curse words before I'm being placed in front of him. When I try to turn around to ask what he's doing, I feel it.

He's rock hard, pressed against my hip.

A tidal wave of realization washes over me, and I laugh. I laugh so hard that Braden cups my shoulders and squeezes, trying to get me to stop. He hisses a plea under his breath when I press my cheek to his chest to muffle myself.

"Yeah. We're leaving," he grunts. "Thanks for dinner, guys. It was great, Lana. I promise that I'll come clean the bathroom or something this week to make up for ditching."

"Go. It's fine. Thanks for coming," Brooks says, his voice a little wonky, a little higher-pitched than usual.

Oh, my God. His dad saw.

Braden doesn't even wait to hear what Lana has to say before he's rushing us out of the room, and I laugh again.

"You just showed your entire family your boner, didn't you?" I stammer, trying not to trip with how fast he's pulling us through the house.

"This is never to be spoken of again," he states, stopping so that we can slide our shoes on. "I mean it, Sierra. Never."

Tears leak down my face as I shake my head frantically. "I can't promise that. No way. This has been the highlight of my life."

He reaches toward me, and his fingers curl into my sides when he says, "Don't make me tickle you, Sierra. I can never face them again. Promise me that this dies here. Tonight."

I squeak in surprise and look up at him with wild eyes. "What do I get in return for this promise?"

"Anything."

I arch a brow. "Anything?"

He dips his chin, looking exasperated. "Anything."

"Take me home."

IT'S easy to forget about your problems when you're lounging in the warmth only true happiness can provide. When what plagued your mind with darkness is washed out by the light that radiates from the person you love. The person who makes you feel content, at peace.

It's a dangerous feeling—letting go. Turning off the switches in your head that allow fear and doubt to grow and fester deep in your belly so that the exact opposite can take shape. Excitement, joy, the good kind of nerves that feel like butterflies flapping in your stomach; they're all good feelings that battle the bad.

Once you shut off the bad—if you can—that's when you're at your best. That's when life seems worth living, worth enjoying. I know that because I'm living with that realization. That reality.

As my mountain of a boyfriend flips on the lights in my apartment, his dark, hooded eyes on me, I feel that excitement, those butterflies in my belly instead of fear nipping at my spine and squeezing my throat.

Right here, right now, he's everything. Braden is my focus, that voice in my head repeating soft, encouraging words. The break in the storm raging inside of me.

He cups my cheeks in his hands and holds me there in front of him, his breath on my parted lips, amber eyes moving from one of mine to the other. I place my open palms against his chest, above the hard, grooved muscles I love so much, before sliding them outward, over his sides, and around his back.

The tension between us makes it hard to breathe. It's like we've been stuck inside of a sealed box for days and have nearly depleted our air supply.

My fingers curl into fists around his shirt as I pull him closer, his hips meeting my lower stomach. I focus on the way his throat contracts with a generous swallow when he tips his head back and a low noise gathers in his chest.

"Sierra," he says, sounding pained in a way that has my knees threatening to wobble. "If you want to wait, tell me right now. God help me, I will turn around and leave this apartment right now if you tell me no. But if you let me kiss you right now, I won't stop until your legs are up by your head and my cock is so far inside of you, you'll feel it for fucking days."

Holy. Shit.

My mouth dries as all of the moisture in my body floods between my legs. I don't bother speaking. I push up on my toes and take his mouth in a brutal, unmistakable kiss of approval.

He responds instantly, sucking my bottom lip between both of his before letting it go and slipping his tongue inside my mouth. Braden kisses me like a man possessed. Like he's spent his whole life not knowing what the inside of my mouth tastes like and is realizing what he's been missing.

His kisses—his *everything*—make me feel utterly desired, like I'm something he needs to survive. I want to live the rest of my life soaking up this feeling, burying it deep inside of me in a place nobody else will find it and dare try to take it away.

Cool air hits my cheeks when he releases them and slides his hands to the back of my head, trying to thread his fingers through the tied-back hairs. With a curse spilled against my wet lips, he digs through the braided bun holding back my hair and pulls out each bobby pin keeping it in place. One after the other, they hit the floor before my hair falls free, and he wastes no time before taking his fill, scratching and pressing on my scalp. My eyes try to roll back at the sudden wave of pleasure his touch evokes.

Braden shifts his hips, rolling them against me. I suck in a sharp breath when I feel him, long and hard against my stomach.

"Bedroom," he orders, tearing our lips apart. I nod once and grab both of his hands, removing them from my hair and using them to pull him toward my bedroom, even though I know he doesn't need help to find it.

We're silent as we walk. The only noise in the apartment comes from the padding of our feet, the hot air blowing from the vents, and our shuddered breaths.

I keep waiting for the nerves to settle in. For them to throw a ruin in the comfort that I've been soaking in since we got home, but they don't. I'm not sure if that's because of how utterly desperate I am for the man behind me or if I've just accepted the prospect of Braden fucking me into next week. Either way, I'm grateful.

The lack of nerves helps give me the confidence to stop in the middle of my bedroom, not even a foot from the edge of the bed, hold Braden's heavy-lidded stare, and pull up my dress. It slips off before falling to a puddle by my feet.

I'm naked besides a strapless nude bra and matching panties. But by the fire in his gaze, I could have forgotten that I wasn't standing naked. His usual amber eyes are nearly black, his pupils so large and dangerous that they've overthrown the warm colour. But it's his tight jaw, the muscle fluttering in his cheek, that gives him away.

I shudder under the intensity of his stare and sit on the bed, keeping my feet planted on the floor. He follows me like a bee to honey, stepping between my spread thighs before stopping, his fingers twitching at his sides.

"Don't make me beg," I whisper, pressing my hands flat to the mattress.

Large hands grab my thighs, kneading them and pushing them even further apart. "Maybe I should," he hums low in his throat. "But I don't think that I can wait that long. Not when I can see how slick and ready your pussy is."

His dirty words have me dropping my head back, exposing my throat as I whimper. My nipples pucker, forming hard buds beneath my bra as I arch my back and push toward him like a fucking offering. I'm handing my body over to him on a silver goddamn platter, and he's just standing there, burning holes into my skin with the heat in his eyes.

Frustration blooms deep in my chest the longer I sit exposed, so slick between my legs that I've most likely ruined my underwear. If he thinks he can say such dirty things, things that he knows will have me clawing for him, trying to climb him like a tree and then make me wait, he's got another thing coming.

With a new determination, I reach for his belt buckle, resting my fingers there for just a second before dragging them over his thick, hard flesh and gripping him. He pulses in my hand seconds before thrusting against my palm, a lip tugged between his teeth.

The look of pure need on his face is enough to have me scooting forward on the bed and tearing at his belt, yanking it from his pant loops and tossing it to the side. His zipper is next. I waste no time in pulling it down, exposing familiar black boxer briefs hanging low on his hips.

With a whimper of need, I shove his pants down over his thick thighs and down his legs before he kicks them away. Towering over me in a black dress shirt and boxer briefs, he's the epitome of perfection. A living, breathing definition of the term.

My heart gallops when I lower my eyes to the massive organ that I know waits behind tight, tight black material. Without hesitation, I reach forward, wrapping my fingers around the outline of him and hearing my breath hitch as clearly as I do his. But it's not enough, and it's with that thought that I'm yanking on the waistband of his underwear and watching with wide eyes as his cock slaps his abdomen, the smooth head red, angry, and wet.

"Fuck, Sierra. Take me in your mouth. Please," he grinds out, his chest heaving.

I want to torture him, to make him feel as helpless and needy as I do, but there's something about the plea in his eyes that has me shoving aside those thoughts and wrapping my lips around him, swallowing as much of his length as I can in one go.

A hand cups the back of my neck as I continue to suck him deep before retreating, flicking my tongue at the head and collecting the liquid pooling there. I wrap my hand around the base and stroke him in time with my mouth.

Two hands get lost in my hair, and his grip becomes more firm, more controlling. His hips thrust in time with every dip of my head, and those fingers dig deep into my scalp. He uses his hold to pull me further down his length with every jerk of his hips. I sputter a breath, spit leaking from the sides of my mouth and moisture collecting in my eyes when he brushes the back of my throat and groans out a noise so raw that I let him continue controlling my movements without complaint.

"You feel so fucking good," Braden growls, continuing to fuck my mouth like a man on the edge of losing his mind. "You're the only one that makes me feel like this."

Tears wet my skin, and my throat burns, but I don't stop. I won't. Not until he rips himself from my mouth and hisses, "As much as I would love to paint your throat with my cum, I need to be inside of you."

16

Sierra

Pushing back on the mattress, I prop myself up on my elbows and lift a taunting brow. His words make my insides roll into themselves. I want him to make good on every promise he's made tonight. My legs up by my head, his cock deep inside of me.

It's been a long six weeks spent full to the brim with insatiable sexual frustration. Every lingering kiss on my neck and brush of his fingers across my chest has made me so high-strung that I worry I'll snap and lose my grip on sanity at any given moment.

I saw it in the way Braden held his shoulders when we got home—heavy like they carried the weight of the world—that he was expecting me to say no and push him back out the door. He has no idea how deep my ache for him goes. But that's going to change. Hopefully, it's already started to.

"Take off your shirt," I whisper while reaching behind my back and unclasping my bra. With no straps, it slides off in one motion, joining the rest of our clothes on the floor.

He unbuttons his shirt with steady fingers, each one

exposing a bit more of the brown hair sprinkled across the hard lines of his chest. Dark eyes move over me in a long sweep. They settle heavy on my chest as he shrugs the shirt from his shoulders and sets his knees on the bed, towering over me.

"Look at you," he says through clenched teeth, sounding angry but looking far from it. No, that's not anger. It's unadulterated lust, an undeniable need that I see in his eyes. For me. The realization has me shuddering into the mattress. "You are the most gorgeous thing I have ever seen."

My lungs tighten, capturing my breath and holding it hostage before releasing it in a wavering puff. Tears pool in my eyes at the sincerity in his words and the way they pry my ribs apart and squeeze my heart.

"So are you," I admit, the words so true that the weight of them sags on my tongue. He shakes his head while searching my face with eyes so hot they could shoot fire.

I swallow hard when his hands cup my calves, moving up over my knees and thighs before settling on my hips. He's towering above me now, the scent of his cologne strong against the heat of his body. Slowly, so fucking slowly, his fingers curl beneath the waistband of my panties, and I lift my butt in the air to help him slide them off.

Now bare, I reach out for him, one hand moving to hold his jaw, the other his trim waist. Warm breath brushes my nose and cheeks as he settles between my legs. My breasts touch his chest, hard nipples against hard nipples, when he drops to his elbows beside my head and runs a knuckle across the length of my cheekbone.

I should speak. Should tell him all the words crashing and burning inside of my head and the reality that I'm hiding from right now. But the moment feels too delicate to risk saying the wrong thing.

I'm pulled from those thoughts the moment careful fingers

part my lower lips, so slick with my arousal that if it were anybody else, I might have been embarrassed. Braden circles the throbbing bundle of nerves once, twice, three times before sliding a long digit inside of me.

Noises escape my mouth that I don't recognize as I clench around the invasion, wiggling my hips, searching for more—begging for it. Sweat breaks out between my breasts as I arch into him, crushing them against him. I cry out when he adds a second finger, pushing them deeper with each in-and-out motion and groaning in my ear.

"Jesus Christ, Sierra."

His face falls to my throat as I croak, "I need you."

Nodding a few too many times to pretend he's not just as desperate as I am, he slips his fingers from inside of me. The absence of his touch only lasts a second before the smooth, round head of his cock rubs along my seam, coating itself in my wetness. "I need you too, baby."

He enters me with a curse, only sheathing himself halfway before retreating and moving again, this time filling me completely. His pace picks up as I adjust to the size of him, and warm, wet lips mold to my throat, moving along the side of it before sucking and grazing my raging pulse with his teeth. I use the hand gripping his waist to pull him closer, encouraging him to pick up the pace.

"Braden," I whimper, lifting my chin, giving his mouth full access to my burning skin. His groans vibrate along my skin, and his fingers press into my hips hard enough I wouldn't be surprised to see bruises there in the morning.

Our bodies move as one, falling in sync as easily as if we were never apart.

"Legs up," he grinds out, pushing back onto his knees. His hands move to my thighs before he's shoving my legs to my shoulders, sliding his palm down to grip my calves, holding them there.

The new position allows him to push in even deeper, hitting a spot inside of me that has stars twinkling in my eyes and my throat burning with a hoarse cry. My head drops to the pillow as I lose the ability to hold it up any longer.

"Do you feel that, little fighter?" he rasps, his lips swollen and red. I grip both of his hands where they hold my ankles. "Do you feel how full you are? How fucking good it feels when I'm inside of your hot pussy?"

Braden's words strike a match to my insides. It's impossible to put it out the flames. A raging inferno with no plans of dying. I let myself burn, loving the way it feels. My heart roars deep in my chest, failing to keep up with the lust ripping through my veins.

"Oh God. Yes. Yes." The release I've been chasing is right there, growing and filling me up like an expanding balloon. Without a second thought, I'm letting go of his wrist and dragging my hand between my legs, sliding my fingers in my arousal. I find my clit and pinch it between my fingertips, gasping at the pleasure that sparks and explodes from the motion.

Braden's eyes glaze over when they focus on my hand, on the way my fingers circle the throbbing bud before pulling at it, again and again as he fucks me harder.

"Shit. That's right," he grunts. "Get yourself there. Need to feel you come around me."

With a few more thrusts, I'm there. My vision blackens around the edges as my orgasm rips through me, sending me flying off the side of a cliff. I'm lost to the pleasure zipping through my bones when Braden comes to a stop, buried as far inside of me as possible. He spits words so dirty I clench around him in approval as he spills inside of me, filling me with a warmth I've been without for too long.

"Holy fuck," he breathes, falling toward my chest, still buried inside of me.

"Yeah," I murmur in agreement.

I don't have the willpower nor the want to be separated from him yet, so I wrap my arms around his neck and pull him toward me, letting out a content sigh when he ducks his head to my shoulder and kisses the wet skin. His next words are so soft and pure that I don't bother hiding the tear that slides down my cheek.

"I can't help but feel like I wasted so much of my life being without you. You're everything to me, Sierra. I won't waste any more time."

I press my face to his throat and force a gentle sigh past my lips as tears pepper his skin.

Tomorrow. I'll tell him tomorrow.

As I tie the strings of my cartoon reindeer–spotted pajama pants tight around my waist, I'm hit in the gut with a punch of appreciation for my family's "comfort over beauty" Christmas rule. And by family, I mean the one comprising Clare, Liz, and me.

Ever since I can remember, we've had a silent agreement to only wear our comfiest clothes on Christmas. Reason being, nobody should have to dress up in clothes that tighten up and tease the threat of suffocation once the turkey settles and your stomach swells up like you've been bitten by an elephant-sized wasp.

My sister and her daughter should be here any minute, and

while that would usually fill me with excitement, I'm terrified instead. I stare at the dresser drawer that I know hides three positive pregnancy tests and try to push back the anxiety festering inside of me.

The high from last night disappeared the moment I opened my eyes this morning and reality swooped in just to take a giant crap on my face. The already wavering support beam I had been standing on collapsed without a worry about what might happen to me afterward. Update: I ended up tumbling into a dark, miserable pit and have thus shrunken back behind my protective seal, where I've been hiding since. Despite the obvious effort I've made to avoid his kisses and all eye contact today, Braden, the stubborn man that he is, has refused to take the hint, never leaving my side.

I didn't miss the way his eyes narrowed into slits of suspicion when he tried to follow me into the shower and I refused to let him join me, or the scoff that followed when I offered to be the one to stop by the grocery store to pick up the missing ingredients Clare needed for dinner when he knows better than anybody how much I loathe spending time at the store. I had just wanted distance, and he knew it immediately.

Guilt burns beneath my skin while I lift my hair off my neck and release a stressed breath.

Keeping this a secret from Braden is far from easy. It's not like I want to shoulder this alone because I really, really don't. But I'm also not about to risk anything by telling him about the pregnancy before I've even gone to the doctor and confirmed what the tiny plastic sticks told me.

With Clare here, it'll be easier. We'll sneak away after dinner, and I'll tell her. Then tomorrow, she'll come with me to the doctors and hold my hand while I'm told what the rest of my future holds. If it's true, if I *am* pregnant, then I'll tell him. I'll crack myself wide open and see if he'll yank my heart from my chest or glue me back together.

Come on, Sierra. I need to think positively, which is the exact opposite of what I've been doing.

Braden won't run. He won't realize this is way more than he bargained for so soon and take off in the night. Maybe it won't be with open arms and a smile, but he will accept this. Right? I keep repeating the encouraging words in my head until they echo in my ears, leaving me with no choice but to believe them.

I'm not sure what compels me to walk, but I'm fumbling with the dresser drawer before I think too hard about it. I rifle through the old shirts and gym shorts with the tags still connected from when I made "work out more" my last New Year's resolution before I nearly keel over and die.

I keep waiting to hear a splat on the floor from where my stomach fell out of my ass, but there's nothing but silence. Eerie, skin-crawling silence. Until I hear him and the forced clearing of a throat coming from the doorway. Where the door was just shut.

My eyes slide shut, and I grab the edge of the dresser tight enough to turn my knuckles white, but I don't turn around. I can't.

Instead, I wait for him to speak, to yell and scream at me. But he doesn't. I keep waiting and waiting and waiting for what seems like hours before he breaks the silence with words that reach down my throat and rip the air from my lungs. That leave me gaping and boneless.

"I'm the only man you'll ever refer to as a DILF again. Got that, little fighter?"

17

Braden

If someone had asked me six months ago what I pictured my life to look like at this very moment, my answer would have been so disgustingly simple.

Women, booze, busted knuckles, daddy issues, and a God complex so intense I would have been choking on it.

That's what my life consisted of before I met her. Before I fell in love and found a purpose—a want to do better and actually achieve something worth a damn.

Life was predictable, flat, but still lively enough to keep me from smashing my head against a brick wall. I was under the pretence that I was happy with the way things were. Every woman that I took to bed and every fight that I didn't deserve to win but somehow managed to added another layer of fog to my smoky mirror. Another stormy night camouflaged as a warm, cloudless morning.

It wasn't until I found a goddamn angel in my bed, halo and all, that that mirror shattered and the mirage cleared, leaving me reeling at the reality of the depressing mess my life had become.

With her beside me, it was easier to captain my sinking ship. I fixed my shit one bucket of water at a time until the deck was dry and I was no longer sinking but merely coasting, swaying gently. Some days I still feel the waves crash against the sides, sloshing overboard and trying to pull me back down, but my ship never fills, never sinks. Not like before.

Six months ago, if I had ever asked myself what I would do if I found out that I was going to be a dad, I wouldn't have had an answer. Actually, I probably would have blacked out and wound up unconscious on the floor of whatever bar I had got shit-faced in.

There's not a doubt in my mind that I would have lost any semblance of reasonable thought and ran once I peeled myself off that floor and was slapped with the reality of it again. I wouldn't have gone too far, or been gone for too long, but I would have run nonetheless. Escape for a little while. I'm ashamed to admit that, but there's no use pussyfooting around the obvious.

Now, I'm no longer that guy, at least not completely. I still have my moments. I'm a fucking far cry from perfect. But as I stood in front of Sierra's dresser this morning—not even minutes after she had left for the store—with one of my old hockey shirts in one hand and a positive pregnancy test in the other, the last thing I wanted to do was escape.

My first instinct was to run *after* her, not away. I wanted to chase her ass down a grocery aisle before throwing her over my shoulder and taking her home. My second was to bend her over the bed and spank her ass for keeping this from me. And my third, well, that one shocked—no, terrified—the shit out of me.

I wanted to sink to my knees in front of her and cry. Not a few silent tears but full-on broken sobs. Fuck, I still do.

Regardless of the fact that my head feels like it's on backward and my chest is so tight that I might as well be wrapped beneath the scales of a giant snake, I can't shake the need to just let it out. My emotions are bubbling up, threatening to boil over and burn everything and everyone in sight.

And it isn't until I stand behind her, watching as she roots through a drawer for something that she won't find, something that currently lives in the pocket of my pajama pants, that I let a string of half-ass flirty words slip from my lips and feel the first splat of that emotion on my skin.

Sierra spins around at the sound of my voice, her expression stricken with surprise and her eyes laced with something that I don't want to admit to myself looks too much like fear.

I can sense it in the air—the moment she realizes what's happening. She starts toward me with hurried footsteps before stopping a breath away, no doubt curling her toes into the carpet in her effort to keep her distance. I shake my head frantically, as if to tell her how stupid it is to keep that fucking space between us when the only thing that I want is to feel her pressed against me, to smell that fresh laundry and men's bodywash scent that clings heavier to her skin the longer I'm around her.

She must understand the urgency in the movement, because slowly, too damn slowly, small arms slide around my waist, and a warm body brushes mine. She holds me like she's scared I'll crumble into a million unfixable pieces if she squeezes too tight, and the thought itself has a muscle in my cheek pulsing in a way it definitely shouldn't.

Expelling a frustrated puff of air, I curl my arms around Sierra and pull her tight, not bothering to brush off how perfectly her body fits with mine, like we're two halves of the same fucking stone. I stopped forcing myself to ignore those things weeks ago, and now it's impossible not to see the spotlights on them.

"I was going to tell you," Sierra whispers.

There's a huge part of me that already knew she would tell me. That she would sit me down and explain what I could so visibly see torturing her. Despite that, there was still that small, barely there part of me buried deep, deep down that had doubted her intentions, doubted that she would open up to me about this and not carry that weight on her own. Yeah, I hate that part. Fucking detest it.

"When did you find out?"

She stiffens in my arms for no longer than a blink of time. "Yesterday."

"With Gracie." It's not a question, but she nods into my chest anyway.

Now, the missing pieces of the puzzle reveal themselves, slipping into their missing slots and creating a much clearer image for me to dissect. I knew it was weird when Tyler told us he was taking Gracie and Sierra out for a few minutes, but it was my brother, the guy who does nothing without a good reason. The first thing I thought was that his wife got one of her insane cravings. Who was I to argue with that? And if Sierra wanted to go . . . I was too excited at the prospect of her getting along so well with my sister-in-law to question it.

Then they got back, and the shift I saw in Sierra was obvious. But I chalked it up to her being in an unfamiliar place. I didn't want to push her, but I should have. And I sure as shit shouldn't have taken her home and had sex with her.

Fuck. I hate that I can taste the bitter anger and resentment on my tongue. Anger at myself for not recognizing the signs for what they were the moment they appeared, and resentment for not being the one by her side when she found out.

"Did you find out alone? Did you have anyone with you?" I ask.

Who am I kidding? She wouldn't have let Gracie watch her

do something so intimate and scary. She did it alone, I'm sure of it.

"Gracie was there before and after," she replies.

An image of a terrified, shaking Sierra staring down at three pregnancy tests with no one there to hold her hand flashes through my mind before I'm gasping for air, truly losing it.

Noticing that my fingers have curled into her shirt, I relax them, moving one flat palm to her lower back, the other wrapped all the way around her shoulders.

"Are you mad?" she asks.

I suck in a breath through my teeth before letting it out gently. "No."

"Are you upset?"

"At you? No. At the fact you have my baby growing in your belly? Fuck no."

She tries to move out of my arms, but I pull her closer, keeping her from looking up at me. "The only thing I'm upset about is that I wasn't there with you. I should have been. Or at least with you after. You shouldn't have come back and sat in silence, Sierra. It fucking pains me to know you were sitting there with me at the dinner table with this knowledge burning a hole in your gut. Fuck, you let me stick my hand down up your skirt while you were digesting this."

I'm the one that pulls back this time, too angry at myself to hold her. There's a whimper of protest from her when I spin around and push my palms into my eyes, rubbing furiously against the static in my vision.

"You couldn't even look at me this morning. Is that why? Did I force you to have sex with me last night?" Bile burns its way up my throat.

I should have waited. I should have said good night and gone back to my apartment after getting her home. The possibility of her hating me for this sits like a grenade in my stomach, the pin already pulled. My hands fall from my face before I set them on my hips and toss my head back.

"No. No, of course not. How could you even think that?"

"How could I think that?" I echo with a humourless laugh.

Sierra's hand on my arm makes me flinch. Yeah, fucking flinch. I'm surprised when she doesn't recoil from that but wraps her fingers around my skin and tenderly pulls me around to face her again. I can feel the burn of her stare on my face, on my scowl and rigid jaw, but I keep staring at the wall behind her, too terrified of what I might see if I look at her.

"Baby," she murmurs while pressing her lips to the place between my pecs. A shiver builds at the base of my spine, but I ignore it. "Look at me."

I can't. I'm furious with myself and how selfish I've been.

More pieces to this unfinished puzzle appear as I start to picture a timeline in my head—our timeline. I was too shell-shocked to notice it earlier, but there was a number on one of the tests. 3+ weeks pregnant. That's what it said.

Apart from last night, we haven't had sex since before she left Vancouver. That was over six weeks ago. My blood freezes. A cold rush slithers up my body. She was either already pregnant when she left or was shortly after.

Fuck, fuck, fuck. What if I hadn't come after her?

I'm suddenly dizzy, my vision spotting for a moment.

"Braden." She says my name firmly, with a sharp edge. Her grip on my arm tightens before she's reaching up and cupping my jaw. "You look like you're going to be sick."

I probably do. I feel sick, but not the way she's thinking. I'm sick with the idea of never having found out, of never getting the chance to be a dad, even if the idea of it has my stomach cramping up and sweat breaking out on my neck. I'm being insane, I know that. There's no way Sierra wouldn't have told me. But I'm not thinking that way right now. Everything is too much—I feel too much.

I sink my fingers into my hair to the point of pain before I finally look at her. There's a look of pure devastation on her face that takes the wind out from beneath me.

I'm being selfish. This isn't about me. This is about her, this baby, and us. Our future. I can't block her out. Not right now, and when she's looking like a visible representation of everything going on inside of my head.

My arms fall to my sides. I walk backward until the backs of my knees hit the mattress. Sitting down on the edge, I press my hands to the unmade bed and exhale slowly. Get it together.

"Come here," I order gruffly. When she doesn't hesitate, a flicker of hope fills me so brightly that I might have squinted on reflex. As soon as she steps between my legs, I'm cupping the backs of her thighs and pressing my forehead to her stomach. "I'm sorry. I'm so fucking sorry, baby."

Gentle fingers run through my hair in slow strokes, nails lightly scratching my scalp. "It's okay, Braden. You did nothing wrong. Not now. Not last night." I shake my head, but she lightly pulls on my hair to stop me and speaks again.

"If we're going to play the blame game here, then I should be the one at fault. I'm the one that didn't ask you to take me to get a test. I wanted your hand up my dress last night just as much as I wanted to be with you afterward. There isn't a thing that happened with you I didn't want to happen."

Her chest shakes against my forehead when she sucks in a long breath. She's upset, but I know better than to interrupt her again.

"I couldn't look at you this morning because I knew that if I did, I would blurt out that I'm pregnant, and I didn't want to do that until I knew for sure. There can always be false positives, and yeah, I know the odds of that are low considering I took three tests, but I needed to be one hundred percent sure. I was going to go see someone tomorrow with Clare. Braden, even if I wasn't really pregnant, I still would have told you. That's a promise."

I'm nodding before her words have even completely sunken in. And once they do, a massive sense of relief hits me dead smack in the centre of my chest.

The weight pressing down on my shoulders, trying to push me to the ground, eases exponentially as I slide my hands up, up, up, settling them on her lower back. I clutch her tight, tipping my head so that my chin rests on her stomach and our eyes meet.

"I want to go to the appointment with you," I say. The roughness of my voice has me fighting back a wince. "Let me be there. Please."

The way her silver eyes soften at my plea makes my mouth tip up in a small smile. There really isn't anything more that I want right now than to stand beside her through this. I still haven't completely wrapped my head around the idea of us—of me, rather—bringing a baby into the world, but I can't deny the intense zing of excitement in my stomach when I think about it either.

"Yes," she says, a slight flush to her cheeks. "Of course you can come."

My small smile grows into a dimpled grin as I nod once and press my lips to her stomach repeatedly.

I can't believe it. Me: a fucking dad.

18

Sierra

Clare's round eyes have never been so narrowed.

My sister watches the man beside me like a shotgun-wielding father standing at the top of a set of porch steps. Braden's grip on my hand tightens the slightest bit, and I swear I just heard him gulp.

"Clare, this is Braden. Braden, Clare," I speak up, moving the hand Braden isn't using as a comfort device between them. "Liz is the little Devil that just took off behind us."

Soft sounds of excitement come from my spare room as my niece makes herself right at home. The thought has warmth expanding in my chest. I've missed her so much.

"It's nice to finally meet you." Braden speaks with confidence, but I hear the brief tickle of nerves he can't hide from me. He sticks his hand out in the distance between us and Clare and waits, letting it hang there as she stares at it for a few seconds. The hand wrapped around mine begins to sweat.

"I would say the same, but I'm not sure if it would be a lie quite yet," Clare replies in a no-bullshit tone. Braden winces beside me before she finally takes his hand and gives it a firm shake. She drops it quickly. "Do your hands always sweat so much?"

"Jesus, Clare!" I sputter a laugh before shutting myself up with a fist pressed to my mouth. I know what she's doing right now, acting so brash and nonchalant. It's what she's done since the very first time I ever brought a guy home. She came dressed in her big-sister supersuit, ready to put Braden to the test.

When Clare finally turns to look at me, her features relax, Braden forgotten for the time being. With a wide grin, she rushes over and gathers me in her arms. "Oh my God. I missed you so much. It's only been six weeks, but I feel like you've been gone for six years."

My cheek smushes against hers, and her familiar smell mixed with the feel of her arms wound around my shoulders has my stomach clenching with nostalgia. "I missed you too, Clarebear."

All too quickly, we break apart, and I force myself to remember that she's going to be here for the next two days so that I don't break down and start sobbing like a child who's had their lollipop stolen. Clare isn't leaving anytime soon. Now is *not* the time.

As if she can read my thoughts, my sister places her hands on her hips and throws a look over her shoulder to the bags sitting by the door. "Help me bring this stuff in? There's more in the car, but I'm sure Braden wouldn't mind making a trip down. Would you, big guy?"

Braden tosses me a look that says "did she really just call me big guy?" before pressing a quick kiss to my forehead and eyeing my sister. "Of course not. What vehicle is yours?"

"Silver Focus parked three stalls from the sidewalk. Here, catch." A key ring cuts through the air before Braden grabs it in a tight fist. Clare's eyes widen for a moment. "Quick reflexes."

He drips his chin. "Thank you." His eyes cut to me when he says, "Be right back."

Braden is barely through the front door when I shut it behind him and pin my sister with a glare. "You're being mean."

She lifts a shoulder before picking up a black duffel bag in one hand and a pastel blue and yellow backpack in the other and hauling them into my spare room. Hot on her heels, I stand in the doorway with my arms crossed, spying Liz stretched out on the bed with a *Geronimo Stilton* book open in her hands.

"I'm always mean to your boyfriends," Clare replies coolly. She drops the bags on top of the dresser and finally turns to face me. There's something in the way she's eyeing me that makes me feel all twitchy and nervous. I don't like it.

"Stop staring at me like that. And you know what I'm trying to say, Clare. You're being extra mean."

She exhales loudly. "You're right. Why don't we go to the kitchen and pop open one of the bottles of sauvignon blanc I bought on the way from the airport. It's still your favourite, right?"

Something churns in my stomach. Maybe guilt? "I'm not thirsty."

"Are you sure? You probably haven't had it in forever. You've earned it."

Yeah, it's definitely guilt. Or nausea. Possibly both? I run a hand over the length of my ponytail and twist it around my fingers.

"Maybe later," I croak. Good God, could I be more obvious? Just come out and say it, Sierra. *I'm pregnant, Clare.*

You're going to be an auntie. Yeah, blunt is good. Blunt is easier. Quick and painless, like ripping off a Band-Aid.

If she's going to be disappointed, there's nothing that I can do about it. She'll just have to get over it and learn to accept that her little sister is having a baby. Of course it will suck not to have her there supporting me through the next several months, but I won't allow her to make us feel bad or like we've done anything wrong.

What am I even talking about? Clare isn't like that. If she's not happy, it won't take her long to get over it. That's how she works. I'm being ridiculous.

If Braden could hear my thoughts right now, he would look at me with that damn stubborn scowl and tell me to knock it the hell off.

My toes are tapping the floor when Clare throws her arms in the air, letting them come down on her thighs with a *smack*. "Oh, good grief! You're pregnant, right? I'm so beyond offended that you thought I wouldn't be able to tell. I can read you just as easily over the phone as I can in person."

What? The world stills for a few seconds.

"You knew?" I wheeze.

Clare's bright blue eyes roll as she reaches for my hands. "Come on. You've been asleep by eight every single night, you've completely forgotten what you were saying in the middle of nearly all of our recent conversations, and you're fucking glowing. Your wine refusal was the last thing I needed to check off before I was completely sure."

"Don't forget the morning sickness that's never actually *in* the morning either," I grumble.

I hear a sharp inhale of breath before soft hands tighten around mine to the point of pain. Smiling sheepishly at her, I let my sister's awed expression drown out all of my previous fears and feelings of doubt.

"You're having a baby?" a soft voice asks, drawing our attention to the little girl watching us gingerly. Her soft eyes peek over the edge of her open book as she continues to hold it in front of her face, using it like a shield.

Something slips between my ribs and pokes my heart. "I still have to go to the doctor to make sure, but we think so, Lizzy."

Cutting a worried glance at Clare, I lift a brow when I find her already watching me with a similar expression. I don't have time to worry about whether the news has upset my niece before she's very carefully placing her book beside her and hopping off the bed, rushing in my direction. She throws her arms around my waist and lights up with a toothy smile.

"Babies are so cute," she exclaims. A thoughtful look flashes across her face before she crinkles her nose. "But stinky."

I laugh lightly and ruffle her light blonde hair, careful to avoid the red beret pinning her bangs to the side.

"It looks like I missed something important."

Liz jumps away from me at the sound of Braden's deep voice. I have to hide my smile in the neck of my shirt when I catch a glimpse of her pink cheeks before she's flopping on the bed face-first.

Braden sidles up to me, a hand curving around my hip. Jutting my chin in the direction of the door, he takes the hint and leads us out of the room, Clare following closely behind us.

As soon as we round the hallway and enter the open area of the living room and kitchen, I notice the pile of gifts and wine bottles set by the front door. Clare follows my gaze, clapping her hands in excitement.

"I thought we agreed that you guys coming here for Christmas *was* my present, Clare," I scold.

I'm torn between wanting to smack her upside the head for spending too much money and feeling excited. Unlike myself, Clare has always been almost *too* good at giving gifts. Even if she doesn't know you all that well, she always seems to pick out something that you'll love. We've always called it her superpower. Meanwhile, I can't choose a good gift to save my life.

I almost smack her when she swipes a hand through the air, shrugging me off. "Me, not bring gifts? It's your fault for believing that I wouldn't bring my own sister a Christmas present." Turning to Braden, she adds, "Thank you for bringing this all up. I'm just going to pop the wine in the fridge before starting dinner."

Braden acknowledges her thanks with a shaky smile—clearly still feeling nervous talking to her due to her cold behaviour—and runs his hand up and down my spine. With a long exhale, I slip my arm around his waist and cuddle into his side, using his presence as my own personal security blanket.

"Let her spoil you if she wants to, baby. You deserve it."

I try not to let his words affect me as much as they want to, knowing that I'll most likely burst into a fit of tears. "I love you."

His words make the hairs on the top of my head flutter. "I love you too. Now, let's go help your sister with this fucking turkey."

My laugh sneaks out before I have a chance to register it. With a lingering kiss to Braden's jaw, I'm detaching myself from his arms, instantly hating the way I feel without him as I join my sister in the kitchen.

As the day comes to an end, I realize that I should probably tell Braden that my sister is really no more intimidating than a small yippy dog biting at your heels. But watching the most calm, cool, and collected guy that I've ever met squirm beneath the glare of someone so much smaller than him has me feeling a bit smug, like an evil villain in a Disney cartoon. Besides, it can't be long now until Clare gives it up and hugs the shit out of the big man. I'm surprised she's even held out this long.

He's passed her test with flying colours—never getting upset or letting her stare keep him from touching me whenever possible, even if it was just brief squeezes of my hand or a fleeting kiss on the cheek. He hasn't frowned or grumbled annoyed words under his breath. He has, in all honesty, been a *perfect* boyfriend. I'm not sure that I can take any more of it before I end up falling all over myself trying to shoo him into bed.

"I want to tell her that if she doesn't stop scowling, her face will stay like that forever, but I don't want her to strangle me in my sleep," Braden mumbles, quiet enough for only me to hear.

He's watching warily as Clare looks up from her half-coloured picture of a Christmas elf and squints her eyes at him, lifting a brow in a "do you have something to say?" kind of way. I bite back my laugh when Liz pinches her mother right below her elbow and grumbles something while stabbing a finger against her own colourful picture.

"It would be more likely that she would strangle you while you're awake. Clare doesn't leave her bed once she's under the covers unless absolutely necessary," I tease.

Braden's body shakes with a laugh. His eyes warm my face like the sun on a clear day. "Who would have thought that a couple colouring books would have slid me into your niece's good graces. I was expecting to be shooting myself in the foot for not buying her a doll or something."

"You chose well, although you really didn't have to get her anything. She gets spoiled enough as it is. Too many more gifts and she'll start thinking that she's the queen of England."

She truly is spoiled, no question about it. Being my parents' only grandchild and my only niece, she gets more than enough presents on any day that ends in *Y*, let alone special occasions. My parents send gift cards in the mail often—seeing as that's all they can give without having to learn a damn thing about her—and I always tried to bring her something every time that I popped by.

Obviously, I don't have the luxury of stopping by on random days after work anymore—a hard truth that unfortunately doesn't become any less painful as time passes—so I've had to improvise. It's safe to say that she'll be taking home a lot more than she came with.

Regardless of how absolutely spoiled the little munchkin is, I can't deny the way my heart grew double its size and attempted to climb up my throat when Braden pulled a Minnie Mouse Christmas bag out from God knows where and handed it over to her with a timid smile.

Liz didn't hesitate before tearing through the tissue paper and letting out a squeal when she pulled out two holiday-themed colouring books and a set of art supplies. I could see a slight dent in the armour Clare threw up earlier and felt the win for both Braden and myself.

"Does that mean that I shouldn't have gotten *you* anything? Because the way you looked at me with those wild, excited eyes after you opened your present made my cock really hard." His voice drops an octave, and his breath brushes the sensitive skin of my ear. An invisible hand cups the area between my legs before I push them together, fighting off the shiver swirling at the base of my spine.

I want to feel surprised by his ability to turn me into a dripping puddle of lust with just a few flirtatious words, but I can't. I've spent months experiencing how easy it is for Braden to make my underwear feel heavy and create an achy tension low in my belly that only he can soothe. I know that his promises aren't empty, and unless absolutely necessary, he wouldn't leave me high-strung and desperate for relief.

At this point, my body has become his to do with as he pleases, and more often than not, I can't find it in me to care.

Suddenly, a wave of exhaustion hits me, and I snuggle into the warmth radiating from his body. A yawn interrupts my train of thought.

He chuckles under his breath. "Do you want me to stay the night? If not, I should get going before you pass out on me."

"If you left, I would chase you down." The power behind my words has me blinking in surprise before I shake it away.

Braden snakes an arm around my shoulders and pulls me into his side. His cheek presses to my temple. "You say that as if I would make you chase me. I would have turned right back around as soon as I heard you coming after me, sunshine."

"That's good. We both know that I couldn't keep up with you anyway." I lift an arm and flex my nonexistent muscles to prove my next point. "I'm embarrassingly out of shape."

Braden squeezes my bicep and lifts the corner of his mouth. "You know that all you have to do is ask and you can join me at the gym. I promise to take it easy on you the first few times."

It's meant to be a joke, but the thought has me feeling both incredibly turned on and intrigued. There's no way that I could keep up with him, but seeing Braden all sweaty and out of breath . . .

"When do we start?" I ask in a rush, nearly panting like a dog in heat.

"Really?" he asks, looking completely shocked.

I roll my eyes. "You make it seem as if I'm a complete bum. I walk to work every day, jackass."

"You're right." He smooths his palm down up and down my arm. "Just tell me when, baby."

Another yawn rips through my mouth as I scoot closer into his hold, nuzzling my head under his chin. My eyelids begin to droop, feeling like I've glued sandbags to them. Sleep sounds like the most beautiful thing, and I stop trying to fight it. Braden's body wrapped around mine becomes the last thing I think about before I let it take me under.

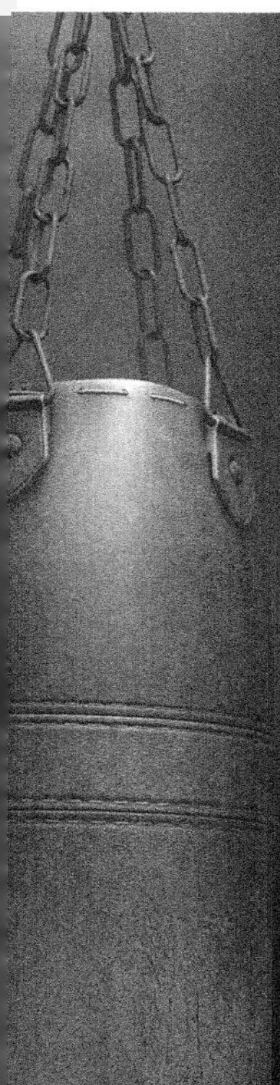

19

Braden

Is it creepy to watch your girlfriend while she sleeps? Probably. Do I care? Not at all.

After carrying Sierra to bed and making sure the duvet is tucked under her like a cocoon, I take two steps to the door before stalling. I shift on my feet and peer down at her sleeping form, feeling a surge of contentment. There's something about knowing that she'll be waiting for me when I crawl into bed, ready to wrap herself around me, that strips me bare, leaving me way too vulnerable.

If it weren't for the intimidating woman waiting for me in the other room, I would shed my clothes and join my girl in bed right now. There's no place that I would rather be than wrapped around Sierra, but the conversation that awaits me might just be the most important one I've ever had.

With that thought, I'm closing the bedroom door softly and stepping into the lamplit living room.

It's almost like being on the receiving end of a swift kick to the stomach when I spot the simple black picture frame housing the photo of Tyler, Oakley, Adam, and me playing college hockey that Sierra gifted me before dinner. It stands by itself on one of the two side tables, looking as if it belongs there —here, in Sierra's place.

That's a dangerous, dangerous thought. One that I don't have the energy to focus on right now.

Luckily, Clare doesn't seem to be a fan of beating around the bush. Her eyes sweep the room before focusing on me. "Are you going to come sit down? I might seem like it, but I don't bite."

There's a brief moment where my breath quickens before evening out again. This is Sierra's big sister. From what I've gathered, sitting down alone with Clare is the equivalent of having a heart-to-heart with a terrifying father. It's better to just get it over with so that everyone can move on from the awkward tension and the occasional fleeting glare. Not that I have even a fucking sliver of experience in that department. The younger version of myself had never cared enough about any of the girls I dated to even consider meeting their fathers.

Wow, talk about what a great conversation starter that would be.

Fighting back a wince, I dip my chin and take a seat on the opposite end of the couch. To keep my legs from bouncing nervously, I pull one over my knee and hold on to my ankle to keep my hands busy.

Clare is looking far too relaxed with her back to the armrest, body turned to face me head-on, and a completely blank stare. I shiver slightly when I start to imagine all of the personal questions and accusations she must have locked and loaded in that head of hers.

She taps her blunt nails on the tops of her thighs and hums in a way that has my hackles shooting straight up. I'm not sure if she's waiting for me to be the one to break the ice, but I can't even seem to muster up a curse to mumble to myself, let alone a decent conversation starter.

There have only been a handful of times where I've felt as uncomfortable as I do right now. Once when I told my parents I was dropping out of school, and the other when I told my old hockey coach that hockey wasn't the sport I was planning on pursuing long term.

Clare decides to cut through the tension before I have a chance to rip chunks of hair from my scalp. "I'm assuming you know how close I am with my sister," she starts calmly. I nod. "So you understand why I'm being such a hard-ass?"

"I do."

How could I not? It would feel almost criminal for Clare not to be so protective of Sierra. I'm grateful for that. It's reassuring to know she has someone else watching her back and looking out for her best interests when I can't be.

"When Sierra told me that she was offered a job opportunity in Toronto, I didn't hesitate to tell her to go for it. As you know, my sister is driven by the idea of success and reaching the goals that she's set for herself. It would have been incredibly selfish of me to tell her that in reality, I was terrified of her being so far away and all alone.

"She probably didn't tell you, but I pushed hard for you before she left. I could see the change in her since meeting you, and I wanted her to keep that glow forever. So I kept trying to get her to just *ask* you to go with her, and if you said no, then, well, that's that. At least she'll leave knowing that there wasn't anything else she could have said or done. But of course she refused to. She was adamant that you weren't the type to follow after a woman. That you weren't interested in a happily ever after."

The contents of my stomach curdle at what I know is coming next. While Clare's admission surprises me, it does nothing to stop the lingering guilt from rising to the surface again like a zit that won't clear up.

Clare exhales slowly while running the pad of her thumb between her eyebrows.

"Sierra kept the details of what happened between you two a secret until a few days after she got settled here. It didn't take a genius to know that you fucked up in a big way, but getting her to open up about it was just about as difficult as convincing my daughter that Santa won't come if she stays up all night sitting on the couch waiting. I'm just ashamed of myself for not being able to decipher the root of her hurt before I let her get on that plane. I assumed that she was upset because she had to leave you behind, but I didn't think that something had happened the night before. I didn't think that you would have been so cruel to her. That's my fault, though, I suppose. For not automatically assuming the worst of you when I clearly should have."

Ouch. There's no hiding the way I flinch.

Clare almost looks apologetic when she catches me doing it, but it's a fleeting expression. "I really don't mean to be so rude, Braden. I just want you to understand where I'm coming from."

"No, I get it. I fucked up. You're just looking out for your little sister," I assure her, even though there's a ball in my throat that makes it difficult to speak. "If somebody had hurt my brother the way I hurt Sierra, I would be doing the exact same thing."

I know better than to expect my admission to earn me any respect in her eyes, but hopefully it helps shine some light on a decent side of me that she hasn't seen. We share a similar sense of loyalty when it comes to family. It's probably one of the only things that we have in common besides our love for the beautiful woman sleeping in the other room.

"I need to ask you something, and I'm hoping you won't bullshit me," she states.

Straightening my spine, I nod once. When she flexes her fingers and smooths her hands down her thighs, my gaze is drawn to the tattoo on her left hand—her otherwise bare ring finger, to be exact. I didn't notice the black ink before now, but after spotting it, I can't seem to look away. A set of initials—the letters *MF*—are written in a thin script on the top of her finger, right where a wedding ring would sit.

Her fingers curl under the intensity of my stare, forcing me to look away, knowing that I've been caught gawking like a weirdo.

"When we got married, Max, my husband at the time, and I were too broke to afford wedding rings," she says, surprising me. A light yet almost pained laugh falls between us. "Max and I were together from the moment we realized cooties weren't real until shortly after Elizabeth was born. I would love to say that our marriage was just as perfect as our dating life had been, but I'm not going to lie to you. Clearly, I'm divorced, so it didn't work as well as we thought it would. However, marrying Max remains one of the best decisions that I have ever made. I wouldn't trade all of the good memories for anything. Not to mention I got Lizzy, and she's the biggest blessing I've ever received."

Her eyes shine, the ghost of a frown on her tight features before she steels her expression. "Too much information, I know. This was a great lead-in to what I wanted to ask you, though, so I'll go ahead and come out with it. Are you planning on marrying my sister, Braden?"

If I tried to get off the couch right now, I couldn't. My brain is nothing but a jumble of unplugged cords and blown circuit breakers. That familiar pinch in my stomach that always seems to appear when the topic of marriage comes up returns with a fucking vengeance. Fighting back a hiss, I genuinely consider bending over just to soothe the pain as the blood drains from my face.

"She wasn't kidding," Clare mumbles, not bothering to hide her disappointment. "You look like you're going to spew chunks."

Her statement pisses me off. Not because it's not true, but because it's *too* true.

"I don't believe in marriage," I grind out.

She arches a near condescending brow and leans forward. "No? So what do you believe in, then?"

"I don't need a piece of paper to tell me that I love your sister and will do everything in my power to take care of her and our baby. Sierra means so much more to me than a damn label meant to convince others that we're in love and happy. If there's anything that I believe in, it's exactly that."

"And I'm supposed to just take your word for it?" she counters, not giving an inch.

I suck in a long breath before pushing it back out and letting my crossed leg drop to the floor. Leaning forward, I rest my forearms on my knees and turn to look at my girlfriend's sister—or my fucking executioner, more like it—with my eyes narrowed.

"If I'm being honest, I don't care what you do with it. All I do know is that I plan on loving Sierra for the rest of my life. Whether she's wearing a ring around her finger or not, it doesn't make a difference to me. She's mine, and I don't plan on ever letting her get away from me again. That's a fucking promise that I would die to keep."

The rapid rise and fall of my chest should be alarming, but I'm too tense to care. Too pissed off at myself for not being able to give Sierra's only real family the answers that she wants.

There's nothing else that I can say to convince Clare of my

feelings or intentions. The ball is in her court now. Either she can let the past go and stand with us as we move forward, or she can hold on to it and let it fester. I'll continue to respect her either way, but I would be an idiot to not hope for option A.

"What if all of that stops being enough, Braden? What if it's either marry her or lose her all over again?"

I look away, sweeping my blank stare across the room. A muscle in my jaw feathers.

"I won't spend another day without her again, Clare. So if those were my only two options, I would marry her in a fucking heartbeat."

20

Braden

Time feels like it's sped up since Clare and Elizabeth flew back to Vancouver four days ago. Between Sierra's first doctor's appointment that confirmed via pee in a cup that she's really pregnant, the sudden influx of potential client calls I've received for the gym while trying to keep a handle on the renovations and deliveries, and my weak attempts at preparing myself mentally for our first glimpse of our unborn baby, each day has felt more chaotic than the last. I feel like I've been running in place, each day stuck in an endless, chaotic loop.

I try to shake those thoughts away and focus on right now. It's the day of our first ultrasound appointment, and like any commitment-terrified man turned first-time dad, I'm trying not to lose my shit. Not in a generic sense where I've found myself pacing back and forth in this incredibly small ultrasound room with my head in my hands, but in a more internal, hidden way where I can't think of anything but the faint ticking noise coming from the bomb implanted in my stomach as it counts down, preparing for detonation.

We've already been told not to get too excited about the idea of seeing much today, that this is just meant to give us an estimated due date and to see how far along Sierra is. The lady on the phone who confirmed our appointment made it clear that we won't be able to see anything yet but a small blob, but I don't care. Blob or not, I'm going to see our baby.

"You need to calm down."

Sierra laughs at me from where she sits on the ultrasound table, dangling her legs off the side. She shifts her butt slightly, which in turn has that ridiculous paper under her crinkling loudly.

I watch her from my place directly beside the table, one hand cupping her knee and the other on her lower back. The ultrasound tech disappeared after leading us to our room and has been gone for so long I've considered the possibility that he decided to take a lunch break across town mid-appointment.

"I am calm." I straighten my back. "I told you that we should have requested someone else."

"Right," she muses with an exaggerated nod. "A female tech, of course."

I don't bother hiding my feelings on the matter. "Exactly."

"I wouldn't worry about that guy. He's most definitely married."

"Married, Sierra. Not blind," I tell her like it's the most obvious thing in the world.

In my defense, the guy we got stuck with isn't nearly ugly enough for me to feel comfortable with his eyes on that section of her bare skin. Her arms? Fine. Her legs? We're getting a bit iffy, but depending *how much* leg, maybe. But her stomach? No. I can feel the vein bulging in my forehead already.

"Either way, he's no competition. Although it will be nice to watch you struggle the way I do when I watch you in the ring, all bare-chested and sweaty. I'm positive that wearing a shirt every once in a while wouldn't keep you from winning matches," she grumbles, lifting her chin defiantly.

I'm grinning like an idiot, but I don't care. "I didn't take you for the jealous type, Sierra." Leaning down, I blow on her ear. "It makes my cock hard."

Her body turns slightly toward me. "You're playing dirty."

"As opposed to what?"

I tower over her, soaking up the easy way she fits to the curve of my body, but it's still not enough. It never is. Maybe it never will be. My addiction to her is everlasting, always growing, evolving. If this is the hill I die on, I'll do it with a fucking smile.

Sierra jolts when three knocks echo through the room, and the door opens, revealing a very unappealing interruption.

"Sorry about that," the not-so-ugly technician says, moving into the room and shutting the door behind him. He plops down on the stool placed in front of a small, four-wheeled desk fit with a massive computer screen, a weird keyboard, and a bottle of hand sanitizer before beginning to type in a bunch of stuff I don't understand. The only thing I pay attention to is Sierra's full name written at the top of the screen beside today's date—December thirtieth.

Sierra's hand covers mine, and I look down to see her already watching me nervously. Despite my own nerves, I throw on a confident smile and give her hand a firm squeeze.

The technician—Marvin, the badge clipped to his scrub top says—moves the desk away from the wall to midway down the bed and spins his stool around to face Sierra. "If you wouldn't mind lying back and lifting your shirt up over your stomach for me, I'll ask you some questions, and then we can get started."

I reluctantly let go of her and take a step back as she follows his instructions. Afterward, she rests her clasped hands on her upper stomach and answers a set of generic questions.

"What is your full name?" Marvin asks.

"Sierra Genevieve Caster."

I snort, and when she turns to glare at me, I mouth, *Gwenevieve?* She pinches my arm, and I swallow back my laugh.

"Your date of birth?"

"June eighth, 1995."

The tech hums quietly before squinting at the screen.

"It says here that we don't have a date for your last period, but you have a general idea of a conception date, correct?"

"Yeah. Early or mid-November. It's hard to guess the exact day, though," I answer for her, puffing my chest like a fucking possessive idiot. Sierra shakes her head at me, but I don't miss the smile she's trying to hide.

Marvin just looks unimpressed. "Either way, we'll have a better idea after today. I'll try an abdominal ultrasound first since we're guessing you're already about eight weeks along." He slides on a pair of gloves and grabs the bottle of blue goo that's been sitting at his station. "I'm going to squirt some gel on your stomach now. It will be a bit cold."

Sierra flinches and grabs my hand again. The gel seems to warm quickly once the tech starts moving it around with a round-ended wand-type thing.

"You can come around and watch the screen if you want," he tells me while continuing to smooth gel all over her stomach.

I look to Sierra for confirmation, not wanting to upset her by seeing something that she can't, but she's already looking at me with a reassuring smile. With a final squeeze of her hand, I'm moving around Marvin and staring at a seemingly empty screen.

Even though I have no fucking idea what I'm looking at, I

can't seem to look away from the screen. Sierra watches me, most likely trying to read my expression to see if I've seen anything interesting.

Marvin wears a blank expression as he continues to do his job in complete silence. I know without even looking at her that his silence on top of not being able to see what everyone else can is only increasing Sierra's frustration.

"It doesn't look like anything yet, fighter," I say, grabbing her ankle. "It's just a sea of bl—"

Lub-dub. Lub-dub. Lub-dub.

A lump builds in my throat when a steady heartbeat floods the room. Sierra's muscles bunch up so tight beneath my fingertips that I get the urge to crawl up on the bed and hold her.

Suddenly, Marvin turns the computer screen to the side, showing Sierra the little blob that's appeared. He points to the grey shape and presses the wand a bit harder to Sierra's stomach to make the image a bit easier to see.

"Is that our baby?" she asks, voice quivering. The emotion in her big grey eyes has mine glossing over.

"That's baby," Martin confirms. "You're about eight weeks along."

Pride swells inside of me. I'm immediately flushing with frustration, needing to kiss my woman and wipe away the tear cascading down her cheek.

"Eight weeks," I echo, my voice no louder than a whisper. Straightening my shoulders, I move my large, rigid body around Marvin and his fucking desk, coming to a stop directly beside Sierra.

I bend down, and she doesn't hesitate to tip her head back and capture my lips in a soft kiss, not caring that there's somebody else in the room. When she pulls away, I link our fingers and bring them to my mouth, kissing her knuckles.

Without thinking, I let my mouth linger above the skin of her ring finger for a few seconds too long.

I'm pretty sure the technician is talking again, but his voice is nothing but static flowing in one ear and out the other. Suddenly, I've found myself imagining the impossible, even just for a minuscule fragment of time.

What if instead of bare skin, my lips had met a cold silver band and a diamond? Would that really have been so bad?

An arctic breeze slams into me, and I fall back into reality.

"Remember that the date won't necessarily be when the baby arrives, but it gives you a good idea. I'll send the results to your doctor, and they'll reach out to talk about what's next."

Wait, what date?

Marvin pulls the gloves from his fingers with a *smack* and moves his desk back before grabbing a white towel, passing it to Sierra. "For the gel," he adds when her curious gaze doesn't stray from me, and I take it from him instead. "I'm going to email you the pictures that I took today as soon as I can. You should get them this afternoon."

I nod numbly. I'm in a daze as I wipe the excess gel from Sierra's stomach and pull her shirt back down. Her eyes are narrowed and hot on my skin, watching me drop the towel in the bin full of other towels and shove my hands in the pockets of my jeans.

"Congratulations, guys. Happy New Year." Marvin leaves, and the door stays open behind him—a signal for us to leave when we're ready.

"Ready?" I ask her. She's clearly upset with how cold I've become but won't say anything here.

"Yep," she replies briskly. "Let's go."

21

Sierra

"What's wrong with you?" I snap once we get in Brooks' car and Braden turns the heat on full blast. He hasn't spoken since we left the clinic, and after a very long, awkward walk to the parking garage, I can easily say that I am *so* done with the silence.

His grip is so tight on the steering wheel his knuckles have turned a ghastly shade of white. I want to reach over and pull apart his scrunched brows before they morph into a single one.

"Nothing," he replies tersely, flicking his eyes to me quickly before looking back at the road. "Is your seat belt on?"

Feeling by my left hip, I realize that I forgot to put it on.

"Put it on."

With a huff, I'm reaching behind me and pulling it over my chest. I clip it in place and mumble, "Yes, sir."

"You can't forget to wear a seat belt, Sierra."

"I didn't do it on purpose."

"Is that supposed to change the odds of something hitting us and you being thrown through the windshield?"

I bristle at his tone. "No. I'll remember next time."

He looks at me again, and I notice that his eyes have softened a bit. "I just want you to be safe. This baby is sucking your brain through a damn bendy straw right now."

"Maybe she'll be extra smart, then."

"She?"

I shrug. "Call it a mom's instinct."

Braden turns to me when we stop at a red light, grabbing my knee. His eyes move around my face before he sighs. "I just got a bit overwhelmed back there. I'm sorry."

I feel the tension in my shoulders disappear at his apology. "It's okay to get overwhelmed. But don't take it out on me. I'm just as scared as you are."

"You don't look like it."

"Trust me, I'm freaking out enough on the inside. I don't need to look like it on the outside."

Braden keeps his hand on my knee, but his stare falls back on the road when the light turns green, and we move through traffic again.

"How *are* you feeling right now, y'know, after actually seeing . . . it."

Something about the way he stumbles over the word "it" has me chewing on my lip to hide my grin.

"Honestly, I feel terrified. I don't think that it had fully set in yet until I heard that heartbeat. Now I just . . ." I hesitate for a few seconds when a feeling of intense, brutal love crawls up my throat. "The reality of it hit me really hard. All of a sudden, I realized that I was really going to be a mom."

I can still feel the way my heart swelled and my stomach tightened up in that exam room once that strong, quick heartbeat filled the silence. There will never be a sound as beautiful as that. Not ever.

And I'm so grateful to have had Braden there with me during that experience. He gave me the reassurance and courage that I needed to keep from turning into a sobbing mess. He handled everything so well, and I don't think that I've ever been prouder of him. But maybe that's why it made me so upset once he flipped that switch and turned cold and detached.

"I thought that maybe you were upset," I confess before he has a chance to say anything. "Today was perfect—at least to me. So when you got so upset, it really, really sucked. All I could think of was, what if this was too much? What if you realized that you couldn't really do this?"

My hand flies to my mouth when the car lurches and swerves to the right. "What are you doing?" I screech, swinging my head to look at Braden.

He flies into an empty parking lot and puts the car in park. "What did you just say?"

Anger is potent in the car, becoming more and more charged until I actually start to worry that it'll shatter the windows. It fills my mouth and burns my throat.

Braden swipes quick hands through his hair, making the ends stick straight up. "It fucking guts me that I've made you think so low of me, baby."

"I'm sorry."

"Don't." The word is strong, leaving no room for argument. "I'm the one who should be apologizing. Fuck, Sierra. I've *never*, not once in my life, felt like I did when we got to see and hear our baby back there." He lays a careful hand on my stomach and watches me with glossed-over eyes. "We *created* that. We *did* that."

Covering his hand with mine, I murmur, "We did that."

"Come here," he commands, sliding our hands to rest on my hip and pulling me toward him. When I'm close enough that our faces are inches apart, he presses our foreheads together. "I'm not sure that I'll ever fully be ready for this, but who is? Being a dad terrifies me, but that doesn't mean that I'm going anywhere. I will not abandon you. We're in this together. Okay?"

"Okay," I whisper past the lump in my throat and blink away the threat of tears. "I love you."

His eyes close softly. "I love you."

"For the record, I think that you'll be an amazing father."

"Yeah? I'll have to be to keep up with their mother. God knows that you'll put every other parent on this fucking planet to shame."

And just like that, my worries evaporate for the time being.

A FEW MINUTES LATER, Braden leads me through a small family-style restaurant with a steady hand on my lower back.

"Your stomach hasn't stopped growling for the past fifteen minutes." He chuckles under his breath and stops us beside a booth, signaling for me to slide in.

I feel a bit bad that I didn't catch the name of the restaurant on the sign outside, but there was only one thing on my mind when he pulled up: food. After sitting down, I see the menus are already resting on the table alongside a metal basket full of condiments and napkins.

"Have you ever been here? To—" My eyes find the name of the restaurant on a menu. "—Supreme Eats? What an awful name."

Braden's laugh is completely unfiltered as his head falls back. "Fuck no. It was the first place that I saw after your stomach started gurgling. Figured it was better than nothing."

"Your romantic gestures never fail to make me swoon," I tease.

He shoots me a wink as an older woman with tight silver curls and thick-framed glasses strolls up to our table, notepad and pen in hand. Her smile is warm and inviting, making me grin in return.

"Good afternoon, sweethearts," she says, the hint of an accent I don't completely recognize peeking through. "My name is Val, and I'll be taking care of you today. I hope you don't mind my candour, but I must tell you how stunning of a couple you make. You make me miss my *marito*."

My brows scrunch together at the unfamiliar term, but before I can ask what it means, Braden cuts in, leaving me a gaping mess. "*Grazie*, Val. My Sierra is gorgeous enough for the both of us. But *sei così bello.* I'm sure your husband wishes that he could be here with you."

Hold on . . . Braden speaks another language? Freaking Italian at that. The fancy words sound way too sensual on his tongue, and I know that I'm in trouble.

I'm openly staring at him with parted lips and an undeniable warmth pooling in my belly when Val says, "Oh my! You speak Italian?"

He shrugs. "A bit. My stepfather's family is from Sicily."

Val nods enthusiastically. "I have only been to Sicily a few times in my life. Have you been?"

"Unfortunately not. Maybe one day."

Val turns to me for the first time since her introduction, and I nearly wave a flag of victory. "Have you, *cara*?"

"No, but it is on my bucket list. I would love to go to Syracuse and visit the theatres. My sister went on a school trip in high school and has so many stories."

Something nudges my foot beneath the table, and I glance over at Braden to see him already watching me with a heated stare.

"You will love it," Val insists. "Anyway, I should be taking your drink orders before the boss man comes and gives us trouble."

"Water for me, please, Val," Braden says, reaching across the table and patting her wrinkled hand.

I smile. "I'll have an iced tea."

With a nod, Val slips her untouched notepad into her apron and walks back to the kitchen. As soon as I'm positive she's not within hearing distance, I'm narrowing my eyes on Braden and asking, "Why didn't I know that you spoke Italian?"

His eyes widen briefly. "I didn't think that it was important. I'm not fluent or anything. I just know the basics."

"Basics or not, I still would have liked to know that about you."

He looks a bit shocked, and I don't know if that should bother me. "Well, I don't speak any other languages besides the French we were required to learn in school, but don't test me on any of it. I can only really remember how to ask to go to the bathroom or how to say hello, my name is Braden."

I find myself laughing before I can stop myself. "That's better than me. I remember how to count to ten, but that's about it."

Braden's expression turns thoughtful. "I didn't mean to keep speaking Italian from you. It just never came up."

"I know," I say on an exhale. Maybe I was a *bit* dramatic. "It sounds kind of selfish, but I just don't like other people knowing things about you that I don't. That's crazy, right? I mean, it's not like you know every single thing about me."

He arches a brow. "And what don't I know?"

Val quietly drops off our drinks, and I take long, greedy gulps of my iced tea. "I don't know. It was just a figure of speech."

"Why don't I believe you?"

"Because you can be a stubborn ass sometimes."

Braden leans forward, his elbows on the table. "Careful, little fighter. Do you remember the last time I led you into a public washroom? I wouldn't want to ruin poor, innocent Val's ears by dragging you inside a stall and fucking the attitude right out of you."

My pulse quickens, and I squeeze my thighs together to try and dull the ache building between them. Braden's threat settles between us as I slide the hair off the back of my warm neck.

Our eyes stay locked, neither of us blinking like we're scared to lose a game we never even agreed on playing. Without realizing, I've started leaning across the table and am now just inches away from feeling Braden's lips on mine. If he just moved a bit closer . . .

A hand curves around the back of my head, holding me steady as he brushes his lips across mine, groaning into my mouth. I'm about to tell him to just kiss me already when he does, softly yet passionately. Gentle yet possessive.

It's over far too quickly, but I'm still left breathless and wanting more—needing more. The only thing on my mind as Val takes our orders and returns a few minutes later with plates of food is just *how* badly I need more. I feel like an addict, yet I can't be bothered to fight off the urge.

My legs remain squeezed shut and my cheeks hot as we eat. By the time we're finished, I'm scared to stand up, not knowing whether I have a wet spot on my leggings.

Braden must be thinking something similar because he pays the bill and says goodbye to Val eagerly, all past playfulness gone and replaced with an urgency that only intensifies the strain of my hard nipples against my bra.

When he slides out of his side of the booth and extends a hand out for me to take, I do so without hesitation and let him pull me up, wet spot be damned. His heat is a welcomed feeling despite my raging body temperature as he leads us past a row of empty booths.

We've almost hit the doors when I feel a shiver crawl up my spine, and an eerie silence envelops the few tables close by. My eyes slide shut when I hear the voice of the only person that could dry the soaked area between my legs so quickly.

"Sierra? What a coincidence. Join us, would you?"

22

Braden

Cole. Motherfucking. Travis.

My spine goes ramrod straight, a protective arm winding around Sierra's waist. She's become as still as a statue after hearing him speak and doesn't melt into me like she usually does. That alone is enough to have my fingers curling into my palms.

I didn't miss the way Cole ignored my presence beside her. But then again, why would he acknowledge me? I'm the competition. The guy he thought he got rid of after bringing her here.

Red mist teases my vision, floating in and out of my narrowed stare when I turn my body and tower over his table. The repulsive smile on his face is enough to have me aching to yank him up by the collar and drop him on the dirty floor.

Expensive black suit, shining shoes that probably cost more than my rent, another diamond-encrusted watch around his wrist. He's cut his hair since I last saw him, trying and failing to pull off a buzz cut. But that's about the only thing new about him.

Cole sits with perfect posture. His hands lie flat on his skinny thighs, head turned in our direction and dark eyes focused on Sierra in a way that makes my stomach roll.

I know that I'm glaring at him, not bothering to hide my feelings toward my girlfriend's pervy boss, but it's semantics at this point. There's no way that I'm going to pretend that I don't hate this fucker's guts.

"Sierra, it's lovely to see you out of the office. How are you doing?" the man I didn't notice sitting across from Cole asks, sounding mighty casual, like he's asked her those questions before.

Yanking my glare from Cole, I let my eyes wander to the occupied booth across from him, asking bluntly, "Who are you?"

The guy has to be about my height but maybe a few pounds lighter. A genuine smile curves his lips. "Mackenzie Thompson. And you must be Braden. I would say that it's nice to meet you, but I'm not sure that you will return the favour."

My brow twitches. "You would be right," I admit, not bothering to beat around the bush. Sierra releases some of the tension from her muscles when my thumb starts making small circles on her hip bone.

"Braden." She clears her throat. "This is Mack. Gretchen is his assistant."

"*Mean Girls* girl?" I ask, remembering the tiny woman I met outside Sierra's office building a few weeks back. I haven't seen her since, but Sierra talks about her all the time.

The Mackenzie guy makes a choking sound before covering it with a cough. "Have you called Gretchen that to her face?" he asks.

I nod, relaxing slightly. This guy could be a threat, but there's something real about him that makes me think he's the opposite.

My thoughts only solidify when he says, "You have a big set of balls, man. I like it."

"Gretchen threatened him, though. So we'll have to see if he risks it again," Sierra puts in, covering my hand with hers where it sits on her hip.

"We should take bets on whether she knees him in the dick or twists his nipples. My money is on the dick," Mack snickers.

"We were actually in the middle of a meeting regarding your job," Cole butts in. His angry words piss all over the light-hearted energy we've created and darken the mood again. "It wouldn't be wise to stay around to listen. I will talk to you Tuesday. Or will you be needing *more* vacation time?"

Sierra stiffens, sucking in a sharp breath. I bite my tongue—hard.

I'm borderline seething, teetering on the edge of letting too many harsh words slip from my lips that could get her fired right here and now. The hatred I feel sizzling in my blood must be obvious because when my eyes collide with Mackenzie's hard stare, the only thing I see is understanding.

My palms burn, and I know immediately that my nails have popped the thick skin.

"It's nothing bad, Sierra," Mackenzie clarifies, looking at Cole with evident disgust before moving his attention to her. "I'm giving him an update on the Waterton Brothers account because he's your direct supervisor. I spoke to both brothers briefly yesterday, and they told me they'll give *you* their update after New Year's."

She squeezes the hand that's still gripping her hip, and I relax it, not realizing how hard I've been holding her. Pressing a soft kiss to her temple, I watch Cole and the way his icy stare focuses on my mouth before caressing her face in a far too intimate way.

"Go to the car, baby," I whisper against the shell of her ear.

The hitch in her breath is nonexistent to anybody but me due to our closeness. "Please just trust me. I need you to go to the car."

A slight nod is all she gives me before she's walking outside without me. I shove the anxiety that erupts inside of me at the thought of her being outside alone behind a door for now. She'll be okay by herself for a few minutes. I really don't need her to see this.

I revel in the way Cole gasps when I spin on my heels and slam one hand to the table in front of him, the other to the booth behind his head, boxing him in. Anger radiates off my body, smothering the air around us.

If I didn't have Sierra outside waiting for me, I would be dragging his ass out back and kicking his teeth in.

"Talk to my girl like that again and I'll rip your vocal cords out with my bare fucking hands," I spit through clenched teeth. "Whatever you thought you were doing with her ends here. Sierra is mine. She'll never be yours. The sooner you get that through your thick fucking skull, the easier it'll be for you. This is your *last* warning."

The deep-rooted fear in his eyes barely settles the storm raging in my head, but I back away and drop my arms anyway. I put extra effort into not looking at him in case I lose whatever is left of my self-control and break his nose.

I catch Mackenzie's blank stare and hope that he can read what I'm trying to say with mine. *Don't let him ruin her career.*

Mackenzie pulls a wad of cash out of his wallet, tosses it on the table, and tips his chin at me. Standing up, he mumbles something to Cole that I don't bother listening to before walking alongside me out of that fucking restaurant.

"He won't touch her career, Braden. You have my word."

A hand hesitantly pats my shoulder before I spill our secret out to him in a wobbly plea. "She's pregnant. I need you to do everything you can to keep him away from her."

Mack doesn't hesitate. "Consider it done."

THE RIDE HOME WAS SILENT. Brutally so.

Sierra sat with her body curled toward the door and her cheek pressed to the cold window for the entire twenty-minute drive home. She didn't even ask me to change the awful music that I purposefully played in hopes of stoking the fire I knew was spreading inside of her. I wanted it to blaze, to shoot sparks in my direction. Anything to get her to cut the silence and talk to me.

The sunshine that had been beaming from her perfect smile as we ate our greasy food and talked about whatever the hell we wanted had been tucked behind thick, dark clouds, and all I wanted was to rip them apart and feel that warmth again.

At first, I thought that she was upset with me for how I asked her to back away from a fight she probably had every intention of taking part in, but Sierra isn't one to revel in her anger without speaking a word. If she were pissed at me, I would have no doubt about it.

So that left two other possibilities. One, she was embarrassed with the way Cole spoke to her in front of someone as high up on the food chain as Mackenzie, or option two, she was hurt.

Regardless of whether I was looking at option one or two, or fuck, even both, they were unacceptable. When I parked the car outside of Sierra's apartment, I actually inspected the steering wheel for my fingerprints, worried that they had become permanently indented into the leather from how tight my grip was the entire drive home.

I press those same fingertips into my thighs as I sit on the edge of her bed, listening to the shower run behind the bathroom door. My temples throb with a headache that I don't doubt has erupted because of the pile of questions running around my skull.

Sierra wanted to shower alone as soon as we got inside the apartment, and for some stupid reason, I let her go instead of prying answers out of her as to what's been eating at her.

Fuck this.

I quickly strip out of my clothes, dumping them in the hamper before walking to the bathroom and testing the door handle to see if she locked me out. When it turns easily, I blow out a breath and push my way inside.

The room is hot, steam twirling in the air like smoke and fogging up the vanity mirror, blocking my reflection. When I see Sierra's clothes forming a small pile beside the sink, the corners of my mouth tug up. *Some habits never die.*

Pulling back the shower curtain, I step in behind her. My arms form a cocoon around her wet frame before I'm pulling her back to my chest and clasping my hands at her middle. She shudders, tipping her head back and out of the water until it hits my chest.

"You don't get to hide your problems from me." My lips brush the tip of her ear. "Your problems are also mine."

Sierra doesn't say anything beneath the steady stream of water, but when I nudge her head to the side and drag my nose along the column of her neck, she falls into me, trusting my strength to keep her upright. The pulse beneath the thin skin beats fast against my lips as I kiss her throat, once, twice. My tongue begs for a taste of her, but I shake those thoughts free when my dick starts to harden against her back.

"I would do anything for you, my little fighter. Just name it."

Pushing the curve of her ass into the base of my erection, she pulls my hands apart and urges one down between her thighs. "Touch me. *Please.*"

I don't deny her. I can't. Even knowing that this is her way of evading the conversation that we need to have.

With her hand on top of mine, I slide my fingers over her wet mound, spreading the lips and drawing circles around her swollen clit. "You're already wet," I groan, plunging two long fingers inside. "Do you want me to take you? Right here?"

Sierra bucks into my hand, nodding frantically. "Yes," she replies in a desperate gasp.

I pull my fingers from her pussy and take a step back. The hot water hits my chest before I have a chance to miss her warmth. "Hands on the wall."

She moves quickly, desperately. Her palms touch the shower tile at the same time mine settle on the smooth skin of her back. I glide them over the sharp ridges of her spine and down to the two identical dimples above her ass before kneading the thick flesh beneath them.

Her choked sound of surprise erupts around us when I spread her cheeks apart and drag my thumb between them, skimming over her puckered hole and pressing it inside her pussy. "Have you ever let anybody take your ass, baby?"

She releases a strained breath. "No."

I fuck her with my thumb. "Would you let me?"

"Let you what?"

I nearly laugh at the way she feigns ignorance. Instead of responding vocally, I ease my thumb from inside of her and slide it back up to her virgin hole, exploring and teasing. Pressing just the tip inside, I swallow a growl at the way she sucks me in.

"One day you'll let me fuck you here. But not today." Wrapping my cock in a tight fist, I line up with her dripping entrance and push inside, sheathing myself in one thrust. "Today you'll come all over my dick," I growl into her neck, breathing in as much of her clean scent as possible. It goes straight to my head, turning my thoughts fuzzy.

"*Yes, yes*. Make me come," Sierra cries over the sound of rushing water. Her fingers are curled against the tile when she drops her head back and whimpers a contorted version of my name.

My thrusts are savage, hard, and quick. I fuck her like a man who has everything to lose and nothing to gain. Like I'm on death row and this is the last time I'll ever be inside of her.

The sounds that escape us are borderline inhuman yet mix together to form a fucking symphony that I want to hear every day for the rest of my life. My balls slap her backside with every thrust, her juices making sloppy sounds where we join.

I reach around to lightly collar her throat and pull her back flush to my chest. With her legs closed, the walls of her pussy tighten around me, strangling my cock. "You're going to come for me, fighter. You're going to own me. Fucking use me."

Sierra's nails are scratching my forearms like a wild animal when I feel her walls quiver around me. *She's going to come.*

I pinch her clit between my fingers, knowing that that's all it will take to send her over the edge.

"I'm coming, Braden. *Oh God*," she screams so loud it echoes off the bathroom walls.

A roar gets lost in my throat as I fall with her, my face buried in her neck, our sweat mixing before getting swept down the drain. My thrusts come to a stop before I gently ease out of her, my heart throbbing when she whimpers.

I try to catch my breath as I release her throat, dropping my hand to the space between her breasts, feeling her raging heartbeat beneath my fingers.

"It's beating so fast," Sierra says softly, spinning around to face me. Warm, silver eyes shine, watching me in a way that has me fumbling for something to say.

Nothing comes, so I don't force it. Instead, I let my eyelids droop and focus on the steady thump in her chest. The feeling of every exhale drifting across my lips.

Time seems to stop as we stand together, two opposites held together by something more palpable than a magnetic force. Something threaded in her soul and mine, binding us together.

Fate seems like an unoriginal and cliché term to use to describe what I think brought Sierra and me together. But for now, it's as good of one as any. For this moment, it'll have to do.

23

Braden

THE WATER HAS RUN COLD BY NOW, BUT NEITHER OF us makes an effort to leave this safe space. I hold Sierra in my arms, giving her any warmth that I have left. She presses closer in my embrace, sighing long and tired.

"I'm sorry that I tried to cut you out. That was just . . . really embarrassing for me." Her words kiss my wet throat.

"Men like Cole Travis shouldn't hold that sort of power over you. You're too strong to be brought down by that guy."

She takes a hesitant step back, just enough to catch my eyes. Her brows lower slightly, as if I've surprised her with my words.

"It's hard not to be. He's my boss, and he purposely tried to make a fool out of me in front of somebody that could fire me without a second thought. Mack is part owner of the entire company—I can't look like a fool in front of him. Especially not when he's already put his back out helping me when he didn't need to."

"Trust me, Mackenzie doesn't give a fuck about Cole. If anybody will be getting fired, it'll be him." If I have anything to do with it.

"I also hate that he embarrassed me in front of you," she says quietly, glancing away timidly. I almost don't hear her over the sound of the shower.

Cupping her jaw, I tilt her head so that she's forced to meet my gaze. There's a pink flush to her cheeks, but it's not from being warm. Her skin is ice beneath my fingers.

"Sierra, I don't care about what that stupid fuck says about you. You're my girl. Never feel embarrassed in front of me."

She nods cautiously, looking like she only half believes me.

"How about we talk about it more after we get you out of this water? You're not getting sick because of that asshole."

I grab her hair in my hands and wring the water out of it before reaching around to shut off the water. She shivers in my arms as I pull back the curtain and grab her towel from the hook. After stepping out and wrapping her up, I place a kiss on her forehead and tie my towel around my waist.

While she runs another towel through her hair, I grab her some clothes from the bedroom and place them on the toilet lid.

Not long after, she's hanging the damp towel and slipping on the clothes that I brought. My chest pulls tight at how gorgeous she is without even knowing it, all smooth skin and perfectly sculpted features. I could watch her for a lifetime and never get tired of what I would see.

"You're right," she says after a few silent moments. I lift a brow, encouraging her to continue. "About Cole. He isn't worth it. I'm sorry that I let him get to me like that. Usually it's easier to ignore his shit."

"You say that like dealing with his shit is a common thing."

She lifts a shoulder, avoiding my scrutinizing stare.

"He just likes to push his boundaries. It's an ego thing."

My shoulders pull tight, scowl deepening. "It's not a damn

ego thing, Sierra. What kind of boundaries does he push? Has he touched you?"

The unmistakable flame of anger flickers across her face before she can hide it.

"Tell me what he did. Now." I seethe.

Sierra's fingers tap her hip. There's worry in her eyes. "Can you promise me that if I tell you, you won't hunt him down and stomp him into the ground?" she challenges.

"No," I say honestly.

"Then I won't tell you."

I laugh once. The sound is anything but humorous. "Simple as that, huh?"

She nods. "You're not getting involved."

"I'm already involved. You're my girlfriend. We're going to have a baby together, dammit!"

I want to pull my fucking hair out right now. Not smashing Cole's face into a brick wall at this very moment almost feels like a punishment of some sort. And the longer Sierra keeps me shut out, the more this feeling of rage heightens, and the harder it becomes to ignore.

I've always been an act first, think second kind of guy. I'm a fighter; I like to feel the surge of adrenaline in my veins before throwing a punch and the burn in my knuckles that follows.

Sitting back and letting things play out on their own is not something that I ever planned on doing. Especially not when it comes to Sierra and that butt plug of a boss of hers. He's crossed the line one too many times. I should have done more than lay a threat down at that diner, but it was too public.

No, the first time Cole is introduced to how I deal with boys who fuck with my girl, he won't have anybody to save his sorry ass. It'll be just me and him.

"Yes, we are going to have a baby together. But that doesn't mean that I need you to fight all my battles for me. I've got it handled," Sierra says, exasperated.

My stare hardens to stone. "Handled it how? By sitting back like a good little worker bee and letting him continue to make you fucking uncomfortable?"

"Don't talk down to me because I won't let you act like a caveman out to save my honor."

I run a rough hand through my wet hair, tugging on it and expelling a harsh breath. "I'm not trying to talk down to you. I just don't want you to keep quiet about this shit. If he didn't touch you, then tell me right now, and I'll drop it. But if he did, he needs to be dealt with. He can't continue to put his filthy hands on you. He won't stop unless I make him." My voice softens. "Guys like him, baby, they don't just have a change of heart and leave you alone. He won't stop until he gets what he wants, and that's *not* okay."

Something I said seems to resonate somewhere in that pretty head of hers because some of the stiffness in her shoulders melts away, and her eyes finally crash with mine.

Her inhale is shaky. "Before you got here, there were a couple of times where he touched me. Just lingering brushes on my arms and sides when we would pass each other in the halls or get pushed together in a crowded meeting."

"Fuck." Red. Deep, blood red. That's what I see when I drop my head back and stare at the ceiling, pulling in a long breath through my nose before puffing it out of my mouth. "And? There's more. I can hear it in your voice." *I don't want to hear any more.*

"There was only one time . . . that he tried for more." She has to pause to clear her throat, blinking a few times. "I was looking for extra sugar packets in the breakroom for my coffee. They're in the bottom cupboard, so I was bent over or squatting, I don't remember. But I felt hands on my ass, squeezing it roughly. I shot up instantly and just froze. My thoughts were scattered all over the place. It took me a few seconds to turn around and see that it was Cole. He had the biggest fucking grin on his face, like he had just won a gold medal for touching me like that. Some intern walked in before Cole had a chance to say anything or touch me again."

A ball gets lodged in my throat before sliding free and tumbling through my insides like I'm a living pinball machine before it lands with a splat at the bottom of my stomach.

"I'm going to break each one of his fingers," I say with a sense of calm that I don't feel. My rage is simmering beneath my skin, begging for a chance to reach a full boil.

Sierra brushes a clump of damp hair behind her ear, and I stop breathing when I see the way her hand shakes. It only takes three steps to reach her and wrap her in my arms, squeezing her tight like I'm trying to pull her body inside of mine. The need to keep her safe and protected is intense, inescapable. Nothing can touch her if she's in my arms, my frame serving as her own custom-made armour.

With her face pressed to my throat, she murmurs, "I felt dirty after. When I got home, I scrubbed my skin until it was red and sore. Gretchen is the only one I've told."

I bury my lips in her hair and breathe in her pure sunshine scent with greedy gulps in an attempt to keep my cool. Sierra needs my comfort right now more than I need to seek retribution.

"If he touches you again, I'll kill him," I whisper. The words are as soft as silk, but the promise peeking out from behind them is too sharp, too vicious to miss. "You're my everything. My one and fucking only. Nobody hurts you or makes you feel like you're less than the fierce, take-no-shit woman who I met in a line outside Sinners. Cole is done.

That's a promise, Sierra." I catch the hitch in her breathing and quirk a small smile.

She feathers a few kisses along my throat, humming against the skin. Vibrations electrify my bones. "I don't want you to get hurt or in trouble. Plus, Clark would never get rid of Cole. He carries Cole's balls in his back pocket."

"Clark isn't the only one in charge anymore. He gave up that right when he agreed to a merger with Mackenzie."

And if I learned anything today, it's that Mack isn't Cole's biggest fan. My gut tells me that there's not much going between him and Clark either beyond a simple business transaction. If I play my cards right, Cole will be on a one-way trip back to where he came from before he has a chance to snatch his balls back.

Sierra pulls back just enough to allow our eyes to collide and noses to brush. My hands travel to her hips, keeping her smashed to my chest. I welcome the constant need to touch her, soaking it up.

"You're a lot smarter than you look," she pokes fun, trapping her bottom lip between her teeth to avoid laughing.

I narrow my eyes, trailing my fingers up and down her side. "You talk a lot of shit for someone so small and . . . ticklish."

Shock invades her features before she's pushing at my chest and scrambling out of the room, a shriek echoing through the apartment. I stay where I stand instead of following her immediately, allowing myself a few seconds to grin and fully digest the swell of happiness that inflates my stomach. Belting out a laugh, I give my head an amused shake and take off after my girl.

Sierra's ability to let go and embrace that little girl inside of her just for me to see is a fucking beautiful thing. Her quick wit and humour is a hidden layer of her personality that I wasn't expecting to uncover but couldn't feel any luckier to have peeled back and bared witness to.

Soon enough, I'll have discovered every single thing that makes up the woman that I love, and she'll have done the same to me.

We have the time.

24

Sierra

When Braden and I first met, there were so many pieces in my puzzle that I had forced to fit in the wrong spots just so the final picture wouldn't be incomplete.

I may have looked like a confident, know-it-all woman who had her life stitched perfectly at the seams, but that's a far-off assumption—a mask I spent too many years perfecting. In reality, there was so much going wrong in my head that those perfect seams were really bursting wide open.

Those pieces that were pushed into holes they didn't belong had begun to look out of place. I was starting to notice them, and they were ruining the image I was portraying on the outside.

My panic attacks are only one of the wrong pieces. But one that had become noticeable far earlier than the rest.

They would shake me to my core over things that had no right causing such disruptions in my head. And had been a regular part of my life since I was young. I guess I just got used to them.

I can admit now—after finally reaching out and talking to

a therapist who I've grown to love—that it was shame that kept me from asking for help earlier. Dr. Tali thinks that the majority of my insecurities stem from my parents' abandonment and lack of love they gave. She believes they were one of the main reasons that I felt the need to force my life into a perfect image that in turn helped blossom my anxiety into what it had become.

I don't think she's very far off.

I met Eliza Tali in the line of a small, local coffee shop on one of the worst days that I've had since I can remember. With my stomach swelling just enough that I could no longer hide it beneath my work blouses and high-waisted skirts, a shine to my hair that I had no idea what to do with, and no more morning sickness, the beginning of my second trimester had been doing me too many favours.

My thoughts were in the clouds. I wasn't paying attention to where I was going after I grabbed my expensive lemonade from the counter and spun around so quickly my glossy hair swung over my shoulder. Right into the chest of the person behind me.

We collided so abruptly that my grip on the plastic cup tightened, and the lid popped right off. And when I tried to steady myself, the bright yellow liquid sloshed right over the rim and soaked the blouse of the woman in front of me.

An intense feeling of embarrassment flooded my cheeks and stained my entire upper body a red so bright that all I wanted to do was hide. The eyes of onlookers felt like pins in my skin. I wanted to get out. I *needed* to get out.

I knew that my hands were shaking as I fumbled through my purse looking for napkins, even though there were stacks just over on the counter. My lungs felt like they were covered in cement. I couldn't breathe, and when I did, it was more wheezing than actual breathing.

Thinking back on it now, a hot flash of shame runs through me. I know how ridiculous I must have looked getting so worked up over spilling my drink on someone, but at the time, it seemed like the worst thing that could have happened. It was such an intense feeling of misery that I yearned for an escape route. I was mortified, and my anxiety had spiked to the highest it had been since I was a teen.

But then a gentle, delicate hand covered the one sifting through my bag, stilling it. When I looked at the owner of that hand, I was met with a pair of round, emerald-green eyes that watched me with a compassion so obvious I was left reeling.

"It's okay. I was never a fan of lavender anyway," the woman had said, a genuine smile tugging at her mouth. When I blinked at her, confused, she only laughed. "My blouse. My mother-in-law bought it for me for Christmas, and I'm just getting back from our monthly lunch date. I figured that I should wear it for her today even though lavender washes me out."

I could feel the red subsiding from my cheeks and the cement cracking around my lungs. The ground stabilized beneath my feet again.

"I'm Eliza Tali." She held her hand out for me to take. I could feel her paying too much attention to how mine shook as I clasped it around hers.

"Sierra Caster," I replied, wincing at the roughness in my voice. "I'm so sorry about your shirt. I don't know what I was doing. I wasn't looking where I was goi—"

"Oh, please. You did me a favour, really. I have such an awful habit of keeping clothes that I know I'll never wear. Now I have a reason not to hold on to this," she said sweetly, as if I really had done her a favour.

I was so confused standing there with that woman, her blouse soaked with lemonade and my heartbeat still thumping in my ears. But then she had confused me even more and handed me a slim, white card with her name and number printed on it. She told me to give her a call the next time I felt like the world was shaking and falling apart at my feet.

I didn't have the words to reply, so I only nodded. And after Eliza squeezed my arm and excused herself to the bathroom, I dumped my empty cup in the garbage and got the hell out of there.

I've seen her three times and called her once over the past four weeks, and although my anxiety hasn't necessarily gone anywhere, it's become manageable and only going to get better.

It's put not only my mind but the minds of the people closest to me more at ease. Especially with my pregnancy. Sophie's weekly check-in calls have transformed from worrying interrogations about how I'm doing and handling everything to gossiping about the latest drama's in the span of those four weeks. She still worries too much, but I don't think that will ever truly stop. Not that I would ever want it to.

"You good, S?" Sophie asks, tearing me from my thoughts.

I blink away the fog in my mind and smile at the image of her on my laptop screen. It's still a shock to the system to see Sophie without her blonde hair. She's been dying her chestnut curls blonde since our first semester of college, so it threw me for a loop when she went back to her natural colour shortly after Christmas.

"I'm good. How are you and your new roommate?"

I sit up straighter against the headboard, adjust the pillow behind me to rest lower at my back, and balance my laptop on my small baby bump. The bedroom window is open again, just the slightest bit despite Braden's complaints.

I can't blame him for telling me not to keep the windows open considering it is early March and it hasn't started warming up much outside, but I'm in a constant state of sweat with this damn baby, so he can suck it up.

Sophie scowls. "I don't know why I did this to myself. I should have just built a cardboard house and slept in a damn alley."

I wince. "It can't be *that* bad."

"Oh, it's that bad. He posted a freaking bathroom schedule on the door. A schedule! Not to mention he went and reorganized all of my toiletries, so now he knows how heavy my flow is and what a menstrual cup looks like."

"Braden did mention that he's very particular."

"Particular my ass. He's compulsive."

"At least he's cleanly and not one of those guys who leaves his dishes in the sink until they mold."

"Cleanly or not, he's driving me up the wall," she sighs before looking at something behind her computer.

There's a tug in my chest at the faraway look in her eyes. "What's really going on? This can't just be about Clayton and his hearty relationship with cleanliness."

She presses the area between her brows with her thumb, and her shoulders slump. "This has just been a lot to deal with. I didn't think that I would be twenty-six with no future, a negative sum in her bank account, and a roommate who has an excessive collection of Marvel comics."

"You do have a future, Soph. It just wasn't at that school. We both know that that dad was out of line. You shouldn't have been the one punished for his blatant hatred."

My fingers curl into fists on the mattress as the reminder of that day bulldozes through my head. I'll never forget the pain in my best friend's voice when she called me after getting cornered in her classroom by one of her student's parents—a big white guy with a love for derogatory and sexist terms—after she had graded his son's test "too low."

The scene blew up, and insults that are far too disgusting to repeat even in my head were thrown until Sophie, being the fearless bad bitch that she is, sucker punched him square in the nose. She was fired the next day for professional misconduct. The dad never pressed charges, but that was only because her student aid had recorded the entire thing, and he was terrified of his job catching wind of how big of a piece of racist shit he is.

Sophie pulls at the elastic holding her hair up in a bun, and brown curls tumble down to frame her slim face. She twists a thick strand around her finger, and her frown deepens. "He did it to provoke me. I shouldn't have punched him and played right into his hands."

I roll my eyes. "If you *hadn't* punched him, I would have been disappointed. He deserved far worse."

Sophie is a proud Latina woman who was raised by an even prouder one. She shouldn't have to back down from anything. Especially not men who think it makes them big and strong to talk down on somebody half their size just because of the colour of their skin. She's just as much of a citizen of this country as he is. As I am.

Not being there with her, especially after that, is really, really hard.

"Anyway. When are you telling your parents that you're pregnant? You're already seventeen weeks along."

She obviously wants to avoid talking any more about what happened, so I let it go. If she doesn't want to talk about it anymore, I'm not about to push her.

"How about never?" It's only partially a joke. "Just thinking about how my mother will react has me checking my skin for a stress rash."

"You just need to rip off the Band-Aid, Sierra. Your mother will have something negative to say whether you tell her tomorrow or a year from now with a baby in your arms," Sophie says sympathetically. "It only makes it worse that you haven't introduced them to Braden."

"That's not my fault. They haven't been in the country since I saw them before I moved," I defend myself.

"Then just FaceTime them and do it. At least then you can end the call when your mother starts to lay into the both of you."

I let out a choked laugh. "Yeah, I'm sure they would leave it at that."

"Look," Sophie says, her voice strong in a *no bullshit* way. "It's your life. It's your baby. It's your relationship. Neither your mother *or* your father has ever made an effort to be a constant in your life, so don't give them this power over you. Don't let the fear of what they'll say or do affect you so heavily. You have so many people by your side, you don't need your parents or their judgment."

I swallow the boulder in my throat and dip my chin, looking at the pillow beside me that has become Braden's. If Sophie wasn't watching me, I would have picked it up and held it close to my chest, maybe even breathed in the smell of him that always lingers on the pillowcase.

Besides our baby, Braden has been the biggest surprise of my life. He's put in so much work and become such a pillar of support for me, especially throughout my pregnancy. It doesn't matter what I ask him to do, he'll do it. Hell, most of the time, I don't even need to ask. It's like he can read my mind and body better than I can. He knows what I need before I do and does it before I even have the chance to question him.

Over the past few weeks, he's been working more than usual—coming home later and leaving earlier. But every single night, he comes home with either dinner from my favourite restaurant or plans for what to cook, curls up on the couch with me to watch *Law & Order*, and rubs my feet to the point of near orgasm.

It's become the norm, the expected. I've grown comfortable with him being with me, our lives fully intertwined. Some days—or more like every day—I think about how lonely I was before him and feel such a deep-rooted sadness. It just helps confirm what I already know.

I never want to spend another day without him or the life that we've begun to grow together.

"You're right," I admit, regardless of the burn in my chest. "There's nothing that my parents can say to me that will hurt more than anything they've already done."

"God, that's so sad. You shouldn't have to feel like that, S. I'm sorry."

I wave her off. "Don't. It's not your fault. Clare is more a mother to me than the woman who carried me for nine months. Her approval is the only one that mattered to me, and I got it."

Sophie's mouth lifts in a sad smile. "And you know that I love you and that troublemaker you're harvesting."

"Harvesting? Jesus, Soph." My eyes roll as a genuine laugh slips past my lips. It's small, but it's real.

"You've got this, Momma. And if Braden does anything to upset you, let me know."

"Oh yeah? And what are you gonna do? Jump on my back and stick your finger in my ear?" a deep, rumbling voice asks.

My head snaps up, and I find Braden leaning against the doorjamb, his arms crossed and a giant grin on his face. I fight to keep the squeal of excitement trapped in my throat as I stare at him, halfway lost in a trance.

He's all muscle and confidence right now, and I want to climb him like a fucking tree. Especially when his eyelids fall to half-mast and his stare slides down my body and bare skin, getting snagged on the edge of the sleep shorts I've worn all day.

The heat in his eyes is evident, making my legs fall open of their own accord.

"And that's my cue. I'll talk to you later, babes. Love you!"

I'm half-aware of the way I say goodbye, too busy watching Braden stalk toward me like a predator to prey, anticipation building low in my belly. A large hand presses my laptop closed before moving it to the floor.

Braden bends down, and I inhale sharply when soft lips make contact with my exposed belly and fingertips brush the skin above my shorts.

"You're so beautiful. I missed you both today," he whispers against my swollen stomach. Tears fill my eyes at the intense, unmistakable look of love on his face.

My fingers slip into his hair, playing with the softness of it. "We missed you too."

He's watching me closely when he says, "I want you to go somewhere with me tomorrow."

"Okay. Do I get to know where?"

With a final kiss to my belly, he's standing back up and running his palm over the top of my head. "It's a surprise. A good one, I promise."

"Everyone says their surprise is a good one. Nobody would agree if you said it wasn't," I tease, tilting my head back to meet his gaze. "But I'll play. It better *really* be good, though. Especially if you're making me leave the house on a Sunday."

He chuckles, shaking his head. "You have my word, baby. Now, come on. I picked up dinner."

"Have I mentioned lately that I love you?"

He shrugs. "Once or twice. Now, get your tight ass out of here while I shut this damn window."

25

Braden

NEVER IN A MILLION YEARS DID I THINK THAT I would be holding hands with my pregnant girlfriend in front of my own gym. But here I am. And it feels fucking out of this world.

The words *Knockout Fitness* are scrawled along the right side of the single-storey building, lit in a hard-to-miss cherry red. A giant window sits on the left side of the door, a few steps from the fob scanner we installed to ensure access to clients anytime, day or night, regardless of our official open hours.

Over the past couple of months, a few more nearby buildings have sold, and businesses have started to take up shop, making the area a lot busier than it was when the renovations began. It's only a matter of time before there's just as much traction in our area as there is a few blocks over.

"This is the gym you've been working at for the past few months?" Sierra asks from beside me after a few long minutes of silence. I nod. "It's gorgeous. Are those solar panels on the roof?" She points to the top of the building, where solar panels have been installed along both sides of the sloped roof.

When I turn to look at her, I'm surprised to see the vivid excitement in her eyes. "Yep. It was a super-last-minute idea, but I think it makes it stand out."

She hums in agreement. "I like that I get to see where you work, but working out isn't really how I expected to spend my Sunday morning. Actually, *can* I even work out? You know . . . since I'm four months pregnant?"

I bite down on my tongue to avoid laughing. I'm surprised she doesn't already know the answer to that question considering how much she loves Dr. Google these days.

"I didn't bring you here to make you work out. But if you want to, you can. I already talked to your doctor and have a list of things you can't do in case you decide that you want to."

Suddenly indignant, she grips her hips. "So you brought me to a gym thinking that I would want to stand back and what? Watch you? Please," she scoffs. "I can work out just fine, thank you very much. If you're working out, then so am I."

I'm grinning by the time she finishes her speech, not to mention incredibly turned on. Sierra has a fire inside of her that burns alongside mine. It makes me want to drag her inside my office and fuck her up against my desk.

"Don't look at me like that. I'm not sure the owner of this gym would like knowing we had sex in the changing room."

I toss her a wink. "I don't think he would care. I heard he's a pretty laid-back guy."

Her eyes flare with curiosity. "Is it someone you know?"

"You could say that." Slinging my arm around her shoulders, I pull her close and walk us to the entrance. With my free hand, I scan my key fob and open the door. The lights are off, but before Sierra can ask why, I'm flicking them on and hurrying her inside.

"We're the only ones here?" Her uncertainty is obvious, but there's no sign of fear. She's staring at the black walls surrounding the entrance. Or, more specifically, the white-painted quotes covering them. "*We can't be brave without fear.* You have that tattooed on your bicep."

"Mhm. Muhammad Ali. It was the first tattoo I got," I confirm. "Come on, I want to show you something." I slide my hand across her back and down her arm until I can link our fingers together.

Nerves tangle in my stomach as I lead her to the back office. We walk silently down the bright hallway, the walls decorated with photos, some personal and some not so much. I'm grinning like a naughty schoolboy when I feel her pull on my hand, her heels digging into the floor.

"Why are there pictures of you on the wall?" Sierra asks cautiously. With her body barely a foot away from the first photo hung on the wall, I can't see her expression, but I would put money down on that adorable little wrinkle being between her brows. "How old are you here? You look exactly the same."

Moving behind her, I hang my arms over her shoulders and rest my chin on her head. She sighs, melting into my embrace like warm butter. Like being in my arms is the most natural thing in the world.

"Exactly the same?" I tsk. "You wound me, fighter. I'm much bigger now."

The photo in front of us was taken at my first real fight, back when I was a sixteen-year-old chump who thought his shit didn't stink.

A much scrawnier version of myself stands with a pair of gold shorts hung around his hips, ending right above the knee, and a mess of long, unruly curls on his head and curling behind the ears. My arm is lifted in the air, my hand in Dad's. I had won the fight by some miracle, but there isn't the hint of a smile nor a stitch of pride on my father's face. Probably because

I had entered the fight behind his back, but that's water under the bridge now.

I could have hung any other photo, maybe one where my dad didn't look like he wanted to leather my ass, but it was my first fight. It was memorable. It's the match that decided everything for me. Sparked the fire that hasn't burnt out yet and hopefully won't for a long time.

"Braden, why are there pictures of you here?" she repeats the question that I ignored, trailing her fingers along the top of the frame.

I'm suddenly hit with a wall of fear that causes my throat to swell and my next words to die on my tongue. I shouldn't be scared to tell her that all of this is mine, but once I do, things will become very real, very quickly. Once Sierra knows, the ball will drop. Owning my own gym will no longer be a dream but a reality. One that I have the ability to fuck up and lose.

I grapple with the handle on my emotions when she spins around in my arms and pushes up on her tiptoes, placing a kiss on my jaw. She nuzzles into the crook of my neck, palming my back with her small hands. I shudder a breath and tighten my arms around her shoulders.

"What aren't you telling me?" she murmurs. Her gentle words do me in.

"It's mine. The gym is mine."

Sierra

"IT'S YOURS?" I sputter. "Yours how?"

He might as well have told me he's a born-again virgin. Surprise doesn't even cover how I'm feeling. The mix of emotions inside of me varies from curiosity, surprise, and a whole shit ton of pride.

The gym—from what I've seen so far—has a factory-like feel and is absolutely beautiful. It feels luxurious yet intimate and not at all intimidating like I was expecting when we were standing outside. With shiny wood floors and freaking chalkboard walls, it feels like a place that I would actually want to spend hours at, and I'm not a gym type of gal. I can't wait to see what the rest of the building looks like.

Braden chuckles, kissing my head. "Mine as in *mine*. I own Knockout. I've spent almost every day here for the past four months getting it ready to open."

My jaw is unhinged, but I don't bother closing it.

"I'm sorry that I kept it from you," he apologizes.

"Don't apologize. I just have so many questions."

"Like?"

"Like when did you decide to do this? What about the gym in Vancouver?"

He backs up and grabs my hand again. "It became a real idea the day after you left. Rampage is now Tyler's. He bought it, and I used the money from the sale to buy Knockout. Well, what's now Knockout. The building was empty when I bought it."

What? My brows fly to my hairline. "It was empty?"

He nods. "Four walls and a killer echo."

"Holy shit."

"Do you have any more questions you want answered right now, or do you want the grand tour?"

"They can wait. Show me. Please." I'm incredibly eager. How did I miss something this big? He was building an entire business from scratch, and I had no idea. Although, to be completely fair, I was under the impression that he was just working here.

"We'll skip the office for now. I might be too tempted to bend you over my desk and have my way with you." With a hard smack, his palm connects with my right butt cheek. "These fucking leggings, baby. I want to rip them off of you."

Heat crawls up my neck. These pregnancy hormones have me acting like a dick-obsessed mess. All it takes is the slightest brush of Braden's skin or that gruffness in his voice to make my panties slick and an empty feeling slump between my thighs. Fuck, I don't think that I can deal with his dirty mouth right now.

"Later," I breathe.

"Later," Braden agrees, but his eyes say something else. They're dark, possessive as they sharpen on me. I can feel the tension snap and crackle in the distance between us, and I want it to suffocate me. He crowds my space, suddenly so much closer than before.

The ache between my legs is distracting. It's pulling my head in the wrong direction. I need to focus on the revelation that just took place, not the way my underwear sticks to my pussy, already so wet with my arousal.

I nearly moan when Braden pushes me against the wall, shaking the picture frames beside me. My thighs spread of their own accord, giving him room to move between them. He picks them up and wraps them around his waist instead.

"Fuck," he rasps.

I've nearly torn a hole in my lip from biting down on it by the time he tilts his hips and brushes the hardness of his cock against my centre. I throw my head back as pricks of pleasure ricochet through me. The thin material of his gym shorts do nothing to hide the ridges of his erection as he grinds against me, brushing my clit just enough to tease.

"Please," I gasp, grabbing his flexed biceps and squeezing.

Lust blazes in his half-lidded stare, warming me all over. With a tense jaw, he moves a hand between our bodies and into my leggings. Oh my God. *Yes.* Fingers slide over my wet panties, and knuckles brush my clit, making me tremble with anticipation.

"Oh *fuck*. Please." I'm shamelessly grinding into his hand, far too desperate to care about anything but getting some relief.

I cry out when he hooks two fingers under the crotch of my panties and tugs them aside before plunging two fingers inside of me. I'm so slick, so needy, that there's no resistance as he starts fucking me with his fingers.

"You have such a greedy pussy, baby. Do you feel how it sucks me in? How fucking wet and swollen you are for me?"

His dirty words do nothing to smother the flames under my skin. They're dousing them in gasoline, and the burn is pure pleasure.

The grip my thighs have around his waist starts to loosen when they begin to shake, my climax threatening to send me toppling over the edge. Braden's thigh slides beneath my ass and rests there.

"Want to watch you," he groans, looking pained. "But I need to kiss you."

Braden's mouth slants across mine, hard and needy. The kiss is far from romantic, but that's not what I need right now. His tongue presses to the seam of my lips, and I open for him desperately. He swallows my moan when his thumb applies a hard pressure to my clit before sliding around the wet, soft skin in quick circles.

My head swims, my heart rate blasting into overdrive. Black dots swarm my vision as I rip my mouth from his. "I'm coming. *I'm coming.*"

"Soak my fingers, fighter," he demands, adding a third

finger just before my walls start to convulse around them. A husky groan falls between us as I ride his hand, my head thrown back, sobs falling from my lips.

After the pleasure subsides, my head falls forward, colliding with Braden's chest. I blink a few times to try and gather my bearings again and shudder when he slips his fingers out of me, wiping them on my leggings before squeezing my thigh.

The squeeze draws my attention to the quivering muscles wrapped around him, and I drop them from his waist, cursing at the soreness that pulses through them.

"Better?" The humour in his voice is thick.

Leaning back, I meet his eyes and smile sheepishly. "You're the worst."

"Your ruined panties would beg to differ."

A blush crawls up my neck as I push at his chest and slip from between him and the wall. Running a hand over my hair, I say, "Give me that tour already. I want to see the rest of this place."

I can't help but watch as he reaches into his shorts and adjusts himself. When my eyes stay locked on his crotch for way too long, he snorts. "Keep looking at my cock like that and I won't be able to give you this damn tour. We'll take care of it later. Right now, I want to show you the rest of my gym."

Nodding, I drag my eyes up to the dimple in his cheek and reach out to lace our fingers together again.

Braden leads us through the hallway, past the men's and women's locker rooms, and out toward a huge open space filled with all sorts of workout equipment. Punching bags hang from the ceiling and form a sort of divider between the normal training area full of things like treadmills and bench presses and what I assume to be the part of the room where you would focus more on boxing. A fighting ring sits at the centre of that half of the room.

Racks upon racks of weights and kettlebells are set off to the side of the workout equipment, and more quotes fill the walls where mirrors don't. There are rows of yoga mats and balls beside bottles of sanitizer and rags off by the hallway entrance. A room labelled as a Training Room sits at the far end of the gym, behind the fighting ring.

Braden's eyes beat into the side of my head as he waits for me to speak, but my tongue does nothing but flop helplessly in my mouth. I'm speechless. Completely in awe of him and this space that he's created. I don't think I could be any prouder of him.

"Sierra?"

Oh my God. He sounds nervous.

I squeeze his hand and force something, anything, out of my mouth. "I don't know what to say." His gulp is audible, and I wince, quickly explaining. "This place is phenomenal. I don't know what to say because I think I'm in shock. This is amazing, Braden. *Really* amazing."

When he tugs me toward him, his grin takes the wind out from under me. Joy bubbles in my stomach, and I giggle when he loops his arms around my waist and hugs me so tight my feet hover above the ground.

"Thank Christ," he blows into my hair.

"Did you think that I wouldn't love it?"

"I figured you would. But it feels fucking out of this world to hear you say it out loud."

Understanding floods my system. I pepper kisses all over his throat, jaw, and face before pulling back and holding his gaze hostage with mine. "You did it."

"I did it," he echoes slowly, like he's finally letting it sink in.

"When do you open?"

"Tomorrow."

Mouth gaping, I pull away. "Tomorrow? You waited until the day before your grand opening to show this place to me?"

He puts his hands—palms out—in front of him. "In my defense, the bags weren't hung until yesterday, and the weights were a day late. I wasn't about to show it to you incomplete. It had to be perfect. And now it is."

"Fine." My lips itch to pull into a smile. "Now, are you going to show me how any of this stuff works? Or do I need to find myself a different trainer?"

His eyes darken at the threat, and he takes my ass in his hands. "Not unless you want to be held responsible for the injuries I give them, you fucking won't."

I laugh loudly, blissfully. "Okay, okay. Only you."

His entire face softens. "Just me."

And it's true. It is just him. I place my hand on my stomach. It's just *us* and our future.

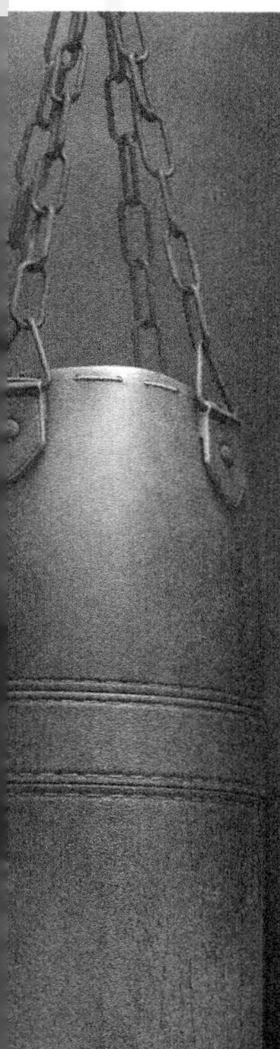

26

Braden

How do baby brands get away with charging five hundred dollars for a stroller? It's straight-up highway robbery at this point. I'm pretty sure a baby doesn't care that the thing pushing it around on the sidewalk has a fancy logo stitched into the handle or a special cup holder for mom and dad.

But it doesn't end there. Stroller after stroller is lined up in front of me and Sierra, and the longer it takes us to pick one, the more my skin itches like a thousand fire ants are trying to burrow themselves beneath it.

Some of them are more like luxury beds with wheels, while others are more clunky and plain. There's cream, black, pink, blue, or beige. Adjustable or nonadjustable. Meant to grow or not meant to grow. Full-sized or lightweight. And what the fuck is a jogging stroller? Oh boy, I'm pretty sure my brain is cramping.

The original plan for today had been to look around a few baby stores to get an idea of what we wanted to add to our registry. However, it's safe to say that that idea crashed and burned the moment we stepped inside the first store and Sierra burst into a fit of tears after catching a glimpse of a newborn onesie with the saying "*Strong like daddy*" written across the chest.

Not even two minutes later, we had an associate in a baby blue polo rushing toward us and whisking Sierra away. Now, a full hour later, my girlfriend is holding a scanning machine, adding items to our in-store registry and waiting on me to help decide which stroller we need to add.

"The first one is fine," I say, staring at the plain black one on the end.

I have no clue how much that one costs, but it looks like it's on the decent end of the spectrum. It's pretty plain and to the point. Nothing too extravagant.

"What about the third one?" Sierra asks, tapping her thigh with her fingers.

The third stroller is beige and lies flat like a bed. Although it doesn't have a fancy brand stitched in the squishy handle, it seems a bit impractical.

"What if the baby throws up in it? Won't it stain?"

She hums. "Good point. I didn't think of that."

I point to the last one. "What about that one?" It's still black but is a bit fancier than the first one I chose with its dual cup holders and decent storage underneath the seat. "The girl said it has a matching car seat that clips inside for when the baby is really small."

"You caught that?" Sierra slants me a surprised look.

I bump her shoulder, smiling softly. "Yeah, I caught that."

There's something about the way she's looking at me—all lovesick and content—that has a warm and fuzzy feeling setting up camp in my stomach. I want to take a mental picture of that expression and tuck it away for days when I really need it.

I try not to show my surprise when she blurts out, "Let's add the last one to the registry."

"You sure? We don't have to pick that one just because I like it."

She cuts a hand through the air. "I'm sure. It's the most practical. Plus less likely to stain."

My smile grows with the small victory when Sierra scans the stroller's barcode and heads toward the crib section of the store. I follow her behind her like a puppy scared of getting lost, my eyes not leaving her back for the rest of our trip.

We spend another hour scanning endless items to our registry before migrating to the outlet mall a few streets over. I've never had to go dress shopping with a woman before, but I'm trying not to act like the idea of it makes me want to take a nap.

A few people walk by us, but the mall is dead for a Saturday morning.

"Do you really not have anything to wear to this dinner tonight? It's not a suit-and-tie type thing, is it?" I ask casually, like I'm not crossing my fingers behind my back in hope that she'll magically remember she has the perfect dress already shoved in the back of her closet.

"It's a charity dinner, Braden." Sierra's arm brushes mine as we walk. "You have to wear a suit, and I need to find a dress that actually zips up in the back and doesn't make me look like a beached whale."

Her last comment makes me frown. Is that really how she sees herself? I can't begin to understand how it feels to watch your body change and grow in the way she is, but it pisses me off to hear her talk that way.

"You don't look like a beached whale. You're five months pregnant and still the most gorgeous woman I have ever seen."

She looks doubtful. "You're supposed to say that."

"Like hell I am," I snap. Grabbing her hand, I tug on it, forcing her to stop walking and face me. When she refuses to meet my gaze, I pinch her chin between my thumb and pointer finger and lift it, forcing her to look at me. The insecurity I find trapped in her silver eyes is enough to put my heart in a choke-hold. I immediately soften my voice. "You were stunning when I met you, and you're even more stunning now. You're growing our baby, Sierra. I've never been as attracted to you as I am right now. I wish you felt the same way about yourself, but until you do, I'll be here to remind you. Okay?"

There's a slight pink tint to her cheeks, but I'm not sure if it's from embarrassment or something deeper down that she won't tell me about while we're in the middle of the mall. Either way, it doesn't matter. The only thing that matters to me right now is making sure that my girl knows how beautiful I think she is so hopefully, maybe, she'll be able to believe it too.

"This isn't the place to talk about this, I know. I'll drop it for now. But you bet your tight ass that we'll be doing a lot more than just talking about it when we get home." I press my lips to hers, feeling them quiver ever so slightly. I swallow the shuttered breaths that brush mine as she tries holding back the tears I find building in her eyes. Brushing my thumb under her lower lashes, I swipe away the rogue tear that escapes and kiss her again before whispering, "No tears."

The only sign of acknowledgment she offers me is the small choked sound that swells in her throat before her spine snaps straight and her chin lifts, this time without my help. And just like that, she's the image of confidence.

"Thank you."

I wear a proud grin when I kiss her temple and say, "Let's go get you a dress, fighter."

I THINK I swallowed my tongue. My hand drifts to my throat and massages the hot skin, like I'm actually searching for it behind my Adam's apple.

The apartment is silent, the air stiff and pulled tight, ready to snap. Lust attacks my senses, so dangerously potent in each quick inhale of air that I suck back. My cock stirs, desperate for attention from the woman walking toward me.

Sierra's hips twist as she moves. The tight black silk wrapped around her curves fits her figure too perfectly, like a damn glove. I want to tell her to go change back into her cookie monster pants and my sweater, but fuck if she doesn't look confident as all hell. It's obvious in the way her lips are quirked up in a seductive smile and her nose stays pointed to the sky even under the intensity of my stare.

I'll happily deal with a hundred sets of wandering, curious eyes following my girl all night if it means that that look stays right where it is.

You could drop a match and set the room on fire with how dense the air feels between us. And I would gladly burn if it meant that I could look at her for a few minutes longer.

Sierra stops a few feet away and spins in a circle, arms splayed out. "What do you think?"

"I think that you're far too good for me," I rasp, eating the distance between us and placing my fingers firmly on her hips. My thumbs draw circles into the silk dress. "And that it's going to hurt keeping my hands off of you all night."

Silver eyes blink innocently at me through thick, black lashes. "It's a good thing that you won't have to, then, isn't it?"

A nearly inhuman groan rattles in my chest when she grabs

my hand and slides it beneath the hem of her dress that she's already lifted to her knee. Smooth, warm skin pebbles with goosebumps beneath my fingertips as she slides them up her calf, her thigh, and to her wet, bare pussy.

"Fuck," I mutter, grazing my knuckles against the slick skin. "Where are your panties?"

She inhales sharply, and her fingernails dig into the top of my hand. "I skipped them. The lines would show in this dress. But if it's a problem, I'll just go put some on—"

I cut her off by digging my knuckles between her lips and brushing the swollen bundle of nerves hiding there, feeling her pussy weep for me. With a moan, her head falls forward, hitting my chest.

"It's cute when you try to beat me at my own game, little fighter. But we both know I'll win every single time." I pull my hand out from under her dress and slip my fingers in my mouth, sucking them clean. "Let's go, Sierra. We don't want to be late."

Her growl has me laughing like a maniac all the way to the door.

27

Sierra

Braden's hand is warm on my back as he leads us past chatting women in floor-length gowns, gawking men crowding an open bar, servers with trays of champagne, and to our designated table in the crowded ballroom. My body is already crying from the heat blasting around us, but I try not to focus too much on the sweat building beneath my arms and more so on not stepping on the hem of my dress and toppling over.

Too many tables to count fill the room, each decorated with elegant pink-and-yellow flower arrangements and a crisp white tablecloth. Number cards are hung from the back of each chair, causing my steps to falter.

"Shit," I hiss, feeling Braden's concern immediately as I dig my heels into the shiny wood floors.

"What's wrong? Did something happen?" he asks with wild desperation, reaching for my stomach.

I offer him a shy smile and urge his hands back down. "No, sorry. I forgot to look at where we're sitting."

Table and seating assignments were sent via email this

morning, but I was too busy fawning over the grey glider chair I wanted for the nursery to pay attention to much else.

I unclasp my clutch and pull out my phone, immediately starting to scroll through my emails. Mackenzie's name is pretty close to the top, so it doesn't take long to pull up the message.

"Seat fifteen and sixteen," I announce, putting my phone away.

"Over there," he whispers, nodding to the front of the ballroom.

We push our way through the sea of tables before coming to a stop at the second table, directly in front of the stage. I bristle when I see Cole already occupying one of the six chairs, his nose in the air and narrowed eyes trained on me—or rather, my swollen stomach.

My pregnancy hasn't been kept a secret by any means, but I've tried to stick with clothes that don't emphasize my bump at work for this very reason. I've already talked to Mackenzie about when I'll take maternity leave, and he volunteered to relay that message to Clark so that I didn't have to have more contact with that man than necessary.

Cole, on the other hand, received an email from me informing him of my pregnancy when he was in Vancouver last week. Chickenshit move, I know. But by the way he's glaring at my stomach right now, as if he would love nothing more than to see it explode in front of him, I can't say that I regret my decision.

Beside me, Braden is a mountain of tight, angry muscles, ready to protect me at the first sign of danger. I know that he doesn't care about where we are or the people surrounding us with pockets so heavy they would sink to the bottom of the Pacific. He's been wanting to have a go at Cole from the moment they met. And with his heightened protectiveness and the knowledge of what happened between Cole and me, it won't take much to make those dreams come true.

I reach for Braden's hand, intertwining our fingers and bringing them to my stomach. A sigh of relief escapes me the second there's something between Cole's glare and my baby.

Braden leans toward me, his nose brushing the tip of my ear. "We can go home. I can tell Mack that you aren't feeling well."

I want to take the offer. *Badly*. But I refuse to let Cole think that he's won something here.

"Mackenzie and Gretchen worked really hard organizing this event. We're not going to let that asshole take away from what tonight is about."

Over the past few months, I've gotten to know Mackenzie Thompson on a deeper, personal level that's made him more of a friend to me than just a boss. Gretchen had more to do with that than Mack or I did with all of her constant pushing, but that's beside the point. After Mack took care of the Waterton Brothers budget problem for me, I was able to help them reach their goals and secured a long-term client. It's been pretty smooth sailing since.

Braden and Mack have also been spending a lot of time together recently. I think Mack has been to Braden's gym every single day since it opened two weeks ago. They've built the foundation of a really great friendship here, and that makes me happy.

We both owe it to Mack to be here tonight. To support him and the Save A Home Foundation, an organization that he holds so close to his heart.

I was shocked when Mack told me about his history with foster care and how hard it was for him growing up in the system. His parents passed away when he was only five, and without any other immediate family, he had no choice but to fall into the hands of the Toronto foster care system.

He explained how grateful he is for his adoptive parents and the way they helped him turn his life around after spending ten years alone, without much comfort or affection. I remember tears filling my eyes and his steady voice explaining how those hard years helped him grow into who he is today.

Mackenzie isn't the type of man who looks back and hates the torments of his past. He values the lessons they taught him along the way instead. Hearing him sound so sure and positive despite everything that he's gone through was what made me realize that I wanted to get to know him. As more than just my boss, but a friend.

Knowing that tonight means so much to Mack made Braden's and my decision to come tonight a very easy one, despite our mutual dislike of this type of social event.

"You're right," Braden agrees, although he sounds pained.

He shifts his body so he stands in front of me and starts to push my unbuttoned jacket from my shoulders. I shrug it off, and he takes it eagerly, laying it over the chair farthest from Cole before pulling it out for me. He drapes his suit jacket across his chair, and we both sit. The chairs are so close together that with Braden's body being so large, we're pressed firmly against each other, thigh to thigh and bicep to bicep.

Braden places one hand on the table and the other on my thigh before giving it a comforting squeeze. He's more tense than I think I've ever seen him. The sharp lines of his jaw are more prominent as it clenches, and his thick bottom lip is thinner than usual, probably from scowling so deeply. My fingers itch to touch all of those tight muscles and relax them. Put him at ease. But it would be for nothing as long as we're here, only a few feet from the root of the problem.

"I noticed the bar when we walked in. Do you want to get a

drink before dinner?" I ask, feeling a bit helpless as to how to help him relax.

"I'm good, babe."

"Are you sure?"

He nods once, and I kiss his cheek, hoping that the subtle affection can help settle him even the slightest bit. His stubble scratches my chin. Even though I've become used to the scrape of his facial hair, it still sends a shudder down my spine that has me leaning even closer to him.

"I see you got your friend into a suit, Sierra. Is that why you were late? You missed the raffle entirely," Cole snarks, one eyebrow lifted in judgment.

A pang of guilt ricochets through me before I can ignore it. Missing the raffle was entirely my fault. After having such a busy morning and afternoon, Braden and I fell asleep as soon as we got back home before either of us could set an alarm. It's a miracle that we made it here before dinner considering we only woke up an hour and a half ago.

"I'm not her friend, bud." Braden laughs coldly. "But you're very aware of that."

Cole slants him a dirty look. "And I'm not your *bud*," he spits, putting extra emphasis on the label.

"Glad we got that cleared up, then."

Cole ignores Braden and focuses on me as he gulps back whatever brown liquid he has in his glass. "You look incredible in that dress."

Bile slithers up my throat. I would rather roll around in a dumpster than be complimented by Cole.

Braden leans back in his chair and grins smugly, like he's in on a joke that nobody else is. A nervous flutter fills my stomach as I think of what's about to come out of his mouth. Only he doesn't say what I was expecting. My jaw falls open when his brash grin morphs into something warmer, and he starts rubbing his thumb up and down my thigh. "Yes she does."

There's nothing dark or threatening in his voice, just a genuine feeling of love and appreciation that makes my heart vibrate like the ground beneath a dozen running elephants. Cole's presence fades to nothing in the background.

A buttery warmth slips over my skin and into my bones as I stare at Braden, surprised by his comment in the best way.

Braden has grown so much over the course of our relationship, and right now, it couldn't be any more obvious to see. I have no doubt that if I looked inside his head, I would find more than one crude comeback that would have pissed off Cole so much more than a simple agreement. And I think knowing that he could have but didn't makes his comment that much more satisfying.

"Thank you," I whisper so only Braden can hear.

His eyes meet mine, shining with so much affection I feel it down to my toes. "Don't thank me, sweetheart. It's the truth." He pinches the silky material of my dress between his fingers and hums low in his throat. "I can't wait to get you home and out of your dress so that I can show you just how strongly I believe it."

"Oh? Is that right?" I quirk a brow, acting tough even as my cheeks flush.

He laughs, so clear and bright, and it's the most beautiful sound in the world. It's a drug, one that I can see myself addicted to for the rest of my life.

"You already know it is. Now hush before I prove it to you right now. I think Mack's about to come on."

Releasing a tight breath, I pull away from him and blink a few times, bringing everything around us back into focus. The ballroom lights have dimmed, the stage now lit. With a megawatt smile, Mackenzie saunters across the stage toward a tall podium.

He's dressed incredibly dapper in a slim-fitting black tuxedo that I would probably puke at the cost of and shining, scuffless black shoes. His hair is buzzed neatly on the sides with longer, curly pieces pushed back on the top. Focused entirely on the crowd and rippling with confidence, he owns the stage, capturing the attention of everyone present and holding it in the palm of his hand.

All chatter ceases to exist as we watch him settle behind the podium, adjust the microphone stand higher, and pull his shoulders back. His chest puffs out as he grips what looks like a notepad and begins to speak.

"Good evening, everyone. I'm Mackenzie Thompson, one half of Brenton and Thompson Marketing here in Toronto. Firstly, I wanted to thank you all for joining me tonight. Secondly, on behalf of myself and Lilah Clevance, the founder of the Save A Home Foundation, we wanted to thank you all again for not only helping us reach our original goal of one hundred thousand dollars, but for going above and beyond. So far tonight, we've raised two hundred and fifty thousand dollars for our Toronto foster care system."

Clapping erupts around us, and Mack's smile grows brighter. I spot Gretchen standing off to the side of the stage, somewhat hidden behind a thick black curtain. Her lip is tucked between her teeth as she watches her boss, a faraway look flickering across her doll-like features.

"He's a good man," Braden whispers, kissing my bare shoulder and drowning out Mackenzie's voice. "I like him."

I laugh softly and lean my head against his. "Me too. Although I don't think we're the only ones."

Braden follows my gaze, and his shoulders shake with a silent chuckle. Gretchen thinks she hides her emotions well, but if you know what to look for, you can see right through her. There's nothing hidden in the way she watches Mackenzie —not now or *ever*—like she would lie down on a bridge of hot coals and let him walk over her just so that he didn't have to burn the soles of his feet.

"He's the same way. Stubborn fucker doesn't even see it."

Unfortunately, he's right.

With a sad shake of my head, I'm looking back at the man in question, tuning back into his speech as he finishes up.

"Dinner will be served in a few minutes, but both myself and Lilah will be around to chat and answer any questions you have. Enjoy the rest of your evening."

He exits the stage quickly before stopping short in front of Gretchen. I catch the tug of her mouth as she speaks before freezing with her lips parted. Then Mack's pulling her against his chest and lifting her feet off the ground, spinning them around.

I'm still watching them like a creep when Braden's phone starts ringing. Removing his hand from my thigh, he slips his phone from his suit jacket and answers it quickly after seeing the name on the screen.

"Hey. Is this important? I can't really talk right now."

Surprise flares in his dark brown eyes, and my spine goes ramrod straight.

"Fuck. Okay, yeah, we'll make it. Keep me updated, okay? Don't go fucking silent on me, Tyler."

I'm smacked with a thousand reasons as to why Tyler would be calling and why Braden looks like he's about to curl over and vomit. My hand finds Braden's shoulder and stays there, unmoving.

"I got it. We'll be there as soon as we can. Go back to your wife. I'll let you know when we're there . . . Okay. Bye."

"What's wrong?" I ask as soon as he pulls the phone from his ear.

Kissing the knuckles of the hand resting on his shoulder, he lets out a shaky breath. "Gracie's in labour. We need to go to Vancouver. Right now."

28

Braden

I'M GOING TO BE AN UNCLE. TYLER IS GOING TO BE A fucking father. We're *both* going to be fathers.

How the hell did that happen?

My head is a jumbled mess as I slip my arms through my suit jacket and help Sierra to her feet, even as she rolls her eyes and assures me she's pregnant, not broken.

I'm pretty sure that I'm grinning, feeling way too excited to get to Vancouver, but my face has been numb since I heard Tyler's voice.

Fuck, it hit me harder than I expected to hear him be anything but the arrogant little shit he usually is. His nerves were evident in the way his words shook and the loud gulps that flowed through the phone. It probably hit me harder knowing that in just a few months, that's going to be me.

"You're not seriously leaving," Cole sniffs, sounding almost offended. Of course he would be. How dare we not stay and soak in his presence all night.

Asshole.

"We have somewhere else to be," Sierra retorts while slipping her arms through her jacket.

Cole rolls his eyes so hard I wonder if they'll get stuck at the back of his head. "Convenient."

"Fuck off, Cole," I grumble.

His chair scrapes across the floor when he stands abruptly. His jaw is clenched so tight I'm surprised he hasn't broken any teeth. Who knows, maybe he's leaving that honour for me.

"Can I talk to you outside, Sierra? This can't wait for Monday morning."

My arm slips around her waist as she stiffens. "We really need to go. Maybe you can email it to me."

That's apparently the wrong thing to say because Cole's eyes flash with something violent, making me push Sierra behind me. My brows climb my forehead, this fucker's entire existence a complete thorn in my side.

"Oh, like you emailed me about being pregnant with this incompetent, wannabe fighter's baby instead of telling me face-to-face? Why would you get yourself into this mess, Sierra? He's nowhere near good enough for you."

His words settle in my stomach like shards of glass. He's so angry, so *bitter*, that I can almost smell his hatred in the air. Flat palms glide over my back, drawing my attention long enough for me to notice the several sets of eyes watching us with such curiosity it makes my skin crawl.

"You know what, big guy? I think taking this outside would be a great idea," I growl, gesturing toward the exit. When Cole doesn't move, I look over my shoulder at Sierra, softening my voice as I say, "Think you could find Mack for me? This shit has gone on too fucking long."

She looks hesitant, possibly a little scared—not like I can blame her. "I don't want to take away from his night with this drama."

I can't help but smile. "Trust me, he won't want to miss this. I'll find you after."

"Okay," she exhales. "I'll get Mackenzie. Please don't hurt yourself. Tyler and Gracie don't need to be worrying about you on top of everything else."

I grab her chin between my fingers and lift, making our gazes lock before I'm capturing her mouth in a claiming, demanding kiss. A shiver moves through her when she kisses me back just as hard. With a nip to her lips, I pull back and glide my thumb along the top of her cheekbone.

"Don't have too much fun without me," she teases lightly before slipping away in search of Mack.

With Sierra gone, I turn my attention back to Cole. Hatred swirls in my blood, making it bubble in my veins. "Either you can walk yourself out of the building, or I can drag you out in front of all of these people. Pick."

He stares back at me with a grin that has my stomach swirling.

"You're quite demanding, Braden. Sierra didn't strike me as the type to enjoy being bossed around, but maybe that's what I was missing. Perhaps I was *too* nice."

"Don't talk about her. This is the only warning you're going to get," I say slowly, with a sense of calm that I sure as shit don't feel. "Let's go."

Thankfully, he starts walking toward me before I have to toss him over my shoulder. He narrows his eyes and bumps past me, taking the lead. I squeeze my eyes shut for a few seconds and exhale slowly before following him out of the ballroom. It's easy to ignore the gawking guests now that Sierra is gone and no longer being scrutinized. She didn't need that shit.

Cole stomps his way through the sliding doors at the entrance of the hotel hosting the gala, and I pick up my pace, meeting him outside before he has a chance to shake me and take off.

The wind is strong tonight, swaying through the trees that bend and curve awkwardly, creating loud *whooshing* noises around the parking lot that sound a lot like when you place an empty paper towel roll to your lips and shout.

I'm surprised when Cole willingly moves along to the side of the building, finding a place in the shadows that the street lamps and headlights can't reach instead of being a pussy and staying in plain view.

"If I didn't know any better, I would think that you've dragged me into the dark with plans of beating *my* ass," I shout over the wind and the few feet of distance between us.

Cole's hands find his hips, his fingers curling. He shakes his head furiously. "You're not going to touch me, Braden."

"I'm not?"

"Not unless you want me to press charges, you're not."

I can't help it. A booming laugh scrapes up my throat, and my head falls back.

"Do you know what a hypocrite is, Mr. Big Shot?" I ask with a wicked grin. Cole blinks at me, unimpressed with my question. "See, if you were to press charges against me for whatever it is I'm going to do to you, then it would be completely plausible to expect Sierra to press charges against you for sexual harassment, don't you think?"

He takes a brave step forward, fists shaking at his side. There's no hiding the outrage burning in his eyes. I've just struck a cord deep inside of him, one that he didn't want me knowing he had.

"I didn't sexually harass her!" he roars, taking another step closer.

"You touched her without permission, you fucking scumbag! She's never given you any reason to think you could lay a single finger on her. But you did it anyway. You took what you wanted because that's what you think you deserve, right?"

I don't give him time to answer.

"Well, now I'm going to break every single bone in your hand so that you won't forget what happens when you touch somebody like that without their permission. The next time you think of doing this again, you'll feel the pain of your bones snapping and hear the tremble in your cries like it's happening all over again. Because it will happen again. Mark my words, Cole Travis. Touch somebody else the way you did Sierra and I'll come back here and fucking end you."

I stalk toward him, watching with the same unwavering smile as he fumbles back a step, and another, and another until he collides with a brick wall. *Stuck*. He's stuck.

"You gave her a promotion, so she owed it to you, right?" My voice is shaking, but I'm not sure if it's from the outrage burning inside of me or the pain I feel thinking about him touching Sierra.

"She didn't tell you no. So in your fucked-up mind, that meant yes, right?"

Against my better judgment, my arm shoots out in front of me, and my knuckles collide with the bricks beside his head. He gasps, eyes bulging while I suck a pained breath through my teeth.

Fuck. I can't wiggle my fingers.

I'm towering over Cole as I tightly grip his right wrist with my non-aching hand and lift it beside his face, pinning it against the scuffed brick. The maneuver is a bit uncomfortable and leaves my entire side open and vulnerable if he decides to fight back, but I'm not about to try and test the extent of my hand injury. I definitely broke something.

"You're not really going to do this," Cole stammers, struggling a bit against the wall. I tighten my grip on his wrist until I know that he'll have bruises the shape of my fingertips in the morning.

"You're right. He's not. We both are, shit for brains," a familiar voice spits, the deep tenor swirling in the wind.

I don't turn around to face Mack—not wanting to risk Cole making a run for it—but I know he's close. Worry threatens to knock me off my feet when I think of Sierra and where she is. Is she here too?

"You can't do shit to me, Thompson. Clark won't let you touch me," Cole spits venomously.

"No? Even if a sexual harassment lawsuit with your name on it threatened to dismantle the entire Toronto branch? News flash, Cole. Clark doesn't give a shit about you. He only cares about what you can do for him," Mackenzie states, coming to stand beside me. "And your value has quickly depleted."

I can feel my friend's eyes on my busted hand but merely shrug in hopes he'll leave it alone. There's nothing we can do about it now. The sooner we get this done with, the sooner I can find my girl and get on a plane to meet my niece or nephew. I'll see a doctor then.

"You're done, Cole. After tonight, we better never see you again." Mackenzie brushes me to the side and replaces my hold on Cole's wrist with his own. When he uses his free hand to pull something clunky and shiny from his jacket pocket, my jaw nearly unhinges. He holds his hand out, palm open and face up.

"Fucking brass knuckles? You're a badass, Mack." I take the unexpected weapon from him and slip the cold brass over the knuckles on my left hand. It's not the first time that I've felt this type of heaviness on my hand, but it's never been on my nondominant hand.

I hesitate for a moment, my muscles growing tense. If

Sierra is nearby, there's no way that I can do this. She doesn't need to see or hear this.

Like he's read my mind, Mack shifts his weight and leans over to me, whispering, "She's already on her way back to her place. Just take care of this quickly."

I nod, relaxing slightly. As soon as Cole realizes what's about to happen, he starts to really resist Mack's hold, struggling and clawing at him. Mackenzie has to pin him to the wall with a forearm to the throat to gain some leverage. It's about time the piece of shit realizes that he isn't getting out of this.

My fingers tingle like they know what's about to happen and can't hold back their excitement. I roll my shoulders back and close my left hand into a perfect fist.

"I warned you back at that restaurant what would happen if you so much as talked to Sierra again, but I never would have given you the chance to walk away so easily if I had known what happened while I was gone. Now you'll pay for what you did to her."

Cole's scream vibrates through the night when the brass knuckles make contact with the back of his hand, crunching the bones, leaving his hand utterly useless. Mackenzie lets go of his wrist and steps back. We watch the tears stream down Cole's face as he cradles his shattered hand and kneels over, vomiting on the pavement.

"Get the fuck out of Toronto, Cole. I never want to see you again," I spit.

My lips curl in disgust as I slip off the knuckles and hand them back to Mackenzie. He silently slips them back into his jacket as we turn around and leave Cole to figure out what to do next before somebody comes to investigate the screams.

"Did she take a cab?" I ask him, finally lifting my hand up under a stream of light flooding the parking lot and wincing at the swollen, bloody mess.

"Gretch drove her home."

I let out a breath. "Thank you. For everything."

Mack snorts. "You're welcome, man. He deserves a lot worse."

"Yeah, he does."

We come to a stop in front of a row of parked cars when he jingles a set of keys between us. "Let's get you back to your girl."

"You're okay with leaving your party so early? I can take a cab," I protest. As much as I hate cabs, I'm not about to steal him away from such an important night.

He lifts a shoulder. "They don't need me. The important stuff is over."

"Alright then. Let's go."

29

Sierra

The second I hear the front door click shut, I'm dropping the sweatshirt in my hands and rushing from the bedroom. With my heartbeat in my ears, I run through the apartment and release a tight breath when I see Braden in one piece, slipping off his dress shoes.

"You scared the hell out of me, you asshole." I'm pissed off, but that doesn't stop me from throwing myself at him or planting kisses all over his face while he binds his arms around me.

"I'm sorry for worrying you, baby," he whispers.

"What happened?" I plant my hands on his chest and push back, searching his face for any sign of an injury. When I come up empty of anything but exhaustion in his eyes, I step back, forcing his arms to drop to his sides as I search the rest of him.

"It's a long story," he replies far too calmly.

Glacier water fills my veins when my eyes fall to his hands. Or specifically, the swollen, bloody mess that's left of his right one. My breath catches.

"What the hell did you do, Braden?" I yell, gently taking

hold of his wrist. He hisses through clenched teeth when I lift it to take a closer look at his hand, but he doesn't pull it away.

His knuckles look like they've stopped bleeding, but the side of his hand is already bruised and swollen enough that his pinky doesn't even resemble a finger anymore. His left hand is a bit red and angry-looking, but nothing that has me even half as worried as his right hand does.

"Got into a fight with a wall. It'll be fine. Once we get to the hospital, I'll get it looked at. But we don't have time to worry about this right now. I'll wrap it up, but then we need to go. My dad already booked our plane tickets, but our flight leaves in two hours."

I scoff but lower his hand, releasing it. As much as I would love to fight him on this, he is right about being on a time crunch. Two hours doesn't leave us enough time to get him to a hospital.

"I'm almost done packing. Let me at least clean it up for you. You can tell me why you punched a wall and what happened with Cole while I'm doing it."

He looks like he wants to put up a fight but thinks better of it. "Yes, ma'am."

I level him with a hard stare. "Sit down. I'll get the first aid kit."

After receiving a fake salute, I go to the bathroom and collect everything I need. Braden has his eyes closed and his head resting on the back of the couch when I return.

"Start talking."

With his eyes still closed, he says, "Cole Travis is no longer someone that you need to concern yourself with."

"That's not ominous at all." I snort, dropping to my knees and digging through the first aid kit. "Care to elaborate?"

After twisting off the cap of a bottle of peroxide, I wet a face cloth and gingerly hold his wrist to keep him still while starting to dab at his blood-crusted knuckles. Braden barely flinches as I clean his hand, but his eyes are beating down on my face, watching me.

"Mackenzie fired his scummy ass, and then I broke his fingers like I told you I would."

My brows fly to my hairline. Braden did what? With my head reeling with this new information, I ask, "Mack fired him?"

He chuckles. "Yeah, sweetheart. He did."

"Did Gretchen know he was going to do that? Because she didn't say anything to me about it when she drove me home."

"Do you really think that she would have been able to keep that a secret if she knew?" I chew on the inside of my lip and shake my head once. He grins. "Exactly. Gretchen didn't know. I promise."

"Okay," I whisper. Cole being gone seems almost too unbelievable. Too far-fetched.

Braden told me that he would take care of it, but I tried not to get my hopes up about it. Cole deserved far worse than a few broken bones and the task of having to find a new job, but if that's what it took to get rid of him, then all I have to say is *good riddance*.

Blowing out a breath, I drop the cloth beside me and lean forward to make sure I haven't missed any blood. I hold back a wince when I focus on the angry bruises that decorate his skin. The swelling and crooked shape of his pinky are the most concerning parts of his injury, though.

"I'll be okay, Sierra. We have more important things to do right now than worry about a potentially broken bone," he says gently, using his left hand to palm my cheek. His thumb traces the length of my bottom lip.

I look up at him and lean into his touch. "You have to

promise me that you'll see a doctor as soon as you can. You can't risk not getting it checked out. You're a boxer, Braden."

"I will get it checked out. I promise. Now please kiss me."

A laugh bubbles up my throat as I use his knees to help push myself up and lean over his lap, pressing my mouth to his. He nips my bottom lip and grabs the back of my head when I try to pull back too soon.

"Not yet, you don't," he growls before his lips are back on mine in a desperate, passionate kiss that has my toes curling in my socks. A steady arm moves behind my back and pulls me closer until our knees are knocking, and my hands slip up his thighs.

My eyes slide shut as I kiss him back, hoping to God he can feel my appreciation for him and what he did through our clash of teeth and lips.

The only person who has ever thought to do something like this for me is my sister. But Braden . . . Braden didn't hesitate to put himself in harm's way to protect me. That realization has the world tilting around me.

I lose track of how long we stay in his position, but once my lungs start to burn from lack of oxygen, I pull back again, and this time he lets me, breathing just as hard as I am.

"Thank you. For everything that you did. I still don't know what to say," I murmur, staring into his warm eyes, soaking up the love shining brightly in them. I'm not sure that I'll ever get used to being looked at like this. Like I'm *everything* to him.

He gives his head one firm shake. "Don't thank me. I would do it a million times over for you."

And without a doubt, I believe him.

GRACIE BATEMAN IS A CERTIFIED BADASS. I'm in awe of how perfect and put together she looks not even twenty-four hours after giving birth to a nine-pound baby boy. Hair held up in a bun, not a stitch of makeup on, and a grimace on her face whenever she moves around, she still looks like a runway model.

On the small hospital bed, Oliver Bateman lies curled up on his mom's chest, a head full of ink-black hair nuzzling her breast over top of her silk, baby pink pyjamas. He's fast asleep in a milk coma as his family watches him closely, several curious faces anxious to get a chance to hold him and kiss his soft, smooth cheeks.

Gracie's brother, Oakley, sits at the foot of the bed, a large inked hand wrapped around her ankle. His wife, Octavia—or Ava as she told me to call her—sits beside Braden and me on the small couch resting beneath the large window with a horrible view of the opposite side of the hospital. Tyler hasn't moved from her bedside since we arrived, and I would be lying if I said that didn't make my heart double in size.

There's such a profound love radiating off the otherwise intimidating man as he stares down at his wife and son, like he's in utter awe of them. His fingers timidly trace the edges of Oliver's face before stroking his head and the soft hair that covers his small, round head.

A quiet knock on the door startles everyone before it slowly opens, revealing another unfamiliar face.

Smiling crookedly, an incredibly wide-shouldered man walks into the overcrowded room. There's a young boy clinging to his back like a spider monkey, but he doesn't seem to mind as he tightens two large hands around the boy's knees and holds him close. With his foot, the man closes the door and joins the rest of us.

"Adam," Gracie squeaks, careful not to wake the sleeping baby. "You made it."

Humour lights up Adam's face. "You doubted me, Little H? Come on."

I must laugh a bit louder than I intended to because it captures Adam's attention. My mouth automatically slams shut when he stares at me, seemingly bewildered at my presence.

"You're actually real," he states, eyeing me with a reserved stare, like he's trying to convince himself I'm not a damn figment of his imagination. "And really pregnant."

"Adam, dude." Oakley cracks up. "Don't be a shit."

Glancing down at my belly, I let out a very unattractive snort. "Yep. Very real and very pregnant."

Braden stifles a laugh beside me. "Did you think I was lying?"

"Can you blame me?" Adam counters. "You go from being allergic to commitment to having a baby in less than a year and expect me to believe you?"

"Everyone else believed me!"

"I did kind of doubt you until Gracie showed me some pictures after Christmas," Ava says sheepishly.

Adam feigns offence. "Why didn't I get to see these pictures, then?"

"You didn't ask."

"How was I supposed to ask when I didn't even know they existed in the first place?"

"Oh God, don't start," Braden pleads. "It doesn't matter. Just tell my girl it's nice to meet her, and go meet my nephew."

Adam's lips tug up in the type of smirk that rivals Braden's. Sly, thrilling, and dangerously attractive. His brown eyes fall on me again, more open than a few moments ago. "It's a pleasure to finally meet you, Sierra. This monkey on my back is my son, Cooper."

I smile warmly. "It's great to meet you both. I really appreciate everything that you've done for Braden and Knockout the past few months."

Adam's large hand cuts through the air. "We're family here. That's what we do for each other."

I nod, deciding not to say anything else as I lean into Braden's side, letting the familiar scent of laundry detergent and a combination of spices that I can never pinpoint make me feel that sense of home that only he can bring me.

Grasping the hand he has resting on his thigh, I squeeze it tight, like I'm scared that if I'm not holding on to him, he's going to somehow disappear. And in all honesty, that's exactly what I'm afraid of.

The feeling of Braden's eyes on me, no doubt bright with curiosity, nearly has me pulling him out of the room and into a storage closet just so that I can kiss him over and over and remind him that he's stuck with me. But I settle for the soft strokes of his thumb on my wrist, knuckles, and palm instead, finding comfort in whatever I can get.

The heaviness of these feelings doesn't subside, though. No matter how badly I wish them away. They're blasting through my head, reminding me that I've handed away a piece of my heart to someone else. Someone who could take it and run.

I've always been fine on my own. The only people that I had grown to need over the course of my life were my sister and my niece. But that's changed so drastically over the past year. Now I don't think that I could survive in a world without Braden. Without his flirty jokes and expert-level kisses. Or his burnt pancakes on Sundays and foot rubs that always lead to us spending hours in the bedroom.

The guy I met at Sinners was only a piece of the man I

know now, and there's no doubt in my mind that I want to spend every day for the rest of my life falling in love with the rest of his missing pieces.

Ava uses the break in conversation to get off the couch and move toward Adam, holding her hand out for the boy that seems to have no intention of letting his feet touch the ground. "Coop, come sit with me so your dad can say hi to Gray and the new baby."

Cooper hesitantly moves his face from where it's hidden behind Adam's neck and looks at Ava with a smile so sweet I have to fight the urge to awe out loud. The young boy is a spitting image of Adam with that thick, dark brown hair that curls behind his ear and round, deep chocolate eyes that hold so much light. He's even got the same natural pout in his bottom lip and soft curve of his nose.

With a quick look of approval from his dad, Cooper loosens his hold and drops his feet to the ground.

"What have you been feeding this kid? He looks even taller than when I last saw him," she says as she walks back to the couch and flops down beside me. Cooper settles on Ava's lap and leans back against her chest.

I offer him a small smile when he turns his head and his eyes slam into mine, surprised and cautious. I'm an unfamiliar face in an even more unfamiliar place, and from what I can tell, he's a shy kid. His long eyelashes brush his skin as he blinks at me before turning away and watching his dad.

Braden's presence slams into me when he presses closer, whispering, "Coop doesn't do well with strangers, baby. Don't take it personally. His mother did a number on him."

My brows tug together. "What do you mean?"

"Later, fighter. Adam doesn't like to talk about her."

Even though my curiosity is piqued, I agree with a single nod. It's really none of my business anyway.

Adam's facing Gracie, Tyler, and Oakley now, but he answers Ava with a clear smile in his voice. "He eats me out of house and home, O. I'm sure he even eats more than your husband nowadays. Ain't that right, Mr. Vegan?" he asks Oakley while smacking his shoulder and squeezing.

"Really, Tyler?" Oakley grumbles, tilting his chin to glare at his brother-in-law. Tyler offers a shrug.

Adam moves around Oakley and kisses the top of Gracie's head. "How are you feeling, mama?"

Dropping her chin to Oliver's head, she sighs happily. "Sore. But it's nothing compared to how at peace I am. I feel complete, ya know?"

He hums in agreement. "I'm glad, Gray. Being a mom fits you."

My hand falls to my swollen stomach and moves in wide, slow circles. I might not know exactly how Gracie is feeling yet, but I have a pretty good idea.

With every day that passes, the connection I have with our baby grows, forming something unbreakable and honestly, a bit unbelievable. My excitement climbs with each kick and roll that I feel, with every baby book we buy and tiny shirt we fold.

The fear that's plagued my mind since the moment I found out that I was pregnant is fading, replaced with an overwhelming sense of longing.

Soon, I remind myself for the thousandth time.

I blink away the blur in my vision and focus on the two fists connecting in the air above Gracie. Adam and Tyler share a long look before they both break out in cheek-splitting grins.

"Who would have thought being a dad would look so damn good on you, man," Adam teases.

Tyler rolls his eyes, acting tough, but his smile betrays him. "Could say the same about all of us guys here."

"Maddox can't wait to meet Oli, by the way," Oakley says.

I shuffle through all of the information Braden shot at me about his friends and their families on the plane ride here before remembering that Maddox is Oakley and Ava's three-year-old son.

"Don't call him Oli," Tyler grunts. "It sounds like loli. Kids at school will be calling him lollipop before he even hits the first grade."

"Sorry, Ty. It's already decided. Good luck trying to convince a toddler otherwise," Oakley retorts.

"I think it's adorable," Gracie chimes in. "Plus, it's only fair. We call Maddox Doxxy, and there's no way in hell I'm going to stop once he gets older and starts to hate it. Nicknames are a family privilege."

Cooper laughs in Ava's arms.

"You think that's funny, do you, Coop?" Oakley teases him.

"I'll always call him Doxxy. Even when he strongly dislikes it," Cooper states proudly, his chest puffed out.

Everyone laughs, and Cooper's cheeks turn a deep red before he's tucking his face in Ava's shirt.

I suck in a sharp breath when the baby shifts around in my stomach and I get an intense urge to pee. After wiggling around uncomfortably for a few seconds, unable to get rid of the feeling without having to leave the room, I give up and stand.

Looking down at Braden and the alarm that flickers across his face, I say, "I'll be right back," and make sure he's relaxed again before leaving Gracie's room, the door shutting softly behind me.

The pungent hospital smell was much fainter in her room—most likely because of how many of us were in such a small space—but now attacks my nose with full force.

There's the faint sound of another baby crying somewhere

on the maternity floor as I walk down the hallway, passing a few nurses in pink scrubs and a doctor with a scrub cap on that reminds me a lot of something I would find on *Grey's Anatomy* before I find the washroom.

I'm humming under my breath when I push open the door and ram boobs-first into something—or *someone*. An apology is on the tip of my tongue before it shrivels up and dies.

The aged scowl in front of me is too familiar. I gulp. "*Mom*?"

30

Braden

My eyes wander to the clock above the door, a weird feeling slithering in my bones. It's been fifteen minutes since Sierra left to go to the bathroom, and I've been sitting here nearly the entire time squeezing my knees.

I know that there's a thin line between being protective and smothering, which is why I've waited this long before chasing her ass down. But as the time continues to tick away, the more intense this gnawing in my stomach grows. Something feels wrong.

"You look like you're the one that needs the bathroom, Braden," Adam teases. "Maybe you should have gone with your girl."

My frown deepens as I look from the clock and to the single dad. "She's been gone a long time, right?"

"She's over halfway through her pregnancy," Gracie says lightly. "It gets harder to do simple things the further you get. Give her a few more minutes."

A rumble fills my chest at the idea of waiting any longer

when I have such a strong feeling that something could be wrong. I should have gone with her in the first place.

"If you're that worried, just go check on her," Tyler pipes up from the other side of the room.

He's holding Oliver now, staring down at his son with a look so warm it could melt ice. There's so much love in his eyes, so much protectiveness. My brother would burn the world to the ground for his wife and baby. Just as I would for Sierra and our baby.

I tear my eyes from them when jealousy scrapes my insides like barbed wire. It's completely irrational to be jealous over something that I will have in only a few months. But I'm getting antsy.

Antsy to hold and smell and love our baby.

Antsy to watch my beautiful woman become a mom.

"Yeah. I'm going to do that. Be right back." I'm off the couch and out the door in a matter of seconds.

My head moves in all directions as I stalk down the hallway in search of the bathrooms. Panic starts to bear its ugly head the longer it takes me to find her. Irrational or not, I can't shake this fucking feeling.

I almost shout in relief when I see the familiar stick person that marks the women's washroom. I lunge for the door, about to whip it open, when I hear a set of hushed voices from behind it.

"Don't. You don't get to say anything about this." *Sierra*. I would recognize that voice anywhere.

The other voice is high in pitch and carries the slightest bit of an accent that I doubt I can pinpoint. It almost sounds like a mix of several different ones.

"You're unmarried, you don't own a home. You've barely even started your life. How could you let something like this happen?"

The silence that follows is haunting. I want to let Sierra handle this on her own, but there's no way that I can stand here and let her be talked to like that. My muscles are taut, pulled so tight I'm afraid they might snap like an overstretched elastic band. Pain radiates from my palms, and I release my hands from the fists they've become.

"You don't know anything about my life, Mom," Sierra exhales, sounding defeated in a way that has my feet begging to bring me to her. "You haven't known anything about me or my life since I was a little girl."

I had a feeling that the posh-speaking woman was Sierra's mother, but hearing her confirm it makes me pull open the door and join the two women in the bathroom. Shock and panic flicker across Sierra's face when she realizes what's happening, but I don't do anything more than wrap my arm around her waist and kiss her temple before facing her mother.

Anger is a dangerous emotion. It almost always has a way of bringing out someone's true intentions and feelings that they've kept hidden. For Sierra and her mother, that couldn't be a truer assumption.

Dina Caster narrows her eyes on me, on the tattoos that cover my bare arm, the scars on my face from years of fighting, and the splint on my right hand. I already knew she wouldn't like me. Wouldn't see me as a worthy match for her daughter. But seeing the disgust in her eyes still feels like a crowbar through the ribs.

"The baby daddy, I'm assuming," she sneers, venom dripping from every word.

Trying not to laugh, I realize that not only does Sierra have nothing in common personality-wise with this woman, but she doesn't look anything like her either.

Sierra's hair is a warm brown, like a cup of coffee with too much cream, while Dina's hair is so dark it's almost black. Her mother's eyes are a steely blue, not the molten silver that I see even in my sleep. Pale, porcelain skin and a bronze tan that comes from being out in the sun for hours on end. Tall and short. Curved and thin. They are complete opposites. In every way.

I don't bother holding my hand out for her mother to shake, knowing full well she would probably spit on it. There won't be any winning this woman over, but hell if I'm not going to try and help her understand the mistake she's making by continuing to mistreat her daughter. It's clear that I have nothing to lose when it comes to this woman.

"Braden, actually. But baby daddy does have a nice ring to it," I say while pulling Sierra even closer and brushing my thumb along the side of her belly. She wraps an arm around my front, keeping us close, not bothering to hide her affection from her mother. "And you're the mother."

Her glare tightens. "Dina Caster."

"Why are you even here, Mom? This is a maternity ward."

"A friend's daughter just had a baby last night. I was dropping off some flowers."

Sierra releases a sound of disbelief. "Wow. Lucky her. I wouldn't know what receiving a gift from my mother feels like."

Dina's lips pull taut. "Don't act as though you ever cared whether you received anything from me. You had Clare growing up. She's all you've needed," she snips. The frown lines in her forehead and between her thin eyebrows are deep, like they've been there for years. There's a thick sense of jealousy in her words that I know Sierra latches onto.

"No." She tips her head back and sucks in a steadying breath. "You don't get to act jealous of my sister. She was there for me when you couldn't be bothered. She was more of a mother to me than you ever were."

A mix of guilt and regret slides across Sierra's face the second those hate-filled words fall between them. Dina Caster gasps, a hand to her chest. The temperature in the bathroom drops.

"Well then." Dina straightens, suddenly wearing a mask of indifference. "If that's how you feel, then I'm glad you didn't bother telling your father and I about your pregnancy. He will be just as disappointed in you as I am when he finds out."

My teeth gnash together, and I have to press my mouth to Sierra's temple to keep from mouthing off. If this was anybody else, I would have shoved them out the fucking door by now.

"I stopped caring about your opinion a long time ago, Mom. You've never supported me a day in your life. Why start now?" My heart splits down the middle at the blinding pain in Sierra's voice. It rocks me, the ground suddenly unstable beneath my feet. "Believe it or not, I don't need a house or a wedding ring to know that I'm ready to take care of this baby. You would know that if you had bothered getting to know me over the past twenty-six years.

"You weren't ever involved in our lives. You've seen Elizabeth a handful of times. I wasn't naive to think you would take a sudden interest in my baby. And you know what? That's okay. Clare and I turned out fucking amazing on our own. And *our* baby"—she peers up at me through wet lashes—"is going to grow up surrounded by so many amazing people and so much love that they will never question how special they are, regardless of if you and Dad are involved."

Sierra finishes on a heavy breath before pressing her forehead to my bicep. A warm wetness forms on the sleeve of my shirt, and I know that means tears. Tears that her mother doesn't deserve. I move my hand from her side, dragging it up her back and cupping her neck. She shudders against me, and a broken sound slips from her mouth.

"You have no idea what you've given up," I mutter, meeting Dina's gaze head-on. "I would do anything for your daughter. It doesn't matter what or why. I would do it without a single reason and with a goddamn smile on my face because Sierra means that much to me. She's fucking *everything*."

I'm dizzy, high on adrenaline and the feel of Sierra's body molded to mine. I wait for Dina to say something, but when she just continues to stare at me, unblinking, I decide to continue, letting everything off my chest.

"I had only known Sierra for a few months before I ended up losing her. I made the biggest mistake of my life, and I paid heavily for it. We were only apart for *three weeks*. Yet in those three weeks, I was nothing more than a husk of who I was after being with her. Sierra makes me want to be a better man. A better person, friend, and now a father. So to know that you are okay with feeling even a shard of the loss I felt when I lost her and that you're *choosing* to feel that emptiness? That tells me all that I need to know about you."

The silence is deafening.

But when Sierra curls into me, her face hidden in my shirt, both hands wrapped around my body in a side hug, I know that she's not upset with me. Her swollen stomach pushes into me the closer she tries to move, making her huff. A laugh rattles my chest as I fold my arms around her as much as I can.

"Sierra," Dina scolds. "You're not going to let him talk to me like this, are you?"

My glare darkens, becoming sharp and unforgiving. I try to keep my anger locked down, but when Sierra's mother places her hands on her hips and opens her mouth again, I growl, "Leave," before I can stop myself.

Dina looks surprised, like she can't believe somebody had the nerve to order her around. "Excuse me?"

"Leave, Mother," Sierra mumbles, looking at her over her shoulder. "There's nothing else that needs to be said."

"I'm not leaving. This is ridiculous," she scoffs.

Sierra's eyes bore into mine with a silent question. I nod.

"Then we'll go."

It's almost painful to let her slip from my arms.

Dina blanches. "Sierra."

"I have all the family I need. People who actually care about me. Blood or not. Your opinion doesn't mean anything more to me now than it did ten years ago. Now, if you'll please move, we are here visiting our friends."

When her mother doesn't move, I level her with a stare that has her fumbling out of the way so we can pass.

As soon as we're out of that godforsaken bathroom, I'm pushing Sierra back against a wall and covering her lips with mine. It's a desperate kiss, a raw and vicious claim. A reminder that I'm not going anywhere. Not today, not tomorrow. Not fucking thirty years from now.

"You're mine," I rasp, nipping at her bottom lip.

Fingernails scrape at my neck, Sierra's voice just as needy and possessive as mine. "And you're mine."

31

Sierra

"Surprise!"

I clutch my chest as I take in my living room, now full of smiling faces, tables, and decorations. There's a large banner hung above the tables with the words *Happy Baby Shower* written in thick pastel yellow letters. The long white tables are covered with frilled tablecloths the same shade of yellow, one stacked with gifts, the other piled with assortments of snacks and desserts. My stomach goes rogue, growling loudly.

Braden's breath is warm on the back of my neck as he holds me to his chest by my shoulders. "I know surprises aren't really your thing, but I figured you might accept this one."

"It's perfect," I whisper and throw him a grin over my shoulder.

Gretchen, Sophie, Ava, and Oakley stand to the side while Gracie practically vibrates between her husband, Clayton, and my sister.

A mix of nerves and excitement taints Gracie's features before I open my arms and close the distance between us. Her embrace is warm and calming, like a sister's should be. The realization that I've begun to think of Gracie as a sister is an electric shock straight to the heart.

"I'm here too, you brat," Clare scolds teasingly.

"And me," Sophie says, beaming at me.

I'm swapping from one woman to the next as I launch myself at my big sister and wrap her up tight. My words are no louder than a soft exhale. "I've missed you so much."

Clare sniffles in my ear before pulling back and holding me in front of her. Her eyes make a long sweep over me. "I missed you more, S. Look at you. I haven't seen you since your birthday, and now you're damn near about to pop."

"It certainly feels like it. You should see my ankles after a long day," I groan as Sophie, Ava, and Gretch rush over and collect their hugs. Luckily, it's only eleven in the morning and my ankles don't resemble tree trunks yet, or I would have already flopped down on the couch with my feet up.

"Oh my God," Ava chimes in. "I was the exact same way with Maddox. I had to sleep with a stack of pillows under my feet to keep them elevated, or else I would be up all night."

Oakley visibly shudders beside her.

"When do I get to meet your little troublemaker? He's not here, is he?" I ask, looking around the apartment that feels entirely too small all of a sudden. With the body heat from so many people combined with the lack of A/C, I'm grateful for the sundress I slipped on before leaving for breakfast. It's early June, and the heat isn't taking it easy on us this year.

Ava shakes her head at me. "He's with my parents for the weekend. Planes and Dox go together as well as orange juice and toothpaste do."

"Not to brag, but Oliver slept the entire flight here," Gracie says, tipping her chin.

"That's because he's not even four months old. Wait until

he hits toddlerhood," Oakley snorts, pinching the underside of Gracie's arm. She yelps, flicking him in the arm.

Braden continues to hover behind me, kissing the top of my head. "Our baby will be the top dog in this group. So embrace it now, Gray."

Tyler laughs loudly, taking everyone but his wife by surprise. "I sure as shit hope your kid doesn't have nearly as much arrogance as his dad does." He gives me a pitiful look. "Good luck, Sierra. You're going to need it."

"She seemed to do a good enough job with Braden." Clare tosses me a wink.

Everyone hums in agreement while I lift a shoulder and grin. I'm not about to deny it. I know Braden isn't either when he cheers, "Fuck yeah she did."

"Okay, okay." Gracie claps her hands. "Enough chitchat. It's time for the guys to leave. This is a *girls-only* baby shower."

"It is?" I ask.

The five women nod.

Braden rotates my body so that we face each other. His stare is so intense it makes my breath pitch. It looks like he doesn't want to leave, but then again, I don't want him to leave either. I'm not sure if general clinginess can be blamed on an unborn child, but that's what I've been going with over the past few months.

I was expecting to find work exciting again after Cole was fired, but to my surprise, it started feeling more like a prison sentence than anything. Being cooped up in my office day after day has pressed on the wrong nerves. By five o'clock, the only things I want are a healthy dose of fresh air and to feel Braden's arms wrapped around me.

My love for my job isn't the problem, I'm positive about that. I adore my colleagues, my clients, and the work that I do. I think I just want to be at home for a while. Relaxing. After working so hard with no breaks over the years, I think I've just become worn out and need to spend some time focusing on the people in my life.

I joke that this is all the baby's doing, but in reality, I'm beyond thankful for the sudden change in thought. The last thing that I want is to become too wrapped up in work and my career that I lose track of the other important things in my life.

Braden's words are gentle, almost raspy. "Try not to miss me too much, baby."

"Likewise."

Pushing up on my toes, I kiss him quickly, not wanting to put on a show in front of so many of our friends. But unsurprisingly, Braden seems to have other plans.

I startle when he nips at my mouth and holds me in place with a strong hand around my nape. His tongue swipes my lips, and a soft growl falls between us when I refuse him entrance.

"Open, fighter. I'm not leaving here with a cheap kiss," he whispers, sealing our lips together again, and this time, I let him in for just a few seconds before pulling back, my cheeks flushed.

Clare gags. "Yeah, I could have gone my whole life without seeing my sister get kissed like that."

Kill me now.

Ava coughs to cover her laugh before she's pushing Oakley out of the room, Gracie doing the same with Tyler. Both guys grab Braden by an arm and drag him out with them.

"Bye, ladies. Don't get into too much trouble!" Oakley shouts seconds before the door clicks shut, leaving us five women alone.

Gracie's blue eyes are pure trouble when she moves to the front of the room. "What do you say? Is it time to get into some mama-approved mischief?"

WITH A VIRGIN MARGARITA in one hand and a mini veggie sandwich in the other, I tip my head back and laugh. My mind is clear, my heart full. Stacks of baby clothes and blankets sit at my feet, surrounded by a mountain of tissue paper that Clare is eagerly stuffing into a garbage bag.

"I didn't even know there were so many brands of bottles," I say, gawking at all of the baby supplies spread along the gift table. "Or soothers."

Ava nods and touches my arm reassuringly. "It can be a bit overwhelming. But once you know what baby likes, it'll get easier."

"I still can't believe that you don't want to know the gender yet," Clare guffaws. "Especially with how much you hate surprises."

"It's such a beautiful surprise, though," Gracie says.

I throw her a smile. "If there was ever a time to make an exception to my 'no surprise' rule, it's right now. Plus, it did make the nursery easier to decorate without having to focus on blue or pink. The yellow we chose is beautiful."

Gretchen leans forward in her folding chair, getting more engaged in the conversation. She was the one who helped pick out the colour of the nursery and started painting after I bailed on our plans and passed out on the couch. She smiles so wide her sparkling white teeth shine. "And the pastel makes it easier on the eyes."

"It's a gorgeous nursery," Ava chimes in. "And you make a good point. I know that as soon as people find out you're having a boy, they assume you want dinosaurs on everything, and if it's a girl, you must want ballerinas or hot pink sparkles. It's easier to just tell them to buy neutral."

"Personally, I think you're going to have a girl." Clare beams, finally setting the full garbage back to the side of the room and plopping down on the arm of the couch. "You might be huge, but you're carrying really high. Plus, it seems to run in the family."

"Don't start with all the hypothesizing." I wag my finger in her direction.

"I could see you having a little girl," Gracie says. The other girls hum their agreement.

"Braden is sure that it's a boy. I have a feeling it's a girl, though."

"Mother's intuition might prove itself after all. You only have a month left. Think you can make it?" Gretchen stretches her legs out in front of her and kicks my foot.

Smiling, I drop my gaze to the giant round belly stretching the material of my sunflower-decorated dress. Excitement swells and blooms in my chest.

"I can make it. We've already waited this long." I rub small circles on my stomach and laugh when something kicks against my palm. Eight sets of eyes focus on me as I continue watching my dress shift with each kick from inside my stomach.

"You said that baby was super active, but I thought you were exaggerating," Clare confesses, slightly in awe.

"I nearly peed myself when I touched her belly and felt a kick for the first time," Sophie blurts out. "I didn't think babies were that strong."

I shake my head. "She gets even crazier when Braden's close by. It seems that we're both a bit obsessed with her daddy."

Gretchen snorts. "A bit?"

I narrow my eyes on her.

"Well, if it isn't obvious enough, Sierra, Braden's utterly

obsessed with you. He looks at you like you're the only woman in the world," Ava says, her eyes sparkling. "I've known him for a long time, and I honestly never thought he would ever love anyone the way he loves you."

Gracie joins in. "I second that. Not to mention the fact he's so excited to be a dad. He's surprised us all, I think."

I'm sure that I look like a schoolgirl who's just found out her crush likes her back right now, but I couldn't care less. I know how much Braden loves me and how excited he is to meet our baby, but hearing it from people who have known him for years and have watched him learn and grow and become the man he is today makes it feel that much more real.

"If I can be the big sister here for a minute, guys," Clare says cautiously, like she's scared of what she's about to say and how we'll all react. Ava, Gracie, and Gretchen look weary. Sophie just looks plain annoyed.

"Clare," Sophie warns. "Just be happy for her."

I shoot Sophie an appreciative smile but shake my head, showing her that it's okay. Clare might not have another chance to tell me whatever is brewing inside of her before she leaves again.

Nodding at Clare to continue, I try to prepare myself for whatever she's going to say.

With a weary smile, she says, "I'm always going to worry about my sister. It's my responsibility to make sure that she's happy and taken care of. And I've seen how happy you are, S, but I'm not going to pretend that I don't worry about Braden's ability to take care of you later down the road when life decides to take a shit all over you both, because it will."

The room becomes eerily silent. An ache starts to build in my gut that I immediately want to rip out and toss away. In my peripheral vision, I see the other women stiffen, their spines ramrod straight. Sliding my eyes shut, I gesture for Clare to continue before I start thinking too hard on what she's said.

"Braden still has his own apartment, right? Have you discussed him ditching it and living here with you? What about marriage? You've always wanted to get married, S. Are you really okay with never experiencing that? With giving up that piece of your future?"

It would have hurt less if she slapped me.

My face is pale, cold. A lump builds in my throat that I try to swallow down but fail. Gripping my knees in a white-knuckled grip, I keep my eyes focused on my yellow-painted toes.

I wince at the scratchiness of my voice. "Braden is here every day. Every night and every morning. For months he's been here. He hasn't given me any reason since coming here to believe he would flake on me and this baby." I fold a protective arm around my stomach. "And as far as marriage goes, I used to think that that meant forever. But I know better now than to believe a ring and piece of paper equate to a lifetime of happiness with somebody that I love."

"Are those Braden's words or yours? Because that was the excuse he told me when I asked him the same thing," Clare says tightly, a cold bite to her words.

"You asked him about marriage? When?" My questions are snipped and just as harsh as I intended.

"Christmas."

I blow out a harsh breath and finally lift my darkening eyes to my sister. Her lips are pulled tight in a scowl, her arms crossed and stiff. She doesn't look the least bit sorry or regretful, and that only fuels the anger sparking beneath my skin.

"I don't expect you to understand my choice, and I especially don't expect you to understand Braden's. But I am asking you to at least remember that I'm not someone who can't think for herself. I know that Braden loves me and this baby. I know that he wants to be with me for just as long as I want to be with him. Sure, I wouldn't complain about being married to such an amazing man, but it's also not something that I'm going to let form a wall between us. If it happens, it happens. If it doesn't, then it doesn't.

"I appreciate you caring so much, Clare. But I'm not a little girl anymore. I can make my own decisions. And being with Braden for the rest of my life is the one that I've decided to make."

My sister nods once, a look of acceptance finally slithering across her face, and I release a harsh breath, taking the small win in stride. In reality, we don't need her or anybody else's approval. But having Clare completely in my corner, especially after what happened with our mother, feels better than I thought it would.

32

Braden

THERE WILL ALWAYS BE MOMENTS IN YOUR LIFE where you want to throw two middle fingers in the air and tell the universe to kiss your ass. But there are also times when you want to drop to your knees and thank whatever god you believe in for blessing you with the life you have and the people you've gotten to meet along the way.

Right now, I'm struggling not to do the latter. At least not while I have an audience.

Sierra's confession has my heart in my throat and my stomach between my legs. I'm gaping at the back of her head like a fucking idiot, but I can't get my feet to move. It's like they've been cemented to the floor in the two minutes since I walked inside the apartment.

The guys were adamant that we should stay out longer, damn near dragging me to a pub to grab a few beers for old times' sake, but all I wanted was to come home and see my girl. And now that I've heard her declare to her sister and all of my closest friends that she wants to be with me forever—everyone else be damned—the few steps between us feel like miles. Too fucking many of them.

Tyler chuckles quietly under his breath before squeezing my arm and giving me a small shove forward. That's all it takes for me to rip my feet from the floor and rush to Sierra.

I round the couch quickly, grinning at the gasp that falls from Sierra's parted lips while scooping her up in my arms and starting to carry her belly-up toward the bedroom.

Her stare is warm with affection, but her touch is blazing hot and greedy as her fingers burn through my T-shirt and brand my skin.

"Thanks for coming, everyone. I'm sure the gifts are great. You can let yourselves out!" I shout once there's some distance between us and everyone else. I turn down the hallway, my steps large and quick. As soon as we walk through the doorway, I'm kicking the door shut behind us and setting Sierra down on the bed.

She falls back, hitting the mattress. Her chest heaves, eyes droopy and clouded with a sheen of need. Pushing up on her elbows, she watches me closely while slowly parting her legs, that fucking dress the only thing keeping me from seeing between them.

I'm beyond caring if anyone's still here and within listening distance. My cock is hard and heavy between my legs—it has been since the moment I heard Sierra declare me her forever. The only thought ringing in my head is to get inside of her and show her that I return her feelings.

With a rumble in my chest, I'm pressing my knees on the bed and sliding my hands up the smooth skin of her legs, from her ankles to her knees. Then I'm pushing her legs up until her thighs brush her belly. Her dress flips up over her stomach, exposing her white cotton panties and the wet spot at the centre of them.

My scruff scrapes the inside of her thighs as I lean in and press kisses along all of that sensitive, silky skin. "Forever is a long time, fighter," I rasp, tonguing the crease of her inner thigh. "Are you sure that's what you want?"

"I'm positive," she breathes, collapsing onto her back, one hand slipping through my hair while the other grips the bedding.

I drag my nose straight up the centre of her slit, groaning when my tongue slips out and follows its path, the taste of her exploding in my mouth. "Then that's what you'll get."

She peels her eyes open, and the barely contained emotion in them has my movements faltering, my thoughts sizzling out into nothing. I stay frozen, knelt between her legs, and can't help but watch as she releases my hair and pushes herself into a sitting position. When she grabs my face in her hands and pulls me up her body, I don't fight. I roll us over instead.

She sucks in a breath that releases as a whimper when I grip her waist and settle her on my jean-clad cock. Silky brown hair falls around her face as she peers down at me and swirls her hips, lips slightly parted and brushing mine. A whisper skips across my mouth. "Are you sure you can handle me for that long?"

My hands drift to her ass and squeeze, using the soft, round flesh to slowly glide her pussy up and down the swell in my jeans. Her breaths are uneven, shuddered. With her pupils blown, she watches me with a deep, predatory hunger that has me grappling for my self-control. It's only been three days since I've been inside of her, but that's a record for us. The last thing that I want is to blow too fast, and right now, with the need I can feel pulsing beneath her skin, that's too big of a possibility.

"Do you doubt how well I can handle you, fighter? Should I remind you?" I ask tightly when quick fingers undo my jeans and gently trace the bulge begging to be released.

Watching me through a blanket of lashes, she yanks down on my waistband, and I eagerly lift my hips, giving her the room to pull off both my jeans and boxers. I hiss when her small hand wraps around my length and gives it two gentle pumps.

"Yes. You should."

I reach toward her, but she shakes her head, tightening her grip on my cock and collecting the bead of precum that's pooled on the head with her thumb before slipping it between her lips and sucking it clean.

"Jesus fucking Christ," I grunt, barely holding on as she sucks on her thumb and moans a sweet sound of pleasure that has my balls tightening. "Fuck me, Sierra. Slip me inside before I come all over your hand."

A rebel brow lifts, and she tilts one side of her mouth. Reaching between us with her other hand, she tugs her panties to the side, exposing her pretty pink pussy. My head tips back, a raspy noise building in my throat when she slips my cock along her wetness, the tip grazing her entrance for the briefest second, just enough to make my head fucking spin and my hips lurch.

"Say please," she orders. I buck my hips again, pressing my fingers harder into her skin.

"Please," I grit out before groaning not even a second later when she sinks down my shaft, whimpering at the sudden fullness. "*Fuuuck* yes."

Sierra's head lolls to the side, her hands planted on my chest as she anchors herself before starting to move, working my cock with confidence and expertise. She moves like she knows I was made for her. Like every single inch of me is all for her and only her.

She's right in that assumption.

I am hers.

Only hers.

"Forever," I choke out, yanking her dress down to expose the heavy tits held behind a silky beige bra. Possessiveness has me pinching at her peaked nipples through the material, craving the sounds she makes when I do. Euphoria sinks deep in my bones and ignites a fury of different emotions, all of which have me gasping for breath like I've just run a marathon.

Swiftly, I unhook her bra and toss it away. Her nipples are so hard they almost look painful, but when I roll them between my fingers, the sound she makes is anything but pained. It's pure bliss.

"Forever," Sierra echoes, tossing her head back and scratching at my pecs and thick-cut abs. I savour the burn her nails leave behind, fighting off the urge to beg her to dig deeper and leave me covered with her marks.

My thrusts pick up speed when she starts to slow, her cheeks flushed and a sheen of sweat glistening across her forehead. Brushing her hair from her face, I grasp her chin and lift, forcing her to look at me.

"Come with me," I whisper, staring fiercely into her eyes, holding them hostage.

Sierra nods frantically and makes a high-pitched noise when I slide a hand between us and apply pressure to her swollen flesh. She tightens around me, damn near strangling my cock, and I know that she's about to reach that peak.

"That's it, baby," I coo before gritting my teeth and grunting as a shock wave of pleasure bulldozes into me. Sierra releases a series of curses and bucks on my lap, her eyes damn near crossing with the strength of her climax.

"Braden. Braden, fuck." It sounds like a prayer.

"Take it, fighter. I'm coming," I rasp and thrust a final time, spilling deep inside of her. My thighs are clenched, pulsing. Sierra's uneven breaths mirror my own as her eyes fall shut, and a small smile pulls at her lips.

"I can't wait until I can just collapse on top of you again." She laughs and pulls off me, releasing a small whimper as I slip from her warmth. Falling back on the bed, she turns her head and stares at me with wonder.

"What?" I ask, tucking myself away in my underwear and grinning wide.

"How long were you standing there listening before you came and stole me away like a caveman?"

I turn on my side and grab her hand, circling her ring finger with my thumb. "Long enough to hear you hand your sister her ass and tell her that you don't need to get married to be happy with me."

"I don't." There's nothing but honesty in her voice, and it makes my heart thump against my rib cage, trying to go to her.

Slipping a hand into the pocket of my jeans, I pull out the shiny silver band that my boys helped me pick out earlier today and swallow my fear. The smallest, almost inaudible gasp escapes Sierra when her wide-eyed stare focuses on the ring.

"Braden, wha—"

I laugh, cutting her off. "It's a promise ring. I know that it's not quite the same as a marriage proposal, but it's a step in the right direction. It means that I *will* marry you one day, my little fighter. If for nothing other than being able to call you Sierra Lowry and making sure that every other man on this earth knows that even on paper, he has no chance in hell with my woman. I swear that I will give you that dream wedding of yours. The one that you told me you dreamed of all those months ago at my father's wedding." Searching her shiny eyes for any sign that points to her not wanting this, I come up empty of anything but contentment and bliss.

A tear slips from her eyes when she nods. "Are you sure? You know that I would never force you into marrying me. I don't need that from you. I know that you love me and that you're not going anywhere," she rushes out.

Clasping her hand, I pull it to my mouth and kiss her knuckles.

"This was all me. I'm not ready yet, but when I am, you will be my wife, and I will be your husband. I was a fool to hold on so tight to the past when my future is so fucking bright. With you by my side. We're surrounded by so many happy couples, all of whom love being married. Both of my parents are happy and have moved on. It's time that I moved on too."

She blinks, and tears cascade down her cheeks. "Oh, my God. I love you."

"I love you too, beautiful." Settling her hand between us, I slip the ring onto her finger and capture her lips in a fierce kiss, one that I hope helps portray the long list of emotions that are zapping through me right now.

Love, excitement, *hope*. Our future's so bright it's blinding.

But I wouldn't dare look away. Not now. Not ever.

33

Braden

Leather screams as strained voices fill the gym. The captain of the Toronto Timberwolves is throwing perfectly timed punches at the pads covering my outstretched hands as Mackenzie does the same exercise with Laslo, one of my trainers. Sweat flows freely down our skin, soaking into our clothes and hair.

We've been here for the past two hours, training and pushing through things we would rather burn off through gallons of sweat and sore muscles than talk about.

It's been a month since I put a ring on Sierra's finger and two weeks since I dumped my apartment and officially moved into her place. There was really no point in keeping a lease on an apartment that I hadn't even been to in forever, so as soon as Sierra brought it up, I didn't hesitate to agree. We had been unofficially living together since I got to Toronto, anyway.

Sierra's due date was three days ago, and we're still waiting for something to happen. The stubborn baby refuses to come out and meet us, and that feels like a really messed-up form of torture.

Sierra's OBGYN doesn't want to induce her until the beginning of next week, which means that if our baby decides to bake for another four days, we have to just sit here and wait. I've been losing my mind, constantly doting on her, needing something to keep me busy. That's why Sierra kicked my ass out of the house this morning.

"Attention to Braden," Kyle says, smirking when I snap back to reality, barely avoiding a punch.

The confidence on the captain's face has me changing up our drills to throw him off. "Go! One-Two-One-Two-One-Two." His lip curls as his punches speed up before ending the drill with an uppercut that has me stumbling back.

"You're a cheeky fucking bastard, Lowry," he hisses, resting his gloved hands on his hips and tilting his head back, trying to catch his breath.

"Is that a compliment or an insult?"

"I'm going to shower." Tearing off his gloves, he shows me his middle finger before stalking toward his water bottle, not humouring me with an answer.

"I want to keep Lo as my trainer," Mack grunts, finishing a defense drill. "You're a fucking hard-ass, man."

I fake a gasp. "Me? Really?"

Laslo snorts loudly. For a new hire and an even newer friend, he sure doesn't hold back. It's why I like him so much. Well, that and the food his mom brings us every day.

"Stop being a pussy, Thompson. Pay attention before I knee you in the balls." Laslo lifts his gloves higher up his six-foot-three body, and Mack follows with his punches.

"Try it," Mack growls.

I shake my head at their bickering and slip the pads off my hands before stretching out my fingers. Heavy steps pound against the floor, and I spin toward the sound only to stiffen completely.

Kyle's face has gone pale—way too fucking pale—as he stares at me, unblinking. I tear my stare from his face and drop it to the phone clutched in his hand, the screen open and glowing.

My stomach plummets, fear turning my blood ice-cold. "What's wrong?" I force the words out.

"Your phone kept ringing in your office." He's holding my phone out for me now. "Baby," he stammers.

It's Mack who speaks up, his tone showcasing how little he cares for Kyle's vagueness. "What do you mean *baby*? As in Braden's baby? As in Sierra is in labour?"

Muffled voices come from the phone's speaker. Kyle nods, his eyes clearing a bit as whatever the fuck is wrong with him slips away. "Sierra's water broke. They're on the way to the hospital."

"Give me the fucking phone," I command, rushing toward him. Once I've yanked it from Kyle's grip, I place it to my ear and exhale deeply. "Sierra?"

"Braden," she cries, the sound alone slicing me in half. "Oh my God. You need to go to the hospital. We're on our way."

"Which one, sweetheart? I'll be right there. How far apart are your contractions?"

A few car horns blare around her voice, and another voice flows through the phone. "Braden, it's Gretchen. Sierra's water broke an hour ago, but now her contractions are five minutes apart and getting stronger. I'm taking her to Toronto General. Tell Mack to drive you. I don't trust you not to get in a damn car crash."

Five minutes apart. Getting stronger. Those are the things I latch onto.

My head feels like it's underwater. I hold my mouth open, trying to get words out of it, but nothing comes. Panic is trying to drag me under and fucking drown me.

"Please get there quickly," Sierra begs, her voice sounding wet and full of so much pain. Hearing her that way has me suddenly bursting out of the gym, not bothering to wait for Mack before heading to his car.

"I'm leaving now. I'll be there as soon as I can," I promise her before tightening my voice and addressing her friend, "Gretchen, text me all the info as soon as you get to the hospital."

"You got it," Gretchen replies as Mackenzie comes busting through the doors and rounds the hood of his car, unlocking the doors. We get in, and he starts the engine when Sierra says, "I love you. I'll see you soon."

I release a shuddered breath and whisper, "I love you, fighter," before she hangs up and Mack pulls away from the curb.

It's time to meet you, baby. About fucking time.

SIERRA'S sob rips through me, tearing my insides to ribbons. She pushes again, for what feels like the hundredth time in the past two hours, and squeezes my hand like it's the only thing feeding her strength.

She's exhausted, her eyes barely open, lips crusted and dry. I keep stroking her damp hair and kissing her clammy forehead, hoping that it's at least doing something to help with the pain she's in. By the time she got to the hospital, she was already too far along to get an epidural.

"The head is almost out, Sierra. On your next contraction, I need you to push really hard," Dr. Spetza instructs, her face firm, concentrated.

"Okay, okay," Sierra breathes, her eyelids fluttering.

"Hey," I murmur, squeezing her hand. "You're almost done, fighter. One more, yeah?"

She dips her chin, and the smallest smile pulls at her mouth before disappearing when the next contraction comes. Sierra pushes hard, a raw yell escaping her as the doctor shouts for her to keep going.

I can't look away from her, not even when the doctor tells us the head is out and the shoulders are next. My heart swells, my knees shaking at the strong tide of emotions that threaten to knock me on my ass.

This is my future wife in front of me, giving birth to *our* baby. I've managed to keep my own feelings on lock while I've been here, not wanting to take anything away from Sierra, but there's no stopping them now.

Tears stream down my face when I hear the first cry, the high-pitched wail that comes from our baby. Sierra collapses on the bed with a smile that I know I'm mirroring.

"It's a girl," the doctor says.

The second the words are said, I'm full-on crying, my shoulders shaking with each sob. My grin couldn't be any bigger as I cut the umbilical cord and return to Sierra's side, kissing her everywhere I can.

"A girl," she cries, grabbing hold of my forearms and bringing me closer until I blanket her entire side. "You were wrong."

I can only nod, not trusting my voice yet.

The baby nurse brings us our girl and lays her on Sierra's bare chest. A tiny pink hat sits on her head, covering a full head of brown hair that I can see peeking out of the sides. She's so tiny that I'm scared to touch her.

Sierra doesn't seem to have that problem as she brushes the knuckle of her finger across the smooth skin of our baby's chubby cheek and coos, "Hi, Tinsley. I'm your mommy."

Our eyes collide when she calls our daughter by her name for the first time, and I nearly choke on a sob. It's like all of the nurses have disappeared and we're the only people in the room.

"It fits her perfectly," I murmur.

I reach for Tinsley's hand and inhale in surprise when she grabs my finger in a tight fist. "I'm Daddy, baby. It's about time you made your appearance."

Sierra laughs. "It was only three days."

"Technically four now," I say, looking at the clock across the room and back at Sierra and the bundle of love cuddled to her chest.

Four a.m. on August fourteenth. That's when our baby girl entered the world and changed my life forever. In the best, most fulfilling way possible.

It's almost fitting that she would make us wait for her arrival, considering her mother had me waiting for her too. And now that I have them both, they're not going anywhere.

"Waiting those four days was more than worth it," Sierra hums, kissing Tinsley's tiny hat-covered head.

I press my lips to Sierra's forehead and whisper with absolute contentment, "Yeah, it was."

EPILOGUE

SIX MONTHS LATER

Braden

Tinsley blows bubbles with her spit as I unclip her car seat and pull her into my arms. She wiggles like a lunatic, as if being held is the last thing she wants, before I try to slip her inside the baby carrier that's hanging open on my chest. I drop her diaper bag onto the curb beside me.

"One of these times, you could at least act like you don't hate being in your carrier instead of scratching at me like a rabid animal," I mutter to the six-month-old, who's trying her damnedest to stay free of the prison strapped to my chest.

Tinsley's only response is to punch me in the chin and blow spit bubbles in my face.

"I was going to give you a few raspberries when we got inside, but after that, I think I'll give you the chicken and avocado purée your mommy sent for you. How does that sound?"

My brow is lifted questioningly as I stare down at a pair of curious blue eyes. Long lashes flutter as she blinks. "No answer to that? That's what I thought. Now, let's go inside before

Daddy gets in trouble for being late to work. I'm the boss, Tiny. I have to set a good example."

I quickly flip her around so that she doesn't have to spend the day looking at me before all but shoving her in the carrier, strapping her in tight so that she doesn't end up on the floor of the gym. I throw her diaper bag over my shoulder and walk us inside Knockout.

It's just after ten in the morning, and the main gym is packed. A remix of "Toxic" by Britney Spears plays through the speakers, making me snort. It would seem that Laslo got a hold of the Bluetooth. Speaking of the asshole, he's already walking toward me, his eyes focused on the little girl on my chest.

As soon as he gets close enough, he's cooing at her. "Tinsley, baby, you are absolutely glowing today."

The little traitor has the nerve to give him a big grin, showing off her top tooth. I glare at Laslo and kiss the back of Tinsley's head.

"Take it somewhere else, Laz. This is a daddy/daughter day."

That's what I refer to them, anyway. With Sierra back to working full-time, we didn't want to have to pay for daycare when it's easy enough for me to bring Tiny to work with me most days. When I train on Mondays and Thursdays, she stays with her grandpa Brooks now that he's working from home, taking care of Knockout's books and finances, but every other day of the week, she's Knockout's little helper. And honestly, I wouldn't have it any other way. I love having her here with me.

"Yeah, okay. According to you, every day is a daddy/daughter day. You can't hog her forever," Laslo teases.

"Wanna bet?" I dare him to argue with me.

Grinning, he throws his hands up in surrender before blowing Tiny a kiss. "Your dad is a lunatic, baby girl. One of these days, I'll teach you how to kick his ass."

"If anybody is teaching her how to kick ass, it'll be me, you cocky shit. Get back to work. I don't pay you to stand around talking all day."

Laslo roars with laughter. "Got it, boss."

"I have to check a few things in my office. Let me know before you go for lunch if I don't see you before then."

With a wave, I'm heading down the hallway, a giggling baby on my chest.

Sierra

I WAKE IN ALARM, drenched in sweat. Flinging my hand out from under my pillow, I come across cold sheets.

"Braden?"

When no response comes, I shoot up in bed, blinking to try and get my eyes to adjust to the darkness blanketing the bedroom. I can barely make out the time on my alarm clock.

3:42 a.m. My lips tug up, warmth building in my chest.

Swinging my legs over the edge of the bed, I slide on my slippers and put on the Knockout T-shirt Braden left on the floor, covering my naked body. It falls to my knees and still smells like his cologne. I fight the urge to bring the material to my nose and sniff, deciding to go find the source of the smell instead.

A small plug-in light illuminates the hallway, just enough that I don't run into anything on my way to Tinsley's room. Her bedroom door is cracked open an inch, another dim light glowing behind it.

As soon as I shoulder it open enough to enter, I smile, placing a hand over the ache growing in my chest. A good ache. The best kind.

A bare-chested Braden sits in the grey glider chair that I spent far too long picking out, a sleeping Tinsley in his arms. Our six-month-old daughter is sucking away on the bottle in her mouth, all five fingers wrapped around Braden's pinky like she's holding him there, terrified he'll vanish if she lets go.

Braden's lips brush her chubby cheek when he whispers, "You eat like your mom, Tiny. Like you're scared somebody is going to take your food away if you don't eat fast enough."

A giggle escapes me, drawing his attention. Those soft brown eyes meet my tired silver ones before drifting along my body, growing more intense the further down they get. My skin heats under his gaze before I manage to reel myself back in. The last thing we need is to keep each other up the rest of the night.

This is Tinsley's only and last feeding tonight, but Braden and I will be up again in a little over two hours when our alarms blare.

I can't even begin to explain how helpful Braden has been during night wake-ups and feedings over the past six months. For some reason, I was worried that I would never get any sleep as a mother with a newborn baby, but when your baby daddy happens to be a guy who doesn't mind swapping every other wake-up with you or rocking a screaming baby back to sleep when you can't take any more, you get more than enough sleep to still be a decently functioning human being the next day.

Although, I'm sure if Braden had the deciding vote in the matter, I would never have to wake up with our girl again. He would do it all without complaint. That's the kind of father and overall *man* he is.

"She's going to hate that nickname. You know that, right?"

I ask softly, walking toward him. His eyes track my movements. When I reach his side, I brush a few stray curls off his forehead.

Tilting his head so that he can still see me, he says, "That's too bad for her."

"Riiight. I'm sure you won't drop it as soon as she opens her wide eyes and flutters those long lashes at you. She already has you eating out of the palm of her hand and she can't even speak yet."

Braden shrugs, eyes sparkling with mischief. "Don't be jealous, sweetheart. You know I'll always eat from your palm. Or anywhere else you want. I'm partial to the paradise between your legs, but semantics."

I roll my eyes. "Okay, Romeo. She's done eating."

Tinsley no longer sucks on the nipple, now in a milk coma, happily curled up in her daddy's arms. Her head of thick brown curls lies messily on her head just like Braden's—another reminder that she got almost all of his genes and so far, not many of mine. We're waiting to see if her eyes lighten from blue to grey or darken to a whiskey brown like Braden's, but if I had to bet, I would say they'll be brown.

My only hope now is that she'll at least inherit my *badassery* as everyone calls it. Sophie bet Clayton fifty bucks that Tinsley will make him cry before her tenth birthday.

"Let me put her down, and we'll go back to bed."

I hum in acknowledgment and kiss his cheek before moving to the side. With heavy eyes, I watch as he slowly gets up, careful not to jostle Tinsley too much, and brings her to her crib. He sets her down like a seasoned pro. She doesn't so much as twitch, just softly coos to herself.

As soon as he turns around, he has me tucked beneath his arm, leading us out of the room and closing the door.

"Have I ever told you that you look good in my clothes?"

he asks, fingers tucking under the sleeve of his shirt and rubbing my bare bicep.

"Once or twice."

"Well, you do. You look almost as good with this baggy shirt on as you do without it. I think I need to take it off to be certain."

The rasp in his voice makes my toes want to curl in my slippers.

"Once tonight wasn't good enough for you?" I nearly purr as we walk into our bedroom, the sheets messy, the blanket lying half on the floor. *4:05*, the clock reads. "We have work tomorrow."

I gasp when he pulls me in front of him and walks us toward the bed. The backs of my thighs hit the mattress before I fall backward. Grinning, I push myself up the bed, yanking the blanket over me and tucking it beneath my chin before he has a chance to make good on his threat.

"You're a little shit." He chuckles and crawls in beside me.

I sigh contently when he pulls me to his chest, my head beneath his chin and arm over the ripped muscles of his abdomen. His heat wraps around me, and my eyes fall to half-mast.

"We won't end up going back to bed at all if you get my shirt off, and you know it."

His hum buzzes in my ear, and his hand slides beneath the hem of the shirt, pushing it up so that he can draw circles on my side. "You make it sound like a bad thing."

"It is when it means I'll be showing up to a day full of meetings looking like a freshly fucked zombie."

"That's my favourite type of zombie." I pinch his side, and he flinches, laughing. "Okay, okay. Just sleep."

I kiss his left pec, the skin above his newest tattoo—Tinsley's name, birth date, and handprint from when she was only a few days old. The cursive writing is the perfect mix of both elegant and simple. I'm still not over it, and it's been months. More often than not, I find myself staring at it, all dreamy like, imagining something similar on my skin.

"I think I want to get a tattoo," I blurt out. "Something for Tinsley. Like yours."

The fingers drawing circles on my side freeze for a brief second before moving again. They start drifting to the area right below my right breast.

"Yeah?"

I nod.

"Okay, fighter. I can call my guy tomorrow."

"Thank you," I whisper.

His calloused fingers continue to stroke the skin over the paw-print tattoo I have beneath my boob.

"You know, I've never asked what your tattoo means. It's your only one."

A small smile tugs at my mouth. "It's honestly pretty stupid. I got it on a drunken night that I don't really remember."

"Tell me anyway."

"A group of football players dared Sophie and I to get matching tattoos at a party our freshman year of college. I remember convincing Sophie that we don't need our names tattooed on each other and that matching pair of paw prints will have the same meaning. Don't ask why I chose paw prints —I'm still not sure why I did. Anyway, she got hers on her left ass cheek, and I got mine under my boob."

Fingers brush the underside of said boob. His laugh is raspy, giving away just how tired he is.

"I really fucking wish I knew you back then. Maybe if I did, I wouldn't have dropped out. Seeing you on campus every day would have been more than enough motivation to keep suffering through class."

My grip on him tightens, and I breathe him in, unashamed with how addicted I've become to how good he always smells. "I still can't believe that we went to the same school. Even if it was only for a few months. Something tells me that you were even more arrogant back then than you were when we met, though. I would have hated how attracted to you I was knowing that you were an arrogant asshole."

"You're right about that. I was awful back then. But that wouldn't have stopped me from pursuing you. Once I saw you, you would have been as good as mine. And once I had you—shit, baby. One night wouldn't have been enough. It never was. I knew as soon as I got you in that cab that I would be back for more."

An overwhelming sense of nostalgia floods through me. That first night in Sinners flashes through my head like a picture reel, bringing back memories that I know will never fade.

"I think I knew it too. That's why I took off before you woke up. You reeked of heartbreak, and I had no clue if I was up for the task of taming a player."

His chest rumbles. "Well? What do I smell like now? From how often you smell me, I think it's safe to say I no longer reek."

I move to pinch him again, but his hand captures mine, holding it tight. A thunderstorm of emotions swells in my chest as I link our fingers and finally let my eyes fall shut.

"You smell like mine."

A shuddered breath slips through my hair like a warm breeze. "Good, sweetheart. I am yours."

Forever.

EXTENDED EPILOGUE

FOUR YEARS LATER

Sierra

I gasp when Braden's glove makes contact with the underside of his opponent's chin, flinging the bulky man's head back as a collection of blood and spit flies from his mouth and hits Braden's face.

My boyfriend's grin is wicked, making him look more like a naughty schoolboy than the thirty-one-year-old father I've watched grow over the past few years.

Overhead lights flood the room, illuminating Braden's body and the elegance and expertise with which he maneuvers it around the ring. Toes tapping silently, arms fixed in their perfect position. He's as skilled as he is cocky—without limits.

I didn't think that it was possible for him to get any bigger than he already was when we first met, but I should have known better. He's a brick wall of powerful, lean muscles that I won't ever get enough of.

Braden never stops working, never stops trying to get bigger and better than he was the minute before. And he has done exactly that. In every aspect of his life.

I've never been prouder of him.

"Finish it!" Tyler shouts from beside me.

Brooks grunts his agreement before adding, "Stop playing with your food, boy!"

I risk a glance at Braden's father and fight back a smile when he grabs the long, grey hairs on his chin and pulls hard enough to wince. My shoulders shake with a silent laugh.

It was a year after Tiny was born that Grandpa Brooks went full silver fox, and he still hasn't recovered it. Our family sure hasn't made it easier for him either. Not with our constant teasing and poking at him for being so old that he can no longer hide his age behind his youthful complexion. But that's just what we do. We tease and poke and laugh, because we're family.

If there's anything that I've learned over the years, it's that blood doesn't equate to family. And the family that I have now . . . it's everything I've ever wanted. Everything I've dreamed of.

With a scowl, Brooks bumps his shoulder roughly with mine and slants me a look. "Stop laughing at my grey hairs."

"Come now, Brooks, I would never," I reply, looking back at the ring with a grin just in time to see Braden's nose spurt blood before he delivers a punishing blow to the other boxer's lower stomach. Subconsciously, I grip the chain—his lucky chain—hanging from my neck in a tight fist. Braden's opponent curls into himself, stumbling back until he hits the red ropes.

An easy win for Braden.

I've watched enough fights now not to be surprised by the bloodshed or moments of brutality, but watching Braden in pain never gets easier. He lets the referee lift one arm in victory before wiping away the blood staining his lips with the other and grimacing. His eyes catch on me, and I wave wildly, relishing in the barely noticeable softening of his expression as we hold each other's stare.

Even with a gruesome-looking nose and splattered with another man's blood, he's the most beautiful person I've ever seen.

"Ready to go?" Tyler asks, turning to face his father and me. I nod, sending Braden a wink that he swiftly returns with the addition of a blown kiss before focusing on his brother.

"What's the time? We should be getting home to Gracie and the kids soon," I say as we start moving through the crowd and toward the locker room, where Braden will meet us.

Tyler and Gracie have been in town for the past two days while the Vancouver Warriors play the Toronto Timberwolves. And with Braden's match landing during their stay, Gray offered to babysit Tiny so I could come watch.

Tyler and Gracie's newest addition to the family is now a year old, and compared to their eldest son, Oliver, Jamieson is on a whole other level of crazy. He's a spitting image of Gracie, inside and out. And with even more attitude.

Add Tiny into the mix, and I don't even want to begin to imagine what mischief they've caused while we've been gone.

"It's not that late," Tyler replies casually, lifting a shoulder.

"She's got Lana with her too. I'm sure those two can handle a few kids," Brooks says.

"You sure about that?" I ask, laughing.

Brooks is silent for a second before he nods, suddenly a lot tenser than he was a few seconds ago. "You're right. We won't be here much longer."

Tyler taps his fingers against his thigh but doesn't say anything else the rest of the way to the locker room. Neither of them does.

A cold wave of nervousness crashes inside of me when we reach our destination and they still haven't spoken. The men in Braden's family aren't always the most outspoken, but they're never this quiet. Especially after a winning fight.

With my brows two hard slashes on my face, I pull open the locker room door and storm inside. The scene in front of me has my knees quaking beneath me.

All of our family and friends are packed into the room, their faces beaming with a sense of unfiltered happiness that I feel like a sucker punch to my chest. A high-pitched giggle that I would recognize anywhere has me searching for my daughter in the mass of bodies.

"Momma," she giggles, bouncing in place.

Tinsley grins up at me from her place between Oakley and Ava's sons, Maddox and Noah, a mess of dark brown curls and red-sucker-stained lips. Her silver-coloured eyes are wild as she watches me expectantly, like she does when she knows something that I don't.

My curiosity swells, reaching a peak when I don't see Braden in the sea of loved ones.

Someone places a large hand on my back, and I look over my shoulder to see Brooks tip his chin, smiling softly. I tilt my head, preparing to ask him what the hell is going on, when the fighter-only entrance door opens and my bloody man saunters into the room.

"What's going on?" I ask him when he walks my way, swallowing the space between us with confident, determined steps. My breath hitches as he comes to a stop a few feet in front of me.

"Daddy!" Tiny shrieks, clapping her hands furiously. Braden blows her a kiss, and she catches it with a giddy smile.

I take a second to inspect him for injuries and release a breath of relief when I don't find anything that I wasn't already expecting. His nose is swollen but doesn't look broken, and all the blood has been wiped away besides a few dried flecks left on the hard curves of his cheekbones. He's grinning at me by the time I finish looking him over, two rows of perfectly white teeth winking at me.

"You seem nervous, fighter," he teases. His grin grows incredulously bigger, and a set of matching dimples pop in his pink cheeks. "I just won. We should be celebrating."

A compelling force has me moving closer to him. "We should. But can you blame me? Why is everybody here? Have they been here the entire time? And why haven't they spoken a word? It's like being in a room full of wax figures."

A snort resonates from somewhere in the room.

Braden gives his head a quick shake, chuckling low and free. Our eyes meet, and the intensity in his has the air solidifying in my lungs.

"They only got here ten minutes ago. And I made them promise me not to speak before I got here. I knew that if they did, one of them would crack and spill my plans."

"What plans? You're not making any sense."

"Well, if you would just give me a second to explain," he chastises me. I throw my hands up in surrender, and he smirks. "I've been planning on doing this for months now, debating how and when. But with Tiny and our busy schedules, I realized that there would never be a time that I thought was perfect enough for this moment. So I decided that this would be as good a time as any. Now I can finally do this."

Shirtless besides his usual pair of gold shorts, he takes a single step forward before dropping to one knee.

My hands are shaking and ice-cold when I bring them to my mouth in absolute awe. The image of Braden knelt down before me becomes blurred when tears fill my eyes.

"What are you doing?" I inhale sharply, shaking my head in disbelief.

We've talked about marriage over the past four years. It's been an impossible topic to avoid. But I was—*am*—still content with the ring already on my finger. There's been no rush. No pressure laid down at his feet. He knew that if we got married, it would be because he *was* ready for it. I have been ready since the moment I fell in love with him.

Even without a marriage certificate and a wedding ring, there has not been a day in the past five years where I didn't know how much he loves me or doubted his intentions for the future.

We've bought our first house—a small three-bedroom bungalow in Scarborough, only a half hour from both our jobs. Tinsley will be starting kindergarten soon, and we've been discussing trying for a second baby.

Braden's sat beside me, holding my hand as my career blossomed into what I always hoped it would, and when I was promoted into the position left empty by Cole Travis' departure, Braden was the one beaming, telling me, "I told you so."

I've gotten to watch Knockout swell in popularity all throughout Ontario while cheering from my place beside him as Braden finally started to understand just how much potential he's always had hiding beneath that thick layer of self-doubt.

My life is perfect. I'm content. The only thing we could have possibly been missing is this. This moment right here and the prospect of what that could bring us.

Braden's hair flops across his forehead, teasing his brows before he blows it away with a harsh breath that I'm sure was full of nerves. I've forgotten Brooks was behind me until he reaches around me and hands his son a dainty, square velvet box.

I'm standing just close enough to the two of them to vaguely make out the warm, hushed words spoken between the two men.

"I'm proud of you, son," Brooks says.

Braden's eyes shine for the slightest second. He centres himself quickly, blinking furiously. "Thanks, Dad."

All too quickly, his eyes are on me again, making me the centre of his attention. Of his world. My once broken playboy, now an amazing father and partner, looks at me with a stare as soft as cotton. A stare that portrays everything he's feeling but hasn't yet said.

He opens the delicate box with long, calloused fingers, revealing a gold-banded ring with a handful of small diamonds nestled around a large oval-shaped one. My chest feels too small to contain my expanding heart when the first tear splashes my cheek.

"Fuck, baby. Don't start crying on me yet," he laughs breathily. His eyes sparkle and shine when I give him a watery smile. "Never in my life did I plan on feeling love like this. The kind of love that both consumes a person and stabilizes them. But you brought me exactly that. You're my strength when I'm weak and my calm when I'm scared. You are every good, honest part of me. And I want you to be my wife. I know that now more than ever."

"Braden," I whisper incredulously.

He shakes his head once. "You changed my life, little fighter. You've been so patient—even though this has taken me far too long. I was serious when I told you that I would marry you one day. And now, I'm more than ready to be your husband. So, Sierra Genevieve Caster, what do you say? Do you still wanna marry me?"

"Yes, of course I do," I breathe. With two steps forward, we're only a finger's length apart, but it's still too far. In this moment, we can't be close enough.

I grab his forearms, pulling him up before throwing myself at him without a second thought. He catches me with ease, as if he was expecting me to wind up in his embrace.

With strong arms, he pulls me in close to his body, holding me tight. Pressing his face into my hair, he exhales slowly before saying, "I fucking love you."

"I love you, Braden." I can't hold back my laughter as it slips free.

After holding me for a few seconds longer, Braden pulls himself free, taking the slightest step back before moving the ring box between us, the lid still open. It's nearly impossible to hold back my tears now as I stare down at the beautiful piece of jewelry that I'm going to wear every day for the rest of my life.

He carefully plucks the ring from its holder before handing the empty box back to his dad. I hold my left hand out for him, and he holds it more delicately than he ever has. The gold-banded engagement ring glides up its designated finger, fitting perfectly. The diamond catches the light, and my heart skips a few beats.

"It's gorgeous," I say, finally looking away from the ring and toward my fiancé. A shiver travels up my spine at the new label. It's going to take some time to get used to that one.

I'm not surprised when I find Braden already watching me. His eyes blaze as he says, "It has to be. Look at you."

I tip my head forward, connecting my forehead to his chest and laughing. His arms bind around me again, trapping me in his hold.

"What would you have done if you lost tonight?" I ask.

His scowl is instant. "Not like that would have been even a possibility, but I still would have asked you to marry me, baby. I just would have been a lot uglier when I did."

I laugh. "You and ugly don't even exist in the same universe."

"You don't have to flatter me, Sierra. I'm already yours." He tosses me a wink.

"Can we speak now, Braden? Because I would really like to

congratulate my sister," Clare says from wherever she's wound up in the crowd.

"Yeah, Mommy. When do we get hugs?" Tinsley asks.

Braden's arms loosen just enough for me to be able to spin around in them. As soon as I do, our little girl is sprinting toward us. She hits my legs and releases a small *oomf* from the impact before wrapping her arms around my knees.

"Hey, baby girl," I murmur and smooth a hand over her unruly curls.

She tilts her chin to look up at me at the same time Braden nuzzles his head into my neck, kissing the warm skin there. Our family starts closing in on us, a symphony of congratulations adding to my bliss.

"Do you get to wear a pretty princess dress now?" Tiny asks.

"I sure do. And so do you," I reply.

She gasps. "I do?"

Braden's laugh kisses my jaw. "Of course, Tiny. Both of my beautiful princesses have to wear their best dresses."

"I will, Daddy. I promise." Our daughter tips her chin to the sky. *Gah*. She's adorable.

My sister is the first of the group of people to reach us. Tiny lets go of my legs when Clare steps in front of me. She doesn't hesitate to bring Braden and me into a tight hug. Tears prickle my eyes again.

"It's about damn time," she mumbles. I can hear the wobble in her voice.

Clare has come around more to Braden over the years, but there was still a lot of distrust on Clare's end. I was beginning to worry it would never go away, but maybe now it will. She should have no doubt now that he doesn't plan on going anywhere.

I wouldn't let him even if he tried.

Braden's body jolts when he's slapped on the back before he's wrenched away from me. Clare drops her arms, and I twirl around to see Tyler, Clayton, Oakley, and Brooks squeezing the life out of my man in celebration.

"How does it feel to know you're about to join the marriage club?" Tyler asks.

Braden's eyes catch mine over the crowd that's formed between us, and his grin is everything. "I've never been more ready for anything."

I soak up this moment with a smile stretched across my face.

If this is how the rest of our lives are going to go, I can't wait.

THE END

This is the end for Braden and Sierra, but the Amateurs In Love series is far from over.

Sophie and Clayton's friends-to-lovers romance is coming late 2023 followed by Clare and Max's second-chance romance in 2024. Both will be stand alones.

Until then, please consider leaving Taming the Player a review on Amazon and Goodreads.

Interested to learn how Gracie and Tyler met and fell in love? Want to get a glimpse at Braden back in his college days, playing hockey alongside the famous Oakley Hutton? Or curious about Adam and his son? Check out my new-adult, hockey romance series!

Keep reading for an unedited sneak peek of Vital Blindside, Adam and Scarlett's love story.

VITAL BLINDSIDE — COMING SEPT 2022

Adam White is many things, but a single dad was one that he never planned on becoming. He was twenty-three when the plan he had for his life crumbled at his feet. In the blink of an eye, he went from a flirtatious playboy just getting his new business up and off the ground to a struggling father of a two-year-old boy that he never knew existed.

Still, he did it. Adam accomplished what he thought was impossible. And now, at the prime age of thirty-three, he doesn't think that his life can get any better. His twelve-year-old son, Cooper, is his world, and his business, White Ice Training, is one of the most known hockey training facilities in Vancouver. But when he posts a job listing for a new hockey trainer, he gets a response that lights a flame inside of him that he never realized was burnt out. One that he refuses to go without again.

One terrible game was all it took for Scarlett Carter to lose everything. After a career-ending injury destroys her chances of ever playing professional hockey again, she finds herself lost in a mess of guilt-stricken "what-ifs" and broken dreams. Moving back home to Vancouver was never in the playbook, but neither was letting herself get tricked into taking a job working for a man who seems to want to stop at nothing to see her play the sport she loves again.

Scarlett wants to forget about the world that broke her, but the single dad refuses to let her move on. The more time she spends with Adam, the harder she's finding it to resist him and the sly grins he seems to only give her. She can't help but wonder why he cares so much about her. And more importantly, why can't she bring herself to make him leave her alone.

CHAPTER 1

ADAM

The lumpy clouds above Vancouver, British Columbia, groan into the sky before opening up to drown us beneath a heavy pour of rain. It wets my hair, making it stick to my forehead as I continue my morning run.

I'm on my seventh mile, and even though the weather just gave me the middle finger, my house is only a couple of blocks away. I can't exactly stop now, even if that means I'll have to listen to my twelve-year-old son scold me for bringing wet clothes into the house as soon as I walk through the door.

Cooper loves to poke at the bear, as long as that bear is me. I can't help but take complete responsibility for that. He learned at a young age that the majority of the time, I'm all bark and no bite, which only makes him enjoy picking on me like a little shit even more.

Our two-story craftsman-style house pokes its head around the eyesore of a spruce tree planted dead smack in front of Mrs. Connell's house. It's almost the size of her entire front yard and looks like it hasn't been trimmed once in its lifetime. I've tried convincing the widow to have it cut down, but she's shut me down each time.

My persistence has no limit, however. I'll get her to agree one of these days.

I jog past the neighbouring yard and toward my house, noticing the open garage door. Cooper's bike is leaning up against my workbench inside, his Marvel sticker decorated helmet dangling from the handlebars. Neither my son nor dog are anywhere to be seen, but I can only assume they're close by. My kid wouldn't dare leave his precious bike out in the open without protection, and Easton doesn't move from his best friend's side for a second longer than necessary.

Slowing to a walk, I move up the driveway, patting the hood of my Camaro when I pass it. I manoeuvre around the array of hockey gear and dog toys scattered on the concrete pad in the garage before shaking my hair free of rain and opening the door that leads to the mudroom, stepping inside.

The mud room is as big of a mess as the garage, with large piles of laundry stacked in front of the washing machine and a collection of shoes everywhere but the designated rack. I've been telling myself I'll get this room cleaned up eventually, but I may have put it off a bit too long.

"Coop?" I yell, slipping off my wet sneakers.

Taking a step out of the mudroom, I wince when my socks make a squelching noise and water seeps to the floor. With rushed movements, I pull off my socks and add them to a pile of dirty clothes before collecting all of it in my arms and tossing everything in the washing machine. I'm throwing in a pod of detergent when I hear the click clack of nails on the floor.

"You're lucky Dad wasn't home to see that, East. You would have had to sleep outside—" Cooper's words cut off when he enters the mudroom.

Chuckling, I start the washing machine and turn around.

Easton, the ninety pound German Shepherd we adopted when Cooper was five, flops onto his back immediately, his tongue lolling out of his mouth and paws folded beneath his chin.

"Yeah, that's not suspicious." I snort and look at Cooper as he rocks back and forth on his heels. "What did he do?"

Cooper is the spitting image of me. Staring at him is like going back in time and looking in the mirror.

His milk chocolate-coloured eyes have the same green flecks around the irises as mine do, and his puffed bottom lip twists to the right just enough to rest in a half-smirk that's gotten me in trouble once or twice over the years. He's tall for his age, coming in at just under five foot four—just like his dad was.

"Uh . . ."

"Cooper," I groan. "Let's do this the easy way, please. What did he do?"

His eyes roam around the room, focusing on everything but me. "He might have eaten one of the jerseys you had lying in that pile." He points to the laundry on the ground.

"He might have? Or he did?"

Cooper gulps. "Okay, he did. But in his defence, he probably thought it was going in the trash anyway. It had been sitting there for at least a couple weeks."

He's not completely off base there. It's been over a week since I brought WIT's spare jerseys home to wash, and they have yet to see even a dollop of detergent. I'm sure they smelled ripe for the picking.

"Did he eat the whole thing?" I ask with a weighted sigh.

Cooper shakes his head. "No. Just the sleeve. And he puked it up in the backyard already."

Flicking my gaze to the dog wrapped around Cooper's foot, I give my head a shake. The little shit is smiling at me.

"Fine," I say. "But make sure he doesn't do it again, Coop. This room is off limits, yeah?"

"Got it, Dad."

I nod before checking my watch for the time and muttering a curse. Cooper raises a curious brow.

"No bike today, Buddy. I'm gonna drive you before you're late for school. Get your stuff and I'll meet you in the car as soon as I change."

My boy doesn't put up a fight, despite how excited he was to ride his bike to school. Instead, he raises his hand in a salute before grabbing his backpack from its hook and slinging it over his shoulder. Once he heads into the garage, I take off toward my bedroom.

Despite the chaos that is our laundry room, the rest of the house is clean and organized. I've never been a messy person, but being a single father is no easy feat. Between chauffeuring Cooper to band practice four out of seven days a week, art lessons another two, and owning and managing a booming business, I've allowed myself just one room to not give a crap about. One room where I can shove everything I don't want, or don't have time to do, away where I can't see it.

Out of sight, out of mind, right?

My bare feet thump against the cold wood planks lining the hallway before meeting the plush carpet in my bedroom. The walk-in closet is too extravagant for my taste, with the built-in maple shelves and drawers, and collection of mirrors that make it impossible to avoid staring at yourself, but it came with the house, and I haven't had the time to change anything yet.

I quickly change into a pair of black track pants and a hoodie, both featuring the White Ice Training logo, before slipping on a pair of socks. Stepping in front of the mirror beside the rack housing my suit jackets, I shake my hair out again and run my fingers through the brown curls.

Every day that passes where I don't find a grey hair on my head is a day to celebrate. Knowing that my father went grey in his early thirties has been hanging over me like a piano on a thin wire since the day I turned thirty. It's been three years since, and every day I count my blessings.

The beeping of my smartwatch has me quickly flicking off all lights and jogging through the house to the garage. Easton watches me run down the hallway from his place on the couch, and I flip him off before heading outside.

Cooper is already waiting for me in the car, and when I slide into the passenger seat, he levels me with a disapproving stare that makes him look far older than he is.

"Are you finally ready, beauty queen?"

With a quick burst of laughter, I reach over the console and ruffle his hair. "Careful, tough guy. I might drop you off on the side of the road and leave you there."

"I dare you," he sniffs, slapping my arms.

I pull back and start the engine. "Triple doggy dare me, and you have a deal, bucko."

White Ice Training is a hockey arena located a few minutes from East Vancouver, housing a half-rink, a full size gym, and several rooms specialized for position specific training.

We coach over a hundred athletes, with ages ranging from five-year-old's learning to skate, players in their late teens preparing for their chance at the big leagues, and anywhere in between.

Besides Cooper, WIT is my pride and joy. My blood, sweat, and bucket loads of tears. I've put everything I am, and have ever had, into building my company, and it still feels like a dream come true to stand here—a handful of feet away from the entrance—and stare up at what I've built in utter awe.

I pull open the heavy glass door and step inside, welcoming the slight chill that settles on my cheeks from the busy rink. I'm very late this morning, and after having to call Banks, my second in command, and deal with his chiding when I asked him to come in early and open the building, I've already determined it'll be a hellish day.

Ever the night owl, Banks doesn't mix well with early mornings. Usually, that benefits me. He doesn't mind coming in after lunch and staying late so I can get home to Cooper earlier and make sure he gets where he needs to go on time. But on days where that doesn't go according to plan, Banks can be a sparking storm cloud ready to shoot off lightning bolts at the first person to anger him.

"Good morning, Adam," Brielle, one of our front desk workers, greets me with a smile.

"Hello, Brie. How was your morning?" I ask, closing the gap between us and leaning my forearms on the half-wall separating me from her desk.

Brielle is a young, single mother of triplets. Her ex-boyfriend left before the three girls were even born, and although she has a lot of help from her parents, I've offered to help her out whenever necessary.

Usually, I offer to pick up her girls for school since I'm already taking Coop in that direction, but she's been adamant over the past couple of weeks that she can handle it on her own. It's not my place to push her on it. Lord knows I didn't love taking handouts when Cooper was young.

Brielle smiles warmly. "It was pretty good. I think we've finally worked out a good morning schedule for the four of us. One that doesn't have me rushing out of the house with my hair still up in a towel and three six-year-olds wearing Halloween costumes."

I toss my head back and laugh. "That's great. But I'm sure they're the life of the classroom in those costumes."

"Oh yes. I've heard all about how much their teachers love chasing child size hotdogs and pickles around during morning announcements."

"I remember when Cooper was in the sixth grade, he went to school on Halloween with one of those Scream masks that was filled with fake blood. The tubing attached to the pump ended up ripping open, and whatever they used to create the blood squirted all over his math teacher. I received quite the scolding from the principal that day."

Brielle covers her mouth with her hand and giggles.

"I know, I know. I'm a cool dad." I wink.

She shakes her head, her lips tugging at the corners. "That's exactly what I was thinking."

I push myself back and plant my hands on my hips. "I better get to work before Banks sees me slacking off. There are three interviews on the schedule today. Just page me to my office when the applicants get here, yeah?" It's been a long search for the perfect addition to our team, and at this point, I'm losing hope that we'll find anybody.

She nods. "Sounds good, boss. Good luck with Banks today. He's already nearly thrown down with Brooklyn Danvers."

Great. One of our best clients and an Olympic gold medalist.

"Thanks, Brie. I'll see ya later." I throw her a grateful smile before spinning around and heading for my office.

As I walk through the busy halls of WIT, I can only hope to make it out of this day in one piece.

Also by Hannah Cowan:

SWIFT HAT TRICK TRILOGY

Lucky Hit — (Oakley x Ava) Swift Hat-Trick trilogy #1

Between Periods (5 POV) Swift Hat-Trick trilogy #1.5

Blissful Hook — (Tyler x Gracie) Swift Hat-Trick trilogy #2

Vital Blindside — (Adam x Scarlett) Swift Hat-Trick trilogy #3

Acknowledgements

Writing a book is never easy, and this one was no exception. Without the team of people that I have around me, surrounding me with so much positivity and encouragement, I wouldn't have been able to show Sierra and Braden the ending they deserved.

My plan for Braden and Sierra was always to have two books. At the end of Craving the Player, they both had so much growing to do. In my mind, they needed more than I could give in a single book. And 180 thousand words later, I can finally say that I am so incredibly proud of how far they've come and what they've both accomplished. I hope you all feel that way too.

The risk that comes with writing a duet is scary, and I'm so grateful for the love that I have received. To every single person that read Craving the Player and fell in love with Braden and Sierra, this one's for you. You gave me the push I needed to finish this story the way I wanted to from the beginning.

I want to say a huge thank you to my beta team for being so excited to help me with this book, and for loving Braden and Sierra so much. Your help meant everything.

I am so happy to have found my editor, Sandra (@oneloveediting). You are such a lifesaver. Thank you for doing such a great job with this book.

To ARC readers, you rock. You help so much more than you know. Thank you for everything.

About The Author

Hannah is a twenty-something-year-old indie author from Canada. Obsessed with swoon-worthy romance, she decided to take a leap and try her hand at creating stories that will have you fanning your face and giggling in the most embarrassing way possible. Hopefully, that's exactly what her stories have done!

Hannah loves to hear from her readers, and can be reached on any of her social media accounts.

Instagram : Hannahcowanauthor
Twitter, Facebook : Hannahdcowan
Facebook Group : Hannah's Hotties
Website : hannahcowanauthor.com

Printed in Great Britain
by Amazon

18719252R00181